A Tango to Die For!

A Culinary Mystery with a Side of Travel

LORALEE LAGO

A TANGO TO DIE FOR!

Copyright © 2020 Loralee Lago

All rights reserved.

ISBN: (9798660065781)

All Rights Reserved. Reproduction or electronic transmission of any part without the author's permission is prohibited.

This book is a work of fiction. Names, characters, businesses, organizations, places and events are either the product of the author's imagination or used fictitiously. Any resemblance to actual persons, living or dead, events or locale is entirely coincidental.

Acknowledgments

Thank you to my fantastic husband Paul for being MY 'Mr. Google' by verifying the facts and adding vital input to make the story more authentic. I'm grateful for your support and enthusiasm in everything that I do. I could never have done it without you Mi Amor!

Thank you to my incredible twin sister, Lynda who read and reread and Beta read the script and offered invaluable insights and input!

A big thank you to my nephew, Cory who is our family 'Mr. Google' with a big heart to match, who offered fun facts to include in the story.

Thank you to my Editors & Beta Readers: Maya Mukherjee, Marry Johns, Elizabeth Thompson, Suzanne Wilson, Angela Osa, Cherrie Hoeft & Amy Sjolund. Your encouragement and direction were extremely appreciated.

Any cat track errors in this manuscript can be attributed to my office assistant, Daisy Blossom, who regularly added her paw prints to the story.

Contents

CHAPTER 1: *Bull-oney!* *1*

CHAPTER 2: *Tango Wars!* *20*

CHAPTER 3: *Feed Me* *40*

CHAPTER 4: *Shocking* *63*

CHAPTER 5: *Mortadella? Como No? (Why Not?)* *81*

CHAPTER 6: *Our Next Stop Will Be...* *93*

CHAPTER 7: *I Heart Bariloche* *105*

CHAPTER 8: *Tierra de Fuego* *141*

CHAPTER 9: *Operation Lighthouse* *167*

CHAPTER 10: *O-so Joyful!* *187*

CHAPTER 11: *Las Rectas!* *203*

About the Author *237*

Bibliography *238*

CHAPTER 1

Bull-oney!

It's nearly midnight as four men stiffly sit in a cold surveillance van. They are huddled around a cell phone, awaiting coordinates to deliver a large duffle bag full of money. The group jumps in tandem as the cell phone ringtone pierces the silence. The man nearest the phone answers it on speakerphone, saying, "This is Lago. Where do we drop it?"

A thick, accented voice spoke quickly, "Leave the money at the base of the large weeping willow tree, located at Longitude -34.60851 degrees N & Latitude -58.37349. Walk through the entrance and up the road alone. You will be given further instructions once you reach the tree. You have 30 minutes."

Click...the line went dead.

Paul Lago, the leader of the group, jumped into action. "Kelly, put the coordinates into the GPS for our rendezvous location and let me know where we're going, pronto!"

"From my calculations, the drop off site is located at the Matador Vineyards, about a 30-minute drive north of here, boss," said Kelly.

"JJ, step on it! We've got less than one hour to deliver the ransom and find the hostages or risk losing them to suffocation," ordered Paul.

Paul and his team had arrived in Argentina a few weeks earlier, at the request of the Director of Interpol, to investigate the murder of an American journalist and his cameraman who had gone deep undercover to investigate the kidnapping of a North American couple. One of the more bizarre aspects of the journalist and cameraman's murders was that they had been poisoned and the bottoms of their feet had been branded with the letters, "O.N." Local authorities had pursued all leads but were unable to make any progress with the kidnappers and had requested assistance from Paul's team in rescuing the two hostages.

Upon further investigation, there were many questions answered, but it also opened up a proverbial can of worms that even Paul could not anticipate. The kidnapping of the couple for ransom just added to the mystery.

Why brand a person? Would the couple be branded as well? What did these people want? Why were these two people kidnapped and held for ransom instead of being killed, like the journalist and cameraman? What message were the murderers trying to convey? What did "O.N." stand for? He thought of all the words that began with the letter "O"- *Orar? (Pray?) No! That couldn't be it. If these people were God-fearing, they would have sought for guidance and not become ensnared with such unsavory people. Oregano? Oranges? No, those were English words. In addition, why were the prime suspects a Miner and a Gaucho (Cowboy)?*

He'd have to think about these matters and many more to make sense of the investigation and proceed further. The couple was being held for ransom, with their captors demanding that $2,000,000 US dollars be delivered in exchange for sparing their lives.

"Okay, men, we are T-Minus 10 minutes before our arrival. Let's have a quick word of prayer for help. I'll say it," said Paul. "Lord bless us with thy protection, and to be able to find these people alive and quickly. Amen. Now let's go with the strength of the Lord, men!"

Paul was dropped off at the entrance to the Matador Vineyard. The rest of the team parked near the entrance and impatiently awaited Paul's signal to proceed. As instructed, Paul walked up the lonely, dark drive to deliver the ransom money next to an old willow tree near the vineyard's homestead. "Okay. I have the tree in sight and am ready to drop off the package," said Paul into his earpiece.

Paul quickly set the duffel bag down and looked around for further instructions mentioned by the kidnapper on the phone earlier. These instructions would lead them to the American couple who he hoped, were still alive. He whispered into his concealed earpiece, "The package has been delivered. I repeat, the package has been delivered. I've located the first clue nailed to the tree. It says, '*Las encontraras donde las uvas son mas dulce*. You will find them where the grapes are the sweetest. Please proceed up the road and meet me where the grape vines are growing near the road.'

JJ, which color of grape is the sweetest? Green, red, black, orange or yellow?" asked Paul.

"BLACK!" Came the response in his earpiece.

"How certain are you that the black is the sweetest grape?" asked Paul.

"I'm only 75% certain, boss!"

"I don't like those stats when all that I can see in front of me are yellow grapes. Verify it. We've got to be certain," said Paul.

"JJ, follow us in the van along the border of the vineyard, so that we have enough light to find the next clue. Keep a lookout for whoever picks up the ransom money. Make certain that your night camera is recording the pickup, JJ; we can't afford to make any mistakes."

"Roger that. We have confirmation from Mariella at Buenos Aires P.D. analytics that black grapes are indeed the sweetest," reported JJ.

"Thanks. Craig and Kelly, come help me locate the black grapes!" said Paul. The men immediately spread out and began scanning the vineyard for the black fruit.

"I've found them!" whispered Kelly urgently.

"Good work, Kelly," praised Paul.

"Craig, you search for the next clue down this row in front of me. Kelly, you take the next row, and I'll take the two rows farthest away." They divided up, each running through the long, narrow rows with flashlights in hand, hoping to quickly locate the next clue.

As they searched, they heard the sound of an approaching vehicle driving on the gravel road. It had quietly pulled up with its lights off at the drop-off site and disappeared within a few seconds.

"The package has been intercepted–I got a ton of glamor shots of the driver and guy who grabbed the bag," said JJ sarcastically. "They won't get far with the tracker that I implanted in the bag. I added a little parting gift bonus of an ink bomb. Within minutes after opening it, they'll all be covered in permanent, fluorescent red ink. The local authorities are on standby now and will be all over them, like bees on honeycomb. They've been instructed to follow the vehicle discreetly to their home base before apprehending them as our governments don't take lightly to groups kidnapping foreigners for ransom."

"The clue is here. I found it!" announced Craig.

"Good, we've now only got about a 25-minute window to find

them," said Paul, checking his digital watch. "The problem is that we don't know what time the couple were buried and how big the coffin is. Those are vital factors in their survival rate. What does the note say?"

Craig read the message in his Western American accent. *"Ear dawn-day los pear-oohs aee-stan al-land-o ahh lah lew-nah.* What does it mean, boss?"

"I'm not sure," Paul said as he jogged up to where Craig was standing. "Would you give it to me, so that I can read it? I could only understand a few of the words. Okay, it says, *Ir donde los perros estan allando a la luna.* Go where the dogs howl at the moon."

"Look around for any signs of dogs!" said Paul. "They can't be too far away—Wait...Quiet...No one move. Listen, I think I just heard a dog howl in that direction." he motioned with the beam of his flashlight. "Everyone move, move, move!"

They sprinted to the far end of the vineyard, where a pack of stray dogs congregated, howling at the moon near a barn. The group easily found the next clue on the fence post but not before carefully navigating around a few growling dogs, who didn't appreciate them crashing the party.

"Anybody got any food on them, by any chance?" asked Paul.

Yeah, I've got a pack of beef jerky in my pocket," replied Kelly.

"By all means, please give the dogs the jerky," said Paul. "I hope that they are Teriyaki lovers. I'd like to be able to read the next clue without being bitten."

"Si va demasiado lejos, seras pisoteado. If you go too far, you'll be trampled." Paul surveyed the large estate and said, "Look over there at the far end of the pasture. There's a cow. No...not a cow, but a huge bull!" realized Paul. "JJ, please bring us the shovels and crowbar now."

Loralee Lago

"Roger that, *Jefe*," (boss) said JJ as he pulled the van up next to the fence of the pasture.

"Craig, follow the fence around to the south end of the pasture. Kelly, you head out in the opposite direction. I'll walk through the middle and meet up with both of you at the far end. Hopefully I won't have any altercations with the bull. By the time we meet up, I think we'll know the exact location where they're buried."

"Good luck with the bull, brother from another mother," said Kelly.

"May the spiritual powers be with you," said Craig.

Each man, with a flashlight in hand, sprinted around and through the perimeter of the bull's enclosure, looking for signs of freshly dug soil.

Within a matter of minutes, Paul noticed uneven dirt piles at the far end of the meadow. He signaled with his flashlight and spoke into his earpiece, "The grave is here! Be very wary of the bull, and come in nice and slow. Keep your flashlights facing the ground."

The men gingerly edged towards Paul, past the bull, and once there feverishly began digging up the shallow grave. After a few minutes of rapid digging, their shovels struck the top of a large wooden box, and they began frantically unearthing the exterior edges with their hands.

"JJ, flash the van's spotlight in our direction, so that we can see better. Kelly, hand me that crowbar, so that I can pry the top off!" ordered Craig.

Paul kept a close watch on the bull, saying, "He's not happy with us for taking over his territory. It's just a matter of time before he charges."

"It's open," said Craig triumphantly as he yanked the top free.

The men put their flashlights together, pointing them into the wooden box's opening, hoping for any signs of life.

Upon feeling the cool breeze on her face, the woman gasped and sputtered for air, then sat up in a terror-stricken haze. Underneath her, a man lay unconscious. Kelly reached down and discovered that he was still warm and had a faint pulse. "They're both still alive!" he exclaimed.

"Quick, get them to the van," said Paul. "Grouchy Señor bull is comin' our way, and he isn't going to give us a warm *Bienvenidos* (welcome) either!" The bull snorted and pawed the ground in frustration and then began taking steps towards them as if he understood Paul's comments.

"He's starting to charge us!" yelled Paul. "I'll do what I can to steer him away from you. Get them out of here now!"

The bull began running at them full speed. Paul took off his coat and waved it in Matador style at the bull, hoping to distract him from the others as they moved to get outside of the fence. The bull took the bait and charged at Paul, who miraculously avoided being impaled on the bull's first pass. The bull charged a second time, catching the arm of Paul's coat with its horns and ripping it out of his hands.

"We're almost out!" yelled Craig as he and JJ dragged the man feet first underneath the lowest fence post, and Kelly pushed the dazed woman through the opening. "We need about five more seconds!"

"I've only got one final chance to keep the bull away. Get them out of the pasture now!" yelled Paul. The bull charged one last time as Paul sprinted for his life towards the back fence, high hurdle-jumping over it just as the bull's horns made contact with the posts with a loud thud. The bull snorted and grunted in rage, its eyes red with fury at its final unsuccessful attempt.

Paul jogged to catch up to the others. Catching his breath, he said, "Well that was an unexpected work hazard–I certainly wasn't trained for that scenario. They might have to add it to our basic training drills in the future. Our HR department isn't going to believe this bull-oney tale," said Paul as he joined the group to help carry the terror-stricken couple to the safety of their surveillance van. "It's a good thing I was on the track team in high school; otherwise, I never would have cleared that fence in one leap. Come to think of it, I've never actually jumped over a hurdle that high in my life. I felt like I was given extra strength to easily clear the fence."

"It's all that good living and praying that protected you for sure, boss," said Kelly. Paul humbly and quietly nodded his head for a quick silent prayer of gratitude for the heavenly assistance that they had received throughout the evening.

"If not for Paul's mad Matador skills and command of the Spanish language, we might never have gotten them out in time," said JJ.

"Thanks, JJ, but *we* saved them as a team," said Paul as he got into the van in front of Kelly. "Wow, that was a close call. Did you notice how long the bull's horns were? So much for my jacket. Good riddance, Señor bull. You can have it! I barely made it over the fence with the seat of my pants on that last jump. It's Team Lago 1 for the win and Señor Bull 0!"

"Yeah... about that," said Kelly. "You might want to check the back of your pants. It looks like Señor bull left you with a little something extra."

"What are you talking about, Kelly?" Paul asked as he jumped up to inspect his pants, only to find a large, ripped off bite mark on his right buttock. In embarrassment, he looked up and said, "Okay. Touché, Señor Bull. The score is now tied at Señor Bull 1 and Team Lago 1. Kelly, May I borrow your jacket, please?"

"Vah-Moose." Craig signaled to JJ to get on the road.

"Don't you mean, *Vamos?* (Let's go)," corrected Paul.

"Yeah, that's what I said! '*Vah-Moose*," said, Craig.

"Okay then. VAH-MOOSE!" said Paul, giving a quick wink at JJ.

"No, it's actually Vah-MOO in honor of Señor bull," JJ chortled as they speedily returned to town.

Safely back in town, the couple was taken directly to the hospital for a total health evaluation. They required hospitalization and were interviewed for further information. The B.A. police easily tailed and apprehended the red-faced men and others awaiting their return at a warehouse. Paul and his team spent the next several days wrapping up their reports and tying up any loose ends needed to mark the case closed.

One week later

Paul is once again waiting for an arrival, but this time it's at the airport terminal for an old friend. As he waits, he thinks about the unforgettable country of Argentina and how it is a traveler's paradise. *One day you could be skiing the Andes mountains and dining on Sea Bass and Steaks seasoned with Chimichurri Vinaigrette, while the next day, you're climbing a glacier with the Magellan penguins and dining on Chorizo (spiced sausages) and chocolate-covered Churros for dessert. Argentina is certainly a land full of opportunity, diverse cultures, and culinary delights.*

He thinks about Argentina's most beloved first lady, Eva Peron, whose tombstone epitaph reads, "Don't Cry for Me, Argentina; I remain quite near you!" Indeed, he had a strong connection and love for this magnificent country, much as she did.

Paul verifies that Celeste's plane will arrive in 20 minutes as he waits at the Ministro Pistarini International Airport in Buenos Aires. She is flying in from Las Vegas, Nevada, USA - the Entertainment capital of the world, home of The Vegas Golden Knights, Las Vegas Raiders, Las Vegas Speedway, and hometown of Celeste Humphries. Celeste is the only person that he knows who is actually a native of Las Vegas. She didn't live at a local casino, as many supposed, but was an attractive thirty-something controller for a local advertising agency living in the Las Vegas suburbs. The last time that he had seen his friend in person was 15 years earlier at a district meeting as a missionary for their church. Paul checks his watch, and nervously drums his fingers on the ceiling to floor windowpane overlooking the tarmac.

Having a few moments to review his life, he concludes that he really hasn't dated much, having immersed himself fully in his career. At that thought, he tugs uncomfortably at the collar of his shirt, rubs the back of his neck to try and relieve his nervousness, and wonders if he's really up for the task.

He runs his hand through his thick brown hair at the thought that he's a bit rusty in his communication skills with women. After all, he mused, *I'm a pro at locating, apprehending, and negotiating with criminals.* He mindfully checks the flight schedule on the overhead display for the hundredth time, making sure that the flight is still on time.

Celeste is flying in on *Arolena* (Airline) Argentina and is due to arrive at any minute. It is funny how just a few minutes can seem like an eternity, while most of the time, a few minutes meant nothing to him. Butterflies begin building up in his stomach.

"Okay, Lago! Get yourself together," he says softly to himself as he slaps the sides of his face repeatedly with both hands. "Focus on something else, anything else." He redirects his thinking by reviewing what he'd learned from the travel guide he'd purchased to reacquaint himself with the best tourist attractions and culinary delights of the country. He slowly inhales deeply and then exhales; saying to himself, *just visualize how you'll respond the moment that you see Celeste.* The soothing breathing exercise allows him to refocus; he feels instantly refreshed as he slowly exhales, thinking, *inhale the good vibes, exhale the bad.*

He mentally checks off a list of things that he'd learned from his crash course about all things Argentina the night before, in

A TANGO TO DIE FOR

preparation for her arrival. *One always needs to be prepared in case there's a lull in the conversation. The first factoids that I'll share with her will be:*

1) Capital of Argentina: Buenos Aires, with a Population of 45,510,000

2) Language – Castilian Spanish

3) Religion: Roman Catholic

4) Argentina is the 8th largest country in the world and the second largest in population and area in South America after Brazil with 22 provinces and one national territory.

5) Argentina is a literal melting pot and has a cultural makeup of Italians (45%) and Spaniards (30%) who settled in the city of Cordoba and are known for their cattle, agriculture and the automotive industry. The French immigrants formed the town of Pigue, not to mention the immigrants from Poland, Russia, Switzerland and Germany, who settled in the Andes Mountains in the city of Bariloche, known for their chocolate and skiing. Bariloche is indeed a miniature of Europe. Besides, there are the immigrants from Wales who settled the city of Trelew, as well as immigrants from Denmark and England who represent the remaining 25% of nationalities present.

6) With the unique combination of cultures and foods, the result is world-renowned beef cattle, delicious pastries, chocolates, grapes, wines, apples and delectable foods with an Italian, Spanish, German, French and Swiss flare. One thing is for certain; you cannot go to Argentina without being surrounded by a multitude of culinary delights. Mouth-watering foods such as *Gnocchi's (*potato dumplings*), Milanesas (*a fried thin meat topped with egg), *Alfajores* filled with D*ulce de Leche* (shortbread sandwich cookies filled with caramel spread), Flan (caramel custard), *Chorizo* (sausage), *Empanadas de jamon y queso* (hand pies made with ham & cheese) or *Carne* (beef) with green olives, a raisin and diced egg to complete

the layers of flavors. The E*mpanadas* are usually fried in lard or oven baked and come in a variety of fillings of beef, cheese or ham, with ham being the most popular, or sweet fillings of jam, caramel or fruit.

Paul is startled by the announcement over the PA system, "Flight 1988 from Los Angeles is now arriving." The flight was a long 12-hours from California. Paul puts his hand up to his face to shield his eyes as he is nearly blinded by the glaring afternoon sun while he looks out of the window for the first glimpse of her plane. *I wonder if she'll recognize me?*

Her plane comes into view as it easily descends from the sky and lands without fanfare on the tarmac. As the plane begins its taxi towards the terminal, he notices with trepidation that the plane's right engine has burst into flames.

"Whoa! What just happened?" he exclaims. To Paul's relief, within a few seconds, the plane's emergency system activates a fire retardant spray, which quickly extinguishes the flames.

Celeste didn't realize that the engine was on fire, but was quickly alerted to it by a woman hysterically yelling, *"FUEGO! FUEGO!"* (Fire, Fire!) By the time she looked out the window for proof, it was already out. A big white plume of smoke rolled out from the plane's engine as the plane taxied to the terminal gate.

She noticed a large banner that read, *"BIENVENIDO"* (Welcome) on the side of the airport's terminal. *That is some kind of welcome!* she thought. She began to mull over why the plane would catch fire but decided that after being in the air for so long, it had likely just overheated.

Celeste was looking forward to meeting up with Paul, whom she met while in her 2nd area of missionary service. They had both served in the *Bahia Blanca* (White Bay) mission, having met at a zone conference in *Mar del Plata*, (Sea of Silver), known as the Latin Riviera. She was serving in the beachside city of *Miramar*

(Look at the sea) while he was assigned to serve in *Mar del Plata,* about 10 miles away. The friends had reconnected through social media last year, on their mission's reunion page. Celeste noticed him first and began Instant Messaging Paul, once she verified with mutual friends in the group that he was single.

Paul was eager to meet up with the beautiful Celeste, who he remembered as a bright-eyed, optimistic soul with a bubbly personality. Those thoughts of her always made him smile. He especially remembered her boisterous nature, cackling signature laugh, and brilliant smile that matched her sky-blue eyes. He hoped that those eyes hadn't been dimmed by time and life circumstances. They had tentatively planned on visiting a few of the cities in which they had served as well as refreshing themselves with the language, customs, and glorious Argentinean food!

When Paul mentioned to her three weeks ago that he was going to Argentina for an Interpol investigation for several weeks, and then invited her on a whim to join him in touring the country after it was completed, she took a bold step in their friendship and accepted the invitation. Celeste knew that it was time to step outside of her comfort zone. She had a few weeks of vacation available at work and quickly booked the flight before she had time to change her mind. That way, they could tour the country as returning Gringos (American Foreigners) together. Her mother, Mary, was concerned about her sudden travel choices, but Celeste reassured her that they wouldn't be staying in the same hotel room or doing anything inappropriate. She even had Paul call and speak with her parents to tell them that he would be honorable and not to worry, although she hadn't lived at home for more than 16 years. His call worked, and her family happily approved of the trip from that point forward.

Celeste's plane taxied up to the terminal. The plane's door finally opened to release the weary and heavy-laden passengers. Paul's legs suddenly felt unsteady, and his palms became sweaty with anticipation.

Get your emotions in check, Lago! You just saved American lives and ran with a bull without breaking a sweat. Why are you so nervous now? he thought. *I sure hope that there is chemistry between us; otherwise, this will get awkward quick.* He figured those questions would be answered shortly. *I'll just enjoy this time with my good friend and worry about the rest as we go along.*

Paul watched attentively as passenger after passenger exited into the expectant family arms with occasional cheers of *"Bienvenido hijo!"* (Welcome son!) He witnessed another family's delight as they welcomed home their missionary and remembered with tenderness his own homecoming when his family met him with cheers and a "Mission Accomplished" banner.

Paul finally spotted Celeste walking out with a larger-than-life smile on her face as she scanned the crowd in anticipation of their meeting.

She hasn't changed a bit–she is more beautiful than ever. At 35, how can she be so unchanged? he thought as he tucked in his shirt, checked his breath for freshness, and then quickly popped in a mint for good measure.

Their eyes met and locked. Paul's breath caught in his chest as time seemed to momentarily stand still. Her gaze was electrifying, and she overwhelmed him with her radiant sky-blue eyes sparkling at him from across the crowd.

She squealed in delight as she ran into his outstretched arms, which immediately enclosed her into a big bear hug.

"Oh, Paul, it is so great to see you!" she exclaimed as she kissed him on the cheek in a customary Latin welcome.

"H-h-h-ow was your flight?" he said still overwhelmed with her presence as he took the carry-on bag from her, grateful that their first meeting wasn't awkward as they walked towards the baggage claim area.

"Great, except for the plane's engine catching fire right after we landed. Did you see that?"

"No! Wait, YES! What was your question?" he said.

"That was so unnerving. One minute we're landing, and then the next minute the plane is burning, and people are yelling fire! I'm just glad that they put out the fire quickly. I feel bad for the lady sitting near me, who fainted when she saw the smoke; although looking at her now, she appears to have fully recovered."

Paul nodded in agreement as he stood back in delight and listened to her enthusiastic chatter.

"I sat by the nicest older couple all the way here, and we only had one crying toddler for a few minutes of the trip. I deem that a flight success—other than the plane's charred engine," she said triumphantly.

"I'm happy that you're here!" Paul said. He was suddenly feeling a bit overwhelmed as to what to say to this lovely woman that had literally walked back into his life. He wished that they could have reconnected years earlier but realized that all things are as they should be and was grateful for the life experiences that made them who they are today. "By the way, these are for you!" he said.

Celeste stepped back in surprise as her eyes fell upon the vibrant bouquet of yellow roses that he'd managed to keep hidden from her until now. "Thank you!" she exclaimed, reaching out and leaning in to smell them. "They're beautiful."

"I just wanted to greet you with a little sunshine to match that sunny disposition of yours."

"Aww, thanks," she said as she blushed and kissed him on the cheek. Now it was Paul's turn to go red in response to her kiss.

"Ahem…Let's get your luggage and get you to your hotel. I'm sure you're exhausted from the long flight." He quickly got back to the business of getting her through the airport terminal and then went in search of the correct baggage claim carousel. With everything retrieved and safely in one place, Paul easily hailed a taxi, as if he'd lived there all of his life. He instructed the cab driver to take them to the Hotel de *Bahia* (Bay), and they were off, speeding through the city.

"Now I remember why I didn't enjoy taking taxis while I lived here," she said.

"Yep, exactly," he said as he gave the taxi driver *the eye* in front of them. "I think that the cab drivers are racecar driver wannabes," he continued as they held on to each other as their driver turned a corner too fast and then weaved in and out of traffic as if he was competing in NASCAR.

"Not much has changed," said Paul. "They still drive without stopping while honking their horns through each intersection, with the largest car yielding to the smaller one."

"I've forgotten how you can take your life in your hands, whether you're a passenger or a pedestrian standing on the corner. I must admit that taking a taxi is a quick and efficient way to get around, rather than taking the bus," said Celeste. "I remember riding the local bus here; it was usually standing room only with people hanging out of the open doors as it sped along to the next stop. I've lost count how many times I had to take the bus with my luggage in tow for transfers. How I managed to survive that as a missionary? I'll never know," she said, shaking her head in disbelief.

In no time, they arrived at the quaint Hotel de Bahia. "I've already checked you in and prepaid for your room," he said. "That way we can bypass the line and get you settled in within a matter of minutes. I hope that you like your room. It has an excellent view of downtown Buenos Aires," he said. "It's not far from where the agency has me staying. Here's my phone number in case you need anything." Paul gave her a quick hug goodbye, saying, "Rest up. I'll be back around 9 pm if you feel up to doing something fun tonight."

"Absolutely and thank you" said Celeste as she nodded in anticipation.

"Great! We can go to this great dinner and dancing restaurant. They're hosting a Tango Dance competition that you won't want to miss–it's going to be epic."

"Sounds exciting," she said as she politely shooed him out of the door; she was in urgent need of a nap.

As she closed the door, Paul put his arm inside it, stopping it momentarily to say, "Don't forget that in few days, I'll be taking you to an Air B&B. It is much quieter than staying weeks in a hotel."

"Bye, Paul, and thanks again for everything. I'm so glad that I'm here with you."

"See you tonight then," said Paul. Celeste could only smile and blow him a kiss in gratitude as she closed the door.

After finding a nice vase to put her flowers in, she allowed herself to decompress saying, "Ah, finally! Time to relax." Celeste reminded herself to make sure that she used both the power and gadget adapters on her blow dryer and curling iron instead of blowing them out on their first use as she had done the first time that she was in the country. *You can't just plug your hairdryer into a 220-Volt adapter with its round pronged outlet as a North American outlet is designed with a flat pronged 120-Volt plug."* A random quote came to mind from one of her favorite seasonal movies, "The Holiday" about a square peg not going into a round hole, which kept going through her head as she prepared to get into the shower.

"*I wonder if this renewed friendship will finally gain some traction?*" Since becoming reacquainted with Paul months earlier, this was a recurring thought in her mind. She stepped up into the fifties-looking, nostalgic bathroom and was immediately transported back in time by its baby blue and white tiles, pull chain toilet, and hand-held shower wand just above it. There was no actual shower stall, just the tiled floor with a sunken drain in the middle of the room.

As she undressed, she was reminded of the importance of having a squeegee to clean everything up and quickly located a well-used one next to the sink before turning on the hot water valve for her shower. She lifted the shower wand over her head, allowing the warm, soothing water to alleviate all of the travel stress and wariness as it went right down the drain. The hot water was relaxing, and she stayed under it for an extra few minutes, relishing in its warmth and comfort.

She remembered a time when hot water propane tanks were in short supply, during her first winter there. She had to heat water on a two-burner hot plate for lightning-fast "bucket" bathing with the limited warm water and then rinse the shampoo out of her hair with the ice-cold tap water, resulting in brain freeze. She shivered at the thought of all of the cold baths that she took that winter.

After her shower, she felt like a new woman as she wrapped her long, blonde hair and body up in large towels and made a beeline for the bed with a sigh. "Ah, this is the life!" she said aloud, plopping down on the bed and burrowing her head under the covers to stay warm for a much-needed siesta. She needed to rest up, knowing full well that she would be going out for a late dinner that evening as the standard dinnertime was between 9-11 p.m. for most Argentine families.

As she drifted off to sleep, she felt at peace that she was back in her beloved Argentina. Celeste recalled with fondness the missionary experiences that changed her life for the better. Being a missionary is not for the faint of heart; it is downright hard. It took lots of rejection, cancelled appointments, walking in the heat, dirt-riddled winds, rain, and cold temperatures to share your testimony of the gospel of Jesus Christ, that she held so dear to her heart. Yes, it was hard, but she learned so much: the language, a love for the people, their customs, to work, serve, pray, study hard, persevere, love unlovable companions and be forgiving of her and their imperfections. She had learned an important lesson in working with each companion as her best, and their best efforts may have been different but were equally acceptable in God's eyes. That was only the beginning of how her mission had changed her life.

Her favorite memories were of the wonderful people that she'd met as they came to know God, were baptized, and willingly changing their lives for the better because they knew where they came from, why they were here, and where they were going after this life. That life-changing knowledge and then adding to the truth that they already had, made life worth living and gave her greater purpose.

Yes, it had been the most difficult thing that she'd ever done in her life, but it was also the most rewarding. Those experiences truly brought out her best self. The thought came to her that *everything worthwhile was worth the struggle and sacrifice involved.* She remembered one of her spiritual advisors telling her that the word, *sacrifice*, meant, "to do something sacred." Indeed, the work was sacred and of upmost importance. With that last recollection, she drifted off into a blissful sleep.

CHAPTER 2

Tango Wars!

BRRRRINNNG! BRRRRINNNG! Celeste awoke with a jolt as her body bolted up in bed, grabbing blindly in all directions for the phone in a fuzzy, sleepy frenzy.

"Hey Celeste, it's Paul. Can I come pick you up in about fifteen minutes?"

"Sure! But how can that be as I'm certain that I just went to sleep a few minutes ago!"

"Yeah, the time has a way of flying by when you are recovering from jet lag," said Paul with a chuckle of understanding.

She focused her eyes on the clock then counted the time she'd slept with her fingers. "I can't believe that I slept for nearly seven hours!" she exclaimed. "Thanks for the call. See you soon!" She was glad that he'd thought to call her; otherwise, she would have slept right on through 'til morning.

Boy, that man understands jet lag and how to politely make sure that I didn't oversleep, she thought. She quickly jumped out of bed in speedy preparation only to find as she looked in the mirror, that her hair had dried in a beehive shape within her towel. *I'm going to have to wet it back down and blow-dry it to fix this mess.* She quickly dressed and put on her makeup. She didn't want Paul to have to wait long.

She successfully utilized the correct adapter for her blow dryer and considered it a major victory that she didn't blow it out on its first use. It was a good thing that she was a pro at the quick hairstyle and no-nonsense make-up, which suited her fair, porcelain complexion that she jokingly referred to as the *skin of royalty,* especially when she got sunburned. Just as she got her jeans and cute baby blue V-neck sweater on, Paul texted her to let her know that he'd arrived.

I'm here! When you're ready, just meet me in the lobby."

Thanks, will do! She texted back, as she added a tasteful necklace, silver glittered hoop earrings, a spritz of her favorite vanilla sandalwood scented perfume and slipped into her practical, comfy leather loafers to complete her ensemble. She was ready and out the door in a matter of minutes. *Lynda will be so impressed with my 15-minute makeover, which is a personal best record. She's going find that hard to beat*, she thought, wishing she had a few extra minutes to call and tell her identical twin sister of her triumph.

As she walked out of her room towards the elevator, she was transported back in time, to a scene from a favorite classic movie "That Touch of Mink." She waited as the elevator slowly creaked its way towards her floor and stepped into a similar looking elevator from the movie. She pretended for a brief moment that she was the elegant, beautiful leading lady Doris Day meeting up with the tall, dark, and handsome Cary Grant as the vintage elevator groaned and moaned its way back down to the main floor.

When the sliding gate door opened up to the lobby, Paul was standing there smiling mischievously with a single red rose in between his front teeth. He took it out of his mouth and gave her a standard Latin kiss on the cheek in greeting. Celeste giggled in delight at his playfulness as butterflies fluttered in her stomach in anticipation of going out on the town together for their first date.

"The rose is so that you are prepared to Tango with Me-Go tonight after the competition is over. Get it? Tango with Me-Go?" he said, laughing at his cleverness. She enjoyed his play on words and quirky sense of humor.

"That is so thoughtful of you," she said. She was looking forward to getting some considerable one on one face-time with this romantic and considerate man. A spark of hope fluttered in her stomach just looking into his handsome, brown eyes, sending a flood of pure happiness into her heart that had been dormant.

Paul suddenly stopped dead in his tracks and just stood there staring at her before saying, "WOW! You look beautiful!"

Celeste's blush nearly matched the color of the rose and said, "Thank you for the beautiful rose," as she inhaled deeply. "Its fragrance is intoxicating."

"My pleasure. Umm, you're intoxicating," he said as he secured the rose in her hair with a few well-placed bobby pins. Paul then gently took her hand in his and then kissed the back of it chivalrously and bowed. "Anything for you, Celeste." She felt her checks flush to match the rose once again.

Paul, noticing her embarrassment, snapped back to business and said, "We've got to get a move on if we're going to keep our reservation tonight at Club Rosita's." He took her hand in his and began walking towards the hotel's front door. "You'll love the atmosphere as it is an old converted hotel that they transformed into a night club, featuring the beloved *Tango after Dinner*. I hope that you don't mind walking with me; the night is perfect for a nice stroll, and the venue isn't too far away."

"These feet were made for roaming these vibrant streets," said Celeste. "Let's go!"

A few blocks away, they crossed the world's widest Avenue, named "Avenida de 9 de Julio," (July 9th Ave.) in honor of the day in 1816 that Argentineans celebrated their independence from Spain. Paul went into tour guide mode as they walked, saying, "The Avenue is 460 feet across from sidewalk to sidewalk, and everything about it is BIG, including the buildings, the billboards, and the trees in this huge capital of Buenos Aires."

Paul and Celeste had to sprint across the Avenue before the next bunch of cars headed their way, as the traffic would not be slowing down for them. Safely across, they stopped to enjoy the beauty of the Avenue with its bustling city life.

"Let's take a selfie to send home to your family so that they know that you've arrived safe and sound," said Paul.

"You're a man after my own heart," said Celeste. "I'm known as the family shutterbug at all of our get-togethers. I cringe at the thought of passing up any opportunity to create special memories through pictures."

"I agree. Isn't it amazing that only a few weeks ago, we were in the middle of spring in the Northern Hemisphere, and now we're walking through colorful, crunchy autumn leaves and enjoying the cool fall weather here in the Southern Hemisphere?"

"Yes, it's truly incredible. I'm grateful for this opportunity to enjoy the fall weather twice this year!"

As they walked hand in hand down the tree-lined sidewalk and crossed the cobblestone street towards Rosita's, Celeste noticed how energized the evening was, with many people out socializing with their neighbors. There were families out walking and enjoying the autumn weather with vendors selling yummy *helado*s (ice creams) on the sidewalk. Her favorite aroma was that of the roasting cinnamon, vanilla, and sugarcoated Spanish peanuts made on sight. They were such a sweet memory of her time spent in Argentina. She took it all in and was certainly renewed by the man holding her hand, as he exuberantly played thumb wars with her as they walked and talked. She noticed that he always let her win, even though his reflexes were considerably faster than hers.

Paul stopped in front of the Spanish peanut vendor's cart as if he had read her mind, saying, "May I buy you some of the best peanuts this side of the equator?"

"Yes, please. I was thinking how yummy those would be to eat about now!"

He quickly bought her the cone-shaped bag of warm toasted sweet nuts and handed it to her to enjoy as they walked.

Celeste put the first few candied peanuts into her mouth and savored the experience fully. "Mmmm…they taste so decadent. I don't think there is anything better that I could eat first than these yummy gems."

"I just love the smell and taste of the Spanish nuts," he said as she passed the bag over for him to enjoy his first taste of bliss.

"I dream about these," said Celeste. "What makes them so special is that they cook them in fine copper kettle pans and use pure concentrated vanilla bean paste, which is added in the final few seconds after they are taken off of the heat. If Heaven had an aroma, it would be this one."

"I agree!" Paul said.

Just then, an Australian Shepherd happily bounded up to Paul with a stick in its mouth, wanting to play. "Hey, he reminds me of my dog Scooby, who our family had growing up in Southern California. I think he wants us to play fetch with him" said Paul.

"Can I throw the stick first to see if Scooby will come back to me?" asked Celeste.

Paul took the stick out of the dog's mouth and then handed it to her. She threw it up against a huge, beautiful, blooming Magnolia tree that had been planted many years before, on the far side of the brick-paved sidewalk. The dog ran and picked it up, but just stood there with the stick in its mouth, wondering which one of them he should give the stick to. Celeste decided that she'd help the dog out by saying, "Come here! Come on, boy!" The dog just stood there with its head cocked to the side with wonder in its eyes.

Paul said, "I think he only understands Spanish. V*en Aqui*!" With that command, the dog happily galloped right back to Paul and placed the stick in front of him for another throw! Paul obliged, and the dog returned again and again after each throw as they continued their walk.

"You are so smart, Paul. The thought never crossed my mind to command him in Spanish." After his final throw, Paul gave the cute pup a few peanuts, which were happily consumed, and off it went trotting down the street, having been paid in full for its playtime offering.

As they neared the restaurant, a friendly-looking Siamese cat came right up to Paul and rubbed its head and body against his leg in adoration. "I think that it has claimed you as its own," said Celeste.

Paul nodded in agreement. He couldn't resist it and bent down and placed his index finger near its nose for a proper introduction and then stroked its back to fulfill the cat's request for some immediate attention.

"Hey, you cute little thing, what's your name?" He shifted the cat's collar to read the heart shaped nametag. "Hey! Her name is Faun! Hi, beautiful Faunie girl! You're such a sweet girl," he said in a baby-like voice, as he showered her in attention. The cat purred loudly in contentment at having her wish fulfilled. Paul meowed his favorite cat food jingle, "Meow, Meow, Meow, Meow. Meow,

Meow, Meow, Meow…" to the delight of both Celeste and Faun.

Celeste couldn't stop smiling and said, "With all of the attention that you're getting from the animals, it looks like you are their favorite human, kind of like a Dr. Doolittle."

Paul sheepishly smiled and said, "Yeah, I sort of am. Animals have always been attracted to me, as much as I am to them."

"Sounds like it is a special gift that you've been given. It shows that you have an inviting, calming aura and kind spirit," said Celeste. "They know that the instant that they catch your scent and come looking for you. That's pretty neat! You are a good soul, no doubt; animals never make a mistake on something like that."

Paul smiled and said, "I've never thought of it that way. Thanks."

As they continued towards their destination, they admired the beautiful European architecture designs of the buildings with small cinder block sidewalks and cobbled stone streets. It was a magical evening with the stars shining brightly as if welcoming them back home. Paul took a moment to point out which stars were out and where. "Look, there is the Southern Cross constellation right there," then out of nowhere said, "Did you notice that the water goes down the drain counter clockwise here?"

"I actually didn't realize that detail," said Celeste. "I'll remember to verify that fact the next time that I flush."

Enjoying the evening sky with this thoughtful man walking by her side made her heart sing for joy. He made her feel so very special, and she wondered why he had never married. She realized that she had never married either, so maybe some things were just worth waiting for, and there was a time and season for all things to occur. Celeste began humming one of her favorite hymns, "To Become as He."

Paul asked, "What song is that? It's beautiful. Would you sing it to me?

"Sure," said Celeste. "I'm amazed to be His child. Yes, I'm amazed I'm a King's child. He walks beside me through every trial. Yes, I am amazed to become as He. He is my Lord, my Savior; my all; through thick and thin and where-with-all. His Love for me is my all in all. Yes, I'm amazed to become as He."

"You have the voice of an angel," he said. "Would you sing the rest of it for me?"

"The King of Kings, He is my Lord. Yes, the King of Kings, He is my Lord; as He guides me to be my all. Yes, I'm amazed to become as He."

"He ministers to me, then I to thee. Yes, He ministers to me then I to thee. He ministers to me and every sheep. Yes, I'm amazed to become as He."

"He walks by me in every change. Yes, I'm amazed that He heals my pain; as He guides me to my eternal gain. Yes, I'm amazed to become as He."

"He is my Lord, My Savior; my all; through thick and thin and where-with-all. His Love for me is my all in all. Yes, I'm amazed to become as He."

They walked the last block to their destination in silence as they contemplated the words to the gospel hymn in wonderment.

As they drew nearer to 'Rosita's', the energy of the evening suddenly increased tenfold, with many people milling around the front of the venue waiting to get in before the dance competition began for the evening. The inviting aromas of the club's cuisine beckoned them in, full of anticipation.

"This is going to be a fantastic evening of duels of the dancing sort–Tango style. I've reserved a little table for two upfront for us to eat and enjoy the competition up close, as I know the owner, Rosita! You're going to be enchanted with the artistry, energy, passion, and pure joy of the Tango, as these competitions are extremely fierce!" said, Paul.

Paul checked in with his waiter friend, Mateo, who said that their table would be ready in about 10 minutes. Since they had a few minutes to spare, they decided to sit outside on the patio furniture and people-watch. Paul said, "Don't you think that man looks like a doctor? Just look at the starched white coat, the way that he holds his head so dignified and walks with purpose."

Then Celeste pointed. "Look over there! That girl looks like she is a dancer, as she walks with the grace of a prima ballerina, plus I think I see evidence of ballet ribbons hanging out of her backpack." They decided to expand their game by making up life stories about each person passing by.

"That couple has five children and are out for the first time together in ages," said, Paul.

"Yeah, for sure. You can tell that they are parents of young children. They have a tired excitement in their eyes and happy contentment to be alone together, as they share their ice cream cone. Looks like they are savoring every bite and holding on dearly to this alone time!" agreed Celeste.

Paul said, "Look, that old man looks like he's going to visit his true love as he is holding a bouquet of blue Hydrangea flowers and walking with a happy gait."

"That teenage couple over there just had a big fight, as she is sitting with her arms crossed with her legs and feet pointed away from the boy next to her. Her face says, *if you say another word, buddy, we're history*!" said Celeste.

Paul and Celeste both chuckled at their creative observations. Still, they mostly enjoyed sitting outside and appreciating the beautiful weather, great people, and the cool vibe of the city.

Mateo finally signaled to Paul that their table was ready. They both jumped up in delight, hardly containing their excitement as they were escorted to their table to be formally seated. As they were given their linen napkins and menus, they saw a few dozen dancers lined up, mentally preparing for the competition.

"The contestant's costumes are Flamenco in style, with many dressed up in the traditional Spaniard attire. You'll notice the men are dressed as Matadors, ready for the charging of the bulls," explained Paul. "Remind me to tell you later about my own bull story that happened recently while on assignment."

The women had on the traditional Flamenco dresses with beautiful white and black shawls with matching laced veil combs in their hair, accented by a red rose. Their fair Spanish skin looked radiant in contrast with their dark brown eyes and hair. Besides the great costumes and dancing, Celeste was excited to be eating the most incredible cuisine on earth; the culinary art that is Spanish, Italian, Swiss, German, and French all rolled up into unforgettable meat dishes and desserts, comparable to the finest cuisines of the world. She could hardly wait to sink her teeth into her favorite *Gnocchis* (potato dumplings topped with a meat marinara sauce) or *Milanesa* (fried thin steak/veal with a sunny side egg on top) with French bread for dinner. And no dinner would be complete without a serving of the beloved *Alfajores (two shortbread cookies between a soft caramel spread and dipped in chocolate)* for dessert. Just the thought of each food made her mouth water in anticipation.

"What would you like to eat for your first meal, Señorita Celeste?" inquired Paul.

"I've got to have the *Gnocchis* first, but I'm struggling with wanting the *Milanesa* as well," she said.

"What if I order the *Milanesa* and you order the *Gnocchis*, and then we can share?" offered Paul.

"Perfect! Thank you," said Celeste.

While they shared their delicious meals, Celeste noticed that Paul thoughtfully gave her the first bite of food from his plate. As their dinner progressed, they spoke of the mission companions that they had served with and reminisced fondly about many of the cities that they lived in and the families that they had met along with a few fun stories.

Celeste shared one of her more memorable experiences of riding her bike following a significant rainstorm in her big blue clunky rain boots around the outer city dirt roads of Miramar one winter.

"One time, I stopped for a moment to pull out my schedule and check the time before our next appointment. As I put my rain boot down to come to a complete the stop, my boot didn't get any traction in the mud and kept sliding in towards the bike, digging deeper into the muddy road until I tipped over with a big splat on the ground. I ended up covered from head to toe in mud!" Celeste just laughed at the memory of not being able to save herself. "Good thing we didn't have cell phones back then, as I know I would have been all over social media," she said, chuckling.

"I recall a time when a sheet of water unexpectedly came pouring down from the sky as I walked on the sidewalk of an apartment building, which soaked me clean through. I later found out that it was a baby's bathwater being tossed out of a window; thankfully, without the baby," Paul said with a laugh.

Celeste mentioned the time when she and her companion were walking in the rain and came upon a mud puddle. "I decided that I'd splash right on through it since I had my rain boots on, but realized too late that it was no small rain puddle, but at least a foot deep," she giggled. "I was covered in mud up to my knees and couldn't stop laughing at how an innocent little puddle could cause such a mess." They relished being near one another and that they could reminisce about the time spent in the country.

"Hey, before the competition begins, do you want to hear a few factoid tidbits about the Tango's origins?" said Paul eager to continue impressing Celeste with his knowledge.

"Sure!" she said, nodding in interest.

"Did you know that the Tango is the second national anthem? It's the country's most authentic form of popular music, where the legendary clubs gave birth to the Tango. The Tango is both sensual and melancholic, so it is intimately identified with Argentina's core. Its exact debut is a mystery, but one thing is certain, it did not take place in reputable company. It most likely came from questionable venues here in Buenos Aires."

Celeste just nodded, amazed at his memory recall and knowledge of the country.

"Did you know the King of the Tango is Carlos Gardel?"

"No, I didn't," said Celeste.

Before he could finish his thought, the emcee announced the start of the competition boldly, *"Bienvenidos muchachas y muchachos para una noche de Guerras de Tango!"* (Welcome ladies and gentlemen, to tonight's Tango Wars).

The competing teams came out two by two, with the women beautifully clothed in dresses of red, white, black and green colors adorned in satin and lace fabrics of various patterns. The details of the costumes resulted in a breathtaking overall effect. Each women's beautiful, shiny, long black hair was pulled back tightly into a low bun with a beautiful red rose added to complete the look. They were mesmerizing. The men were also decked out as Matadors from Spain and Italy; they were truly delightful to behold as well.

The emcee introduced the first couple of the evening, as the Bandoneon player (Argentinian/Spanish instrument similar to an accordion) and guitarist began to play the vibrant staccato (sharply detached notes) Tango music and the competition was off to an exciting start! *"Empezamos la guerras de Tango ahora!* (Let's begin the Tango wars now!)"

The first couple began their intense dance of love, rejection,

Loralee Lago

reunion, and passion. The man machine-gun tapped his feet as the señorita clapped her hands while holding a retracted red lace fan over her head as she gracefully strolled around him. They embraced quickly, and then began dancing, their feet rapidly weaving effortlessly between one another in choreographed perfection. They strode cheek-to-cheek in reunion, ending with a low dip for the grand finale. The couple's dance was flawless and they received a standing ovation from the wildly appreciative crowd.

"Wow!" Paul exclaimed. "They set the bar high for the remaining couples. This is a dancing war in every sense of the word." They noticed as men eyed men in fierce rivalry, and the women did the same with the other women as each couple danced exuberantly with the music.

"I wish I were one of the women competing tonight," Celeste said to Paul, as she got caught up in the excitement of the competition and entrancing music.

"I want to compete in the Tango as well, but I'm afraid I have two left feet," said Paul. The evening was filled with fierce passion as the competition kept them on the edge of their seats, wondering how the next duo could possibly outdo the prior dancers to claim the 20,000 Pesos grand prize ($5,000 USD) and bragging rights for the next year.

Before they knew it, the emcee was announcing the final couple competing for the evening. "Please clap your hands in appreciation for our final couple competing this evening, Señor Carlos and Señorita Graciela!"

They began their dance of love and passion, much like the other couples, but there was something different about these two dancers. They seemed to be supercharged as they danced with so much energy, passion, and even fierce anger in their eyes! Their feet seemed to be on fire as they danced their tangled web of love and passion, and there appeared to be vapors of smoke coming from their shoes.

Paul leaned over and whispered into Celeste's ear, saying, "I think these two are going to take it. They are incredible!" Celeste nodded in agreement.

At the end of their dance, the Matador dipped his señorita into final submission, but let her fall to the ground to the surprise of all the spectators as both partners erratically jumped and screamed in agony. Each dancer was now on the ground unsuccessfully trying to get their shoes off!

The music came to an abrupt stop as they screamed, *"Fuego! Fuego! Por favor, ayuda me!"* (Fire, fire! Please help me!) Before the audience knew what had happened, the couple were desperately clinging to each other and expressed their unwavering love for one another saying, *"Te quiero mi amor"* (I need you my love) before dying in each other's arms as they collapsed motionless in a crumpled heap over one another.

The audience simultaneously gasped in bewilderment at what they had just witnessed. Paul sprang into action, leaping over their tabletop in a single bound and began administering CPR. His efforts were of no avail, even as the onsite paramedics continued with the CPR to try and revive the lifeless dancers. People were paralyzed with fear as they realized something was very amiss to have both dancers die during the final performance of the evening.

Paul, accustomed to taking matters into his own hands, quickly took his napkin from their table, and carefully took the shoe off from the body of Graciela, the fallen Flamenco dancer. To his utter shock, seared into her sole were the initials O.N. He then took the shoe off Carlos's foot, which revealed that he also had the same initials branded onto his sole. *"Why would someone want to brand and kill these dancers?"* wondered Paul. *"And how does this relate to the other murders and the American couple that we just rescued?"*

Paul looked over the acid engraved feet of Graciela and Carlos, quickly assessing that this was a homicide investigation and immediately ordering the staff to cordon off the area. He had to make sure that no evidence tampering occurred before the police arrived. They would need to talk to any witnesses and the other competing couples. Celeste wondered who would want to kill the Tango dancers and why. What did O.N. mean, and why did they die in such a horrific manner? She pondered what else contributed to their deaths, as they wouldn't instantly die from acid-engraved feet.

Paul instructed Rosita, "Close all the doors. Let no one in or out except the Police–we need to keep everyone inside, but away from the dancers. We need to keep anyone from coming into the crime scene and let the police interview everyone here to determine any motive in the painful and rapid demise of Graciela and Carlos." He wondered, *Was there a motive of hate, revenge, a lover's triangle, or previous dancing competition scuffles that might have instigated such a murder?*

Celeste wisely stayed out of the way once Police Captain Lucas, Lieutenant Sosa, Detective Molina and a slew of other officers arrived at the murder scene to begin the arduous task of interviewing everyone as a forensic team analyzed and photographed the crime scene. Celeste could tell that it was going to be a long night.

Paul wondered what other factors contributed to their deaths, as he recalled seeing the smoke coming out of their shoes and began going through which chemicals could both severely burn the skin and get into the blood stream so quickly in his mind. These and other questions raced through his head as he began writing down each question in rapid succession in a pocket-sized notebook that he always carried on him, so that he could try and make sense of such a painful demise.

As the police interviewed people, Paul overheard a couple that had competed testifying to Captain Lucas, "There was a big fight between Carlos and Graciela just before the competition began, about his work on the Susaniche Ranch. Graciela disapproved of his long working hours and not having the time and proper preparation for the dance competition, and especially that he did not have time for her. She yelled in his face, 'IT'S OVER! WE ARE THROUGH AFTER WE DANCE!'

"Carlos had asked her to quiet down and that they would discuss it once the competition was over. She told him, 'There is nothing more to discuss, as we've fought about this countless times with no resolution! You will never change; I can see that. I am a fool to believe otherwise. We're through!'"

Another couple in the competition had witnessed Carlos and Graciela fighting and chided them for arguing publicly, saying, "If you can't get yourselves together before the competition, you might as well bow out now, because we're going to smoke your socks off." That challenge added fuel to the fire, making them want to win the competition more fervently.

Interestingly enough, "Carlos and Graciela's last dance was the best Tango of their lives," commented one of the judges, "They certainly deserved the grand prize," as their anger and passion-filled emotions fueled their dance to epic proportions. The crowd had gone wild with their applause, witnessing the fire in their eyes and smoking feet. They had danced flawlessly, cheek-to-cheek and side-to-side with rapid-fire foot movements and clicks. It was truly a performance of a lifetime for them, until their untimely death by Tango.

Rosita issued orders to the her staff to serve calming Chamomile tea and Mate with bread, making sure that all inside remained subdued until the authorities could interview them. Each patron at the club just wanted to go home, but remained seated and quiet as instructed to help the investigation move forward more rapidly. Celeste found it interesting to watch the police methodically go through the crowd of people, taking down pertinent information in detail and then continuing the process over and over again.

There were more than three hundred people packed inside the club for several hours. Lieutenant Miguel Sosa divided the people up into groups of persons of interest and persons of no interest.

Those persons of no interest were soon dismissed, with a caveat that they should stay in the city, as further questions may be forthcoming. Paul and Celeste remained with the persons of interest group and spoke with Police Captain Cory Lucas, whom Paul had worked with previously while finishing up his own Interpol investigation.

Captain Lucas said, "Thank you Paul, for securing the area. Would you stay and answer additional questions to assist us in preparing a timeline of the events leading up to their deaths? We're short-handed tonight, due to the *"Tus Ojos son Mis Ojos"* (Your eyes are my eyes) concert." Paul was pleased to help and offered to assist in the investigation in whatever way that they needed.

Paul quickly pointed out Celeste to Captain Lucas in introduction, to which Captain Lucas responded by saying, "*Muy bonita es tu novia.* (Your girlfriend is very beautiful) *Mucho gusto,*" (I'm pleased to meet you) he said, as he extended his hand with a quick handshake and slight bow. "I am sorry that we've met under such unfortunate circumstances."

This made Celeste flush, as she wasn't anyone's girlfriend at this point in the friendship, although, with a start, she realized that she wasn't opposed to it in this case. Paul quickly hemmed and hawed, then regurgitated the same random facts to her as before to cover up his embarrassment saying, "Did you know the Tango is the second national anthem, called "Mi Querida Buenos Aires? (My dear Buenos Aires) It is the country's most authentic form of popular music where the legendary clubs gave birth to the Tango. The Tango is both a sensual and melancholic music, so it intimately identifies with Argentina and its nerve center."

Celeste just nodded methodically before redirecting the conversation by asking, "So, what's next?"

Paul told her that the process of interviewing everyone, including every last detail of their time at the club and the day's activities leading up to the competition, took significant time. They gained all pertinent information and detained and interviewed anyone even remotely suspected in their deaths, which would likely take most of the night. Once that was accomplished, Captain Lucas, Lieutenant Sosa, Detective Molina and other officers would take the remaining persons of interest back to the police station for further questioning and evaluation.

Captain Lucas particularly placed his focus on the couple that was seen chiding Carlos and Graciela, who said they'd "Smoke their socks off!" He made sure to leave no stone unturned within the critical first few hours of the investigation. Celeste knew that they would be among the crowd, taking a free ride to police headquarters.

Celeste, who was always one to be prepared and cringed at the thought of missing a meal, wrapped up and stuffed the few remaining French bread baguette slices with packets of *Dulce de Leche* (caramel spread) left on their table into her purse. She knew that it would be quite a while before they'd be able to eat. Many questions at the crime scene kept going over in her head as to why someone would do such a thing in such a horrendous way to these two dancers.

As expected, they were detained and escorted via police cruiser to the police station for further questioning. The only thing that the department could offer them to drink was *Mate*. After all of the questioning and re-questioning, Celeste gratefully accepted the *Mate from Detective Mia Molina* and then pulled out the four crumbling baguette slices and *Dulce de Leche* packets from her purse. She politely shared her meager meal with Paul when he came back briefly with updates, as well as with the kind lady sitting next to her who was eyeing her food hungrily.

Hours later, Paul returned from talking with Captain Lucas for the last time, and told her that they were free to leave. To brighten up a bleak morning, Paul mentioned, "How about we go for a nice relaxing Brunch of Pastries, French bread with *Dulce de Leche*, a few Alfajores and Café Malta to wash it all down? There's a café nearby on the corner. Then, we can walk the few blocks back to your hotel, so that you can get some much-needed rest."

"Yes, please," said Celeste. As tired as she was, the mention of eating at the *Panaderia* (bakery) sounded like just the ticket. "Who can ever say *no* to Alfajores and pastries?"

Once Paul dropped her off at the hotel, he jogged the short distance to his apartment to help clear his mind and try and get some sleep. Celeste found it next to impossible to get any rest, as too many unresolved questions swirled in her head. She decided to write out a timeline of facts on her own, to help make sense of it all in hopes that it would allow her mind to settle and doze off to sleep. In her observation, it didn't appear that the police had found a clear motive or murder suspect among the crowd. She wrote:

1. Why were these people killed? Greed? A lover's triangle? Revenge? Did they just happen to be at the wrong place and time, or were they part of something much bigger?
2. What does O.N. stand for? Why would that be seared on their feet? Why would someone go to such extreme efforts to make them suffer and die in such an excruciating manner?
3. Why did he work so far out of town?
4. What could the couple have been arguing about that caused their fight in the first place? What was it that she said? "You never have time for me anymore."
5. What was he doing that took so much time away from her?

After writing these questions out on the hotel's stationery and reviewing the scene in her mind for additional clues, she was able to make peace with her busy brain and drifted off to sleep for a few minutes until the phone rang. *BBBrrriiinnnggg*! She bolted up towards the ceiling in sleepy astonishment! She fumbled to find the phone and the correct speaking side of the receiver, answering, "Hello? I mean…hola?"

"Celeste." It was Paul. "Are you up? I can't sleep and need to talk, to try and make sense of everything."

She fibbed, trying to save face, and said, "Yeah, I'm up." Celeste quickly pulled out her notes that she'd left on the night stand by the phone and then shared what she'd written to see if Paul had any other ideas to add that might help them both make sense of it all. Together they came up with a timeline of events of the evening, in hopes that it would shed some additional light on the murders.

Paul added, "The couple's fight appears to be a key point to the investigation. Something is happening on the Pampas (grassy plains) that is the cause of their very public break-up before their untimely deaths." Paul also mentioned, "Tomorrow, I'd like to drive out to Carlos's employer and ask additional questions with permission from Captain Lucas, as he had a feeling about a few more possible motives once they got a better feel for what was going on."

"Sure, I'd be happy to go," said Celeste.

Once Paul was talked out, he paused to think for a moment. The phone connection became eerily quiet on his side of the line and all that she could hear was heavy rhythmic breathing, followed by a steady snore. She supposed that Paul had finally felt that enough information had been talked through and fell fast asleep. Celeste gingerly hung up the phone and immediately fell into a deep sleep.

CHAPTER 3

Feed Me

Early the next morning, Celeste awoke to the chant of the paperboy, singing *"Diario"* (newspaper) repeatedly in the streets as he walked selling the morning paper. Celeste knew what would be on the front page of the paper. She appreciated the calming melody, as it reminded her that life did go on, even amid a time of crisis.

Her stomach loudly growled in complaint that it needed food *pronto* (immediately.) She groggily got out of bed and went into the bathroom for a much-needed shower to wash off all of the sad events of their evening out. Celeste was grateful to be alive another day and for her family and friends that cared and loved her. She appreciated living a life that was not in constant fear of someone seeking to take it and that she was blessed to have her faith and family to keep her grounded. Looking at the vibrant blooming yellow roses gave her confidence that all was still right with the world, which comforted her.

She knew that making right choices, along with daily prayer, scripture study and service to others, kept her life in balance and fulfilled. As she brushed her hair, she sang a favorite children's primary song with vigor: "I can do hard things, with the strength of the Lord. I know He's with me, as He's been before. For I know the right from wrong and I can be forever strong with the Savior by my side. For I can do hard things with the strength of the Lord." She made a mental note to call her family more often to tell them of her love, as she realized that you could never say those words enough to those that you care about the most. *You just never know when it might be your last day of life, and I want to live it with as few regrets as possible,* she thought.

Once she was ready to go, she planned to take a little walk to the corner *Panaderia* (bakery), which was nearly on every corner in the city for some breakfast. One thing that she knew for certain was that Argentineans lived on an abundance of proteins and carbs. She could hardly wait to sink her teeth into her all-time favorite *Pastellitos de Mil Hojas* (Thousand-leaf pastry). She nearly collided with Paul, who was rapidly walking in just as she stepped out of the front door.

"Celeste, I'm glad that you're already up. Will you come with me to Cordoba now? It is a town established by the Spaniards, where Carlos has been working for the last few years," said Paul.

Celeste barely had time to respond. "Yes, I guess, but... I'm really hungry!" As she was promptly escorted to the waiting car without her favorite breakfast, which was *NO BUENO*! (Not good!) Somehow, she would have to get something to eat and soon before she got extremely hungry! *Note to self,* she thought, *it appears that Paul doesn't fully understand the importance that a woman never goes hungry,* as they sped down the Avenida de Argentina towards

Loralee Lago

Cordoba.

"I really need to get something to eat, Paul. I get the shakes and become irritable if I don't," she said urgently.

"Sure. Sure...no problem." Paul said, only half listening and nodding his head to appease her, completely missing the importance of her request. He was focused solely on fulfilling Captain Lucas's request, especially since he had his hands full interviewing all of the persons locally and had specifically asked Paul to investigate several leads that were of vital importance to the case. Captain Lucas had stressed that they could not wait even an extra few minutes before the trail went cold.

Celeste barely got in a, "Where are we going again?"

"We're heading to Cordoba, in the Pampas, the home of the *Gaucho* (cowboy) who is compared to the modern-day cowboy. I need to interview the owner of the Ranch where Carlos worked. Captain Lucas has asked that I find out what he knows about what happened, get a feel for the area and why Carlos worked so far out of town each week." As he continued explaining the assignment in detail, Celeste's mind drifted to what she had studied about the Pampas.

The Pampas are world-renowned for their beef herds consisting of Aberdeen, Angus, Hereford, and the famous Holando breed of cattle, which is only bred in Argentina. Her stomach growled loudly in complaint, reminding her that it was way past her normal breakfast time. She began thinking about eating her favorite ragu sauce with *Gnocchis* and quickly decided to divert her thoughts back to the subject of the Pampas to keep from getting irritated at Paul for not bringing snacks! *How could he not bring snacks? Doesn't he know anything about women? Sheesh.... Okay,* she thought, *calm down and think about the Pampas, with its prairieland, cattle, ribs, chicken... Pampas, Sopapillas (fry bread), Thousand-leaf Pastry, Chocolate Flan, Rolled Steak... ah, get back on track!*

To divert her mind to other things, Celeste pulled up the travel guide app on her phone and began reading about the Pampas. "Paul, do you want me to read to you what my travel app says about this area?"

"Sure," he said enthusiastically.

"The grassy heartland of the Pampas is the terrain that Argentina is most known for, with its fertile plains, home of the Gauchos and is the foundation for the largest percentage of the nation's economic health." Celeste knew that they had a long travel day ahead of them as the ranch was a few hours from Buenos Aires with its wide diversity of scenery and climates, as most of Argentina lived within a very moderate temperate zone for the Southern Hemisphere.

"The area is best known for grapes and oil in the Central western sections of San Juan, Mendoza and San Luis. The Gaucho stands as one of the best-known symbols of Argentina. They are the rough, free-riding horseman of the Pampas and proud cousin of the North American Cowboy. The main identity of the Gaucho is that of a horseman. It is said that when a Gaucho was without his horse, he was without legs. Nearly all of his daily chores, from bathing to hunting, were on top of his horse. The first Gauchos hunted with lassos and boleadoras, both borrowed from the Indian culture. The boleadoras consist of three stones or metal balls attached to the ends of connected leather thongs. They are thrown with great accuracy by the Gaucho to trip the legs of a fleeing animal."

As she mulled this information over, Paul suddenly interrupted her thoughts and said, "I don't know if I'd ever really have a desire to take a bath on a horse. Did you know that Butch Cassidy and the Sundance Kid fled to South America? They were known as the Gringo (American foreigner) outlaws. Some historians say that Butch Cassidy went to the town of Esquel, in the foothills of the Andes Mountains. Butch Cassidy and the Sundance Kid chose this place to hide from the law for its remote location at the end of the world. They took up temporary shelter in Argentina while they were

Loralee Lago

on the run from Pinkerton's agents after their famous holdup of Argentina's Rio Gallegos Bank in 1895. They were on the run until the Bolivian police allegedly killed them, although it is speculated that they may have actually survived and returned incognito to the western U.S. Other members of Butch Cassidy's gang, who remained in the region, were ambushed and shot to death years later by the Argentine constable."

Celeste mentioned that she had never realized that Butch Cassidy came this far South, having supposed that he'd just gone to Mexico to hide out after running from the law in the United States and assuming that he'd been killed there. All that she knew about Butch Cassidy and his partners were that they were outlaws, and that their story made a great movie starring Paul Newman and Robert Redford. She remembered that not only was Paul Newman a great actor, but also made delicious spaghetti sauces and salad dressings and thus began the battle of mind over stomach once again when she said, "Do you think we have time to stop at that Panaderia on the corner to pick up something quickly? I'm ravenous!"

Paul said, 'I'm very sorry; we just don't have the time, but I promise, Scout's honor, that I'll take you to eat something as soon as we can get there and speak to his employer Señor Susaniche."

Celeste begrudgingly accepted this final verdict but began to fume inside, hoping that she wouldn't lose her cool and become the dreaded HANGRY (hungry + angry) girl! She made a mental note to carry more snacks in her purse in the future for any upcoming unexpected excursions. She suddenly remembered that she had a few packets of honey-roasted peanuts and pretzels from her flight still in her purse and began fervently digging through it to see if they could be found.

Paul queried, "What are you doing? You look obsessed about finding whatever it is in your purse!"

Celeste did her best not to snap back by saying, "I just remembered that I have a little something in my purse from my flight that will help with my hunger pangs." What she wanted to say was, *You are the reason why I'm acting like a bat crazy woman looking for any remnant of food.* Her thoughts got away from her, and she suddenly blurted out, "YOU are to blame for all of this!" as she continued to search in her purse for the packets. In her search, she found some breadcrumbs from the sliced bread she'd stowed away at Rosita's. She tried to wet her fingertip to press down to extract the crumbs, but nothing substantial was edible.

"Ewe, yuck," she said as she pulled out a breadcrumb crusted, hair covered breath mint and then quickly stuffed it back into her purse again. Finally, locating the coveted peanut and pretzel packets with a huge sigh of relief, she flippantly said, "Found 'em," as she attempted to open each packet without spewing the contents all over the car. She practically growled as she held her food close to her in protection. She was successful at opening each one, only spilling a few peanuts in her purse as she opened the last packet.

Celeste looked over a Paul in a defiant glare and said, "I'm NOT sharing," as she quickly poured the entire contents of both packets into her mouth in one swoop, and then chewed loudly, like a voracious wolf!

Paul was shocked and just looked at her with his jaw open, wondering what had happened to the sweet woman sitting next to him. He made a mental note to always bring snacks and to feed her often so that this frenzied woman would not ever appear again.

They finally arrived at the beautiful ranch just outside of Cordoba with a half mile of fenced cattle lining the lane that went into the Ranch. Celeste saw that the gate entrance was inscribed with the name O.S. Ranch, and she remembered seeing that a similar-looking "O" font initial had been seared into the soles of Graciela & Carlos' feet.

"Maybe we'll find out the link between the initials and the name of this Ranch too," said Celeste, as Paul nodded in agreement. He was deep in thought with his own analysis, going over the same information in his head, trying to put the puzzle pieces together. They pulled up to a breathtaking estate with a large ranch house, lush flower gardens, a horse training track, a barn and stables with beautiful Arabian horses painted on the front.

Paul said, "It looks like they raise not only cattle but also Arabian horses, which are bred not only for their beauty but are also considered a great symbol of wealth and status which were brought over by the Spaniards. They are an extremely versatile breed and make great racing horses."

As a side note, Paul mentioned that once his father retired, he further pursued his love for oil painting, saying, "He would paint Arabian horses to sell to the Equestrian loving tourists who came to town for the horse shows, as a way of earning a little extra income. My father's paintings were very popular with the tourists and always sold out quickly since he mainly painted single Arabian Horseheads."

"I love that memory of your father! I've always wanted to learn to paint snow capped mountains, happy trees and fluffy clouds and then make some 'big decisions' (about where to put those happy trees and clouds on the canvas) like Bob Ross always talks about on his PBS series *The Joy of Painting*," Celeste said.

"I admire Bob Ross' painting techniques too! My favorite Bob Ross quote is, 'We don't make mistakes. We just have happy accidents.' My dad cleverly invented his own tracing technique by using an overhead projector, which he'd use to follow the outline of a picture of an Arabian horse's silhouette for the correct dimensions and then would paint it to perfection, thereby creating breathtaking pieces of art quickly and accurately. It was a real time-saver, and I know that he was ahead of his time with that technique."

"How ingenious. He sounds like he has both an artistic and inventive nature," said Celeste.

"Yeah, he did! He was inventive in other areas too. He and I built and painted an epic doghouse castle for Scooby. He also used his skills to build a boat port for our bright orange Kayak that we'd take out fishing in the ocean. Those were cherished times I spent with my dad," he said with an air of nostalgia.

"I remember one time when I was around seven, I took out the kayak for some fun and decided, spur of the moment, to go out to sea. My father, who had been watching me from the shore, realized that I had gone out too far for him to swim after me, and frantically called the Coast Guard to go get me. I vividly remember the Coast Guard boat pulling up next to my kayak and the captain saying, "Where are you headed, young man?"

"I simply told them that I had planned to go to Japan for the day to see a certain super-sized *Gojira* (Godzilla), who hung out frequently in their harbor. The crew of the boat nearly double over in laughter at my plans, but somehow, most of them kept only amused smirks on their faces, as they carefully got me and my kayak safely back to shore and into the arms of my anxious father. I think that my dad nearly had a heart attack over it, especially about how he was going to explain it all to my mom. Come to think about it, I didn't think to bring snacks or lunch with me then too. Sheesh…Sorry, Celeste."

"You've been forgiven, Paul and I'm sorry that I was inconsiderate and didn't share my snacks with you," said Celeste. "What a great memory of your father, and I love the part in your adventure when you go in search of *Gojira*, as the Japanese call him. I'm a big fan of the King of the Monsters myself, although my favorite *Gojira* ally is Mothra who is a Japanese *Iamago* (caterpillar) and is considered more of a protector of the island. Are both of your parents still living?"

"No," Paul solemnly remarked. "My parents had me later in life, and both of them have been gone for almost a decade." As they got out of the car, he mentioned, "My favorite memories are of my dad and I fishing on the jetty in Redondo Beach. One time we caught so

Loralee Lago

much fish that the family feasted on it for a week!"

As he was about to tell her a little bit more about his home town, they spotted a ranch hand as he quickly poked his head out and back in from the stable, and instantly, Paul was all business, forgetting about his life in California and his sea adventures. Paul clapped his hands twice quickly to summon anyone there who would speak with them about Carlos.

"I love the tradition of clapping your hands outside of a home and then saying 'Con Permiso' (with your permission) as you enter a home instead of knocking on their front door in the more rural towns," said Celeste.

The same ranch hand that had looked out momentarily appeared from the stable with a branding iron in hand and drawled, "Hola Gringos, que quieres?" (Hello American foreigners, what do you want?)

Paul could easily have been mistaken for a native with his brown hair and eyes and flawless Castilian Spanish accent. The only reason that he looked out of place was that he was tall, as most men in Argentina were around 5'5" and women were around 4'9". Both Celeste at 5'7" & Paul at 5'11" towered above the ranch hand and definitely could be identified as *Gringos* with Paul's height and Celeste, with her height, blonde hair, blue eyes and American accented Spanish. The man seemed to be mesmerized with her sky-blue eyes and golden hair as he just stared at her, listening half-heartedly to Paul.

Paul said, "*Tenemos que hablar con su jefe, por favor.*" (We need to speak with your boss, please.) The ranch hand slightly nodded and tipped his hat with his hand, as he led the way to speak with the owner of the estate. As they walked towards the stable to speak with the owner, Paul mentioned under his breath, "Keep your eyes and ears open to others watching, in case we get a chance to speak with them."

Celeste mumbled back, "There are several workers staring at us now, so it might be a bit difficult to discern what their intentions and who to speak to first."

"It might be best to speak with everyone we meet," said Paul. She agreed. Celeste decided to follow Paul's lead and just go along in a supportive role. Her Spanish was pretty rusty and she would never be mistaken for a local with her *Gringa* accent.

A well-dressed man, who they supposed to be Manuel Susaniche, came out of the stables walking with one of the horses. The horse was saddled up and anxiously shifted its feet as if ready for a good ride. Paul extended his hand and introduced himself and Celeste to Señor Susaniche, who unabashedly said, *"Encantado de conocerte, Paul y guapa Celeste,"* (It's nice meeting you, Paul and beautiful Celeste), as he lifted her hand and kissed the top of it gallantly! He stared unapologetically into her eyes and said, "Your eyes are like sparkling stars on a moonless night!"

Celeste blushed a bright red at such a compliment and rewarded his gesture with a big smile.

Not knowing how to react to another man's attention towards Celeste, Paul immediately went into interview mode and explained the situation, asking him, "What can you tell us about what happened to Carlos? Why would anyone want to kill him?"

Señor Susaniche mentioned, "Carlos has been an unreliable ranch hand who's worked for me for the last few years. I am saddened to hear of his untimely death but am willing to help out in any way that I can in this investigation."

As Paul asked Señor Susaniche additional questions, Celeste found herself drawn to the striking horse standing impatiently by his side. She gently put her hand out to stroke its face. The beautiful midnight black Arabian stallion just whinnied in delight, nodding his head in eagerness to the attention that she gave him as she patted his head and mane. She noticed on the harness the name, "Oso" (Bear).

She began quietly whispering the horse's name in his ear, and he immediately nuzzled up next to her contentedly.

Señor Susaniche winked at Celeste. "Looks like my favorite riding horse's preference for you is a positive indication that you are a very good soul." He then added, "Oso always has great taste in people, and if Oso trusts you, then I can trust you." He handed her a few apples to the delight of both her and Oso, who ate them out of her hand politely in two bites.

"Good boy, Oso," she whispered again. "You're a handsome one!" Then remembering to speak Spanish, "*Que Guapo Oso!*"

"Celeste," said Señor Susaniche, "The next time that you come back here, you can ride Oso. He's taken rather a strong liking to you."

"I'd love to ride him," Celeste said eagerly.

"Then come back whenever you wish. You too, Lago."

"Thank you very much, Señor Susaniche. We will be pleased to take you up on that offer."

The men began casually walking down the lane with Oso in tow towards the main road for a bit of privacy, as they were deep in serious conversation. Celeste decided to walk towards the stable to look at the other horses and to greet anyone that she might see. As she looked towards the stable, she saw two men anxiously watching them and her. Once they noticed that she noticed them, they quickly dispersed and went back to their work, grooming the horses and cleaning the stalls. Celeste decided that she'd just casually walk inside to see what was making the ranch hands so nervous.

Inside the immaculate stables were a dozen majestic speckled, white, black, and brown Arabian horses, each more impressive than the next. Each of their names was engraved on plaques, which hung on posts outside of their stalls, and she noted a few of the names: Oso, Negro, Rocco, Rico, and Oro.

A Tango To Die For

Wait, what? Oro? She thought to herself. *Could the initials be the name of one of these beautiful stallions and a clue to this investigation? Would someone want to kill for these horses?*

She decided to get over her fear of her diminished Spanish and went up to the man mucking out Oro's stall. *"Buen dia muchacho!"* (Good day friend!) The man barely lifted his eyes to acknowledge her as he worked, probably hoping that she'd get the picture that he did not want to speak to her. But she persisted and said, *"Mi nombre es Celeste, y usted?"* (My name is Celeste, what is yours?) He mumbled that his name was Pablo. *"Mucho gusto* Pablo," (Pleased to meet you, Pablo).

With that, he lifted his head and slowly offered his hand in a polite handshake. She looked into his eyes; he was just a teenager. He had seemed so much older from a distance, and she realized that he had probably worked for Señor Susaniche for much of his life, as she could see hardened callouses on his weather worn hands from years of hard work.

"What a gorgeous horse! How did Oro get his name?"

Pablo mentioned, "There's gold in this area and Oro was named for that reason."

Celeste asked, "What does the O.S. mean in the O.S. Ranch?"

He said, "It means the O*ro de Susaniche* (Gold of Susaniche). I've tried many times to dig for gold in the area. If I can get enough collected, then I can apply to be formally schooled as a horse trainer. I feel like I am truly happiest when I am here. So far, I've been unsuccessful, as panning and digging for gold takes a lot of time and expensive equipment. It just isn't possible for someone like me to have the time, let alone the money, to be able to make a living. It takes a great deal of effort to get even one ounce of gold collected into a vile, as even that amount of gold requires sifting through piles and piles of dirt and rock, as well as the knowledge to process it correctly."

Celeste nodded in understanding and said, "Yes, that is true. My grandfather dug for gold for over 40 years in Eldorado Canyon in Nelson, Nevada. That area is known for gold along its riverbanks and throughout the canyon as far back as the Spaniards coming to the area to find gold. Grandpa Harris was a local miner, who spent the bulk of his life mining for gold in the cold, dark, claustrophobic and dangerous caves to be rewarded with only a few ounces of gold at a time. It is not something that you do in a day or even in a month, as it takes a great deal of patience, work, danger, tenacity and sheer luck to find a significant gold vein in the mines. It also requires pure grit and passion for the work to end up with enough gold to make a gold bar."

Celeste sympathized with the teen, knowing how difficult and utterly impossible it was to have the time and resources to be able to mine in the hills and pan for gold in the river. "I admire your educational goal, Pablo. Don't lose hope in fulfilling your dream." Still, she persisted with her most urgent question. "Is there any reason why someone would be branded with O.N?"

He paused looking around nervously, then whispered, "Yes" then quickly mentioned *"Tierra de Fuego"* (land of fire) before getting back to work once he noticed the other ranch hand angrily coming in their direction.

With that information, Celeste wondered why he'd even mentioned *Tierra de Fuego,* which was located at the Southern-most tip of Argentina. It was literally at the end of the world, where the penguins, sea lions and beavers lived and the ice-cold gritty winds constantly howled. Celeste built up the courage and quickly asked, "Pablo, do you know why someone would want to kill Carlos and Graciela?"

"Yes." As he began to answer, his eyes filled with fear as they darted back towards the other ranch hand, whom Pablo mumbled was named Rafael, coming towards them as he angrily waved a red-hot branding iron at her.

To try to defuse his anger, she extended her hand out to Rafael in greeting, nervously saying, *"Hola Amigo! Soy Celeste. Me alegro de conocerte!"* (Hello friend. I'm Celeste. I'm pleased to meet you!)

Rafael disregarded the greeting and began profusely swearing at her in anger as he continued to wave the branding iron in the air at her. She knew enough Spanish cuss words to know that she needed to leave immediately or face being kicked out by force and promptly turned around and ran out of the stable.

Once she was clear of the stables, she saw Paul and Señor Susaniche walking back towards her, appearing to have wrapped up the interview. Relieved, she quietly rejoined them, as they had hardly noticed that she'd been gone amidst their intense conversation. Her anxiety eased as she once again happily smothered Oso with added attention, grateful for the safety of being by Paul's side.

Celeste looked over her shoulder one last time and saw Rafael peering sternly at her along with a fearful Pablo in the background, looking nervous as he wrung his hands in anxiety. Celeste wondered what all of this meant, how it related to a dance contest, and why Carlos and Graciela were killed over it. Could that branding iron that Rafael had in his hands have been used to apply the acid to the soles of Carlos and Graciela's shoes or something similar? Did the 'O' font match the "O" on the victim's soles? Was Rafael even at the dance competition?

These questions swirled in her head, with no "definitive" conclusions. She decided that she'd just keep that information close at hand and speak to Paul further about it on their way home. Hopefully, he had more information that would help put the pieces together.

As they got into their car to leave, suddenly the magnificent stallion "Oro" ran out of the stable, as if he had been whipped, swiftly galloping by them as he headed towards the main road. Modern day Gauchos Rafael and Pablo were seen jumping onto an ATV, with lassos in hand in hot pursuit. As the two ranch hands sped by, Pablo, turning his body so Rafael couldn't see him, held up his hands in front of his stomach and put his fingers up in the form of a "T" and then held up seven fingers.

Paul asked, "What was that all about?" Celeste recounted everything that had happened inside of the stables and mentioned to Paul that somehow it was all related, and to add Rafael onto the list of "persons of interest."

Paul wrote down everything that she reported to him in his notebook in addition to the information that he'd recorded from his interview with Señor Susaniche and said, "This is just the tip of the iceberg. I think these leads will help point us in the right direction. I don't remember seeing Rafael at the dance competition, but there were so many people there-he may have conveniently gotten lost in all of the chaos. I'll speak to Captain Lucas about what we've learned, and then we'll get an early dinner since I thoughtlessly deprived you of breakfast like an oaf! I'm profoundly sorry for not taking your needs into account today. After all, we are supposed to be on vacation. I don't know what happened, as it has become more of a working vacation. Are you okay with that?"

Celeste said, "As long as we can do it together and you remember to feed me on time, I can handle it. I'm thoroughly intrigued and want to know whodunit!"

Paul agreed, saying, "We only have a short window of time before the leads will grow cold, so time is of the essence. If not, vital evidence will be destroyed, and more lives could be lost if we don't find the answers soon!"

Celeste agreed that time was of the utmost importance but said, "Can we stop at the corner bakery once we get back into Cordoba to eat something? I'm dying for my favorite syrupy sprinkled Thousand-Leaf Pastry! My mouth is just watering in anticipation of that first honey and sprinkled messy bite of heaven."

As Paul sped towards town, he overwhelmingly agreed, saying,

"Your wish is my command, *Madame*! I'm ready to eat a few of my favorite Alfajores too!"

"Yeah, I could eat a few of those as well," said Celeste. They both smiled with delight once they arrived back in town, pulled over at the first bakery that they saw and practically trampled over each other running through the door for their beloved treats and eats. The sweet and yeasty fragrance of the baking loaves of bread wafting throughout the bakery was exhilarating. As they ordered their sweet treats and sandwiches, Celeste felt like she needed to ask the bakery worker, "Do you know what T7 is?"

The woman just shook her head in confusion and said, "No śe!" (I don't know!)

Then Celeste thought that maybe it wasn't a "T", but a Cross + 7 and tried again, "Do you know what or where Cross 7 is?"

With that combination, the bakery worker's eyes lit up and said, "Si, Si! It is the Cross 7 Mine that is just outside of town. Most of the men in the area work there."

As she served Paul his Alfajores, he immediately thanked her for the Cross 7 information and then promptly asked for directions to the mine.

As they drove back outside of town, they realized that the turn off to the O.S. Ranch was about a mile before the Cross 7 Mine's turnoff. Paul asked with amazement, "How did you figure out that Cross 7 was a place?"

Celeste mentioned, "Pablo told me about the name of the ranch and how he wanted to mine for gold to earn money to become a certified horse trainer one day. He's been unable to search for gold consistently, as he lacks both time and money."

"I see." said Paul thoughtfully. "I hope that he will be able to reach that goal one day. I like that he's got a dream and is willing to work towards making it a reality."

Loralee Lago

Once they arrived at the mine, they were met by men standing around eating *Pan* (Bread) and drinking Mate as they poured hot water from a kettle into a cup, added sugar, then passed it around to enjoy. As they caught sight of Celeste, they began "SSSSS" and "Ch ch ch-ing" to get her to look at them.

Embarrassed, Celeste kept her head held high and expression neutral until they were able to find the supervisor of the mine in a small shed-like enclosure, near the entrance to the mine. She looked over in frustrated disbelief at Paul, who seemed not to notice the catcalls coming her way, undoubtedly lost in his thoughts again.

The supervisor, a short man in his late forties, introduced himself as Jefe Gamero and asked, "What can I do to help you two lost Gringos?"

Paul quickly went into police business mode and asked about the mine and if he knew Carlos.

Señor Gamero said, "Everyone knows Carlos. He's worked here every spare minute when he wasn't working for Señor Susaniche or betting on the horse races."

Paul asked, "Can you provide me with any insight as to why Carlos and Graciela may have been killed?"

Señor Gamero said, "Carlos was a very disruptive worker, always missing in action in the mines, which is both frustrating and dangerous in our line of work. One time he got himself stuck up there"— he pointed— "in one of the air shafts, and we had to climb three stories high to clear the rocks from the area in order to retrieve him, nearly costing the lives of the other workers in the rescue.

"Against my orders, he continued working on a very unstable area. It seems that he found a new gold vein and was bent on following it, even though it would compromise the integrity of the cavern. He didn't care who got hurt and kept at it until he finally got pinned down when it caved in.

"I forbade him from following that vein again, to keep all of our lives intact. This business is a widow maker, you know. The men work long hours in pitch black with only candles, in tight spaces. Constantly breathing the mine dust into their lungs requires most of them to retire by the time they are 40 primarily due to respiratory, eye and ear problems. This is not a profession for the faint of heart; the men are required to manually drill and painstakingly drive holes up to three stories high up and down the main tunnel shaft. It is a very dangerous job on the best of days."

Paul asked Jefe Gamero, "What do you think could have caused the massive burns and ultimate cause of death of Carlos and Graciela?"

Jefe Gamero lifted his hand to his chin to think and then mentioned, "There are many toxic chemicals and stripping agents we use to purify gold. Any two of them combined could be responsible for Carlos and Graciela's seared feet and would have gone directly into the bloodstream. It would cause death within minutes, once their feet began heating up in their shoes. There was probably a protective layer put into place to activate once their body temperature reached a certain level."

Paul asked, "May I get a list of these chemicals?" Jefe Gamero wrote down several probable substances on a piece of paper and handed it to him.

"If you put these two together" — he pointed on the list, —"they quickly turn deadly."

Paul and Celeste exchanged glances as they saw him pointing to the Muriatic acid and Nitric acid.

Jefe Gamero said, "If those chemicals were taken in any significant amount from the mine, I'd know it because I keep a strict inventory of when and how much we use daily to process the gold that we've mined. Purifying gold is a very labor intensive and costly process and cannot be done without proper protocol and control.

Loralee Lago

Paul and Celeste were amazed to learn that to purify gold, it required approximately 20 different steps, which included those same toxic chemicals. If used incorrectly, it could cause serious bodily injury or death.

Paul asked, "Would you check your inventory within the last month for anything that appears to be out of order?"

"Sure. I've got my control records here." he said as he walked over and grabbed a well-worn book. "There are very few of us authorized to purify and process the gold who have access to the chemicals." As Jefe Gamero scanned the inventory book, he said, "Everything looks good except..." His finger rested on a cell blotted out in dark black ink. "That's weird; there was an extra 1/2 ounce taken from both of the Muriatic and Nitric acids by...I can't tell. It's covered by black ink and I can't read the name. In that small amount, it wouldn't raise any red flags as missing from the inventory. Last month before it was blacked out, I notated the difference as a slight concern in my review but did not feel a need to take any action. Someone, who knew that I had already taken inventory for the month, must have come back in and blackened the name."

Paul asked, "May I interview those authorized persons involved in this process?"

"Yes, but I believe it was either Filipe or Marcelo, who may be responsible for taking these extra supplies. I will allow you only a few minutes to interview them and the remaining men on the list.

Paul particularly wanted to speak with Filipe and Marcelo, who may have been responsible for taking the extra half-ounce from the inventory.

"Our lunch break is almost over, and I will not allow them to take off even a minute from their work, as time is money," said Jefe Gamero.

Now Paul and Celeste had a list of purifying agents that they could submit for analysis to verify that their suspicions were correct. Carlos and Graciela were burned and likely killed by one or both of these toxic chemicals.

Before returning to the car, Paul asked one last question, "Who is the owner of the mine?"

"Why, it's my uncle, Antonio Gamero."

"Is he here?"

"Oh no, he's retired now and lives at his ranch a few miles down the road. He rarely comes to the mine anymore."

After quickly interviewing each of the men who had authorization to purify the gold, Paul and Celeste were on their way to the Ranch to see if they could speak with Señor Gamero. Thankfully, as they left the Cross 7 Mine, there were no men in sight to harass Celeste. The break was over and all of the men were already back inside working in the cold, dark and lonely mine to finish the last four hours of their shift. Celeste was reminded of how difficult and hard it is to be a mineworker and how generations continued the tradition of being miners. The lucky ones like Pablo were able to get work in town or at the O.S. or Gamero ranches.

After going to the Gamero ranch, they were told that Señor Gamero lived at both the ranch and had an apartment in Buenos Aires; he was currently at his apartment for a few days on personal business. Within minutes, Paul and Celeste were able to get the street address from Señora Gamero and were headed back before 4 pm.

Once they returned to Buenos Aires, Captain Lucas updated Paul on their interviews, which added more information to the little black book that Paul kept to record important details of the investigation. Celeste was very interested in reading it but kept that thought to herself, although she did catch Paul doodling P+C in it as he added additional information he learned from Captain Lucas.

After the briefing with Captain Lucas was complete, Paul and Celeste were famished and went for an early dinner of *Choripan* (Chorizo sausage sandwiches) and papas fritas (French fries) at a local diner. They ate and talked about the case and life in Argentina until they couldn't eat anymore!

As Paul paid the bill, it began to rain cats and dogs outside. "We'd better get you back soon, or we'll be floating home without an oar in this little car I rented. I didn't expect it to rain and didn't bring an umbrella," he said.

As they got up to leave, Celeste looked out the window and was stunned to see a man glaring directly at her. She looked away for just a second to grab Paul's attention as he was leaving a tip on the table. When she looked back, the man was gone. Pointing, Celeste said, "Did you see anyone just now?"

"No," he said as he turned his head to look out the window.

"Never mind, it was nothing. I'm tired and must be seeing things," she surmised.

Paul looked around and still didn't see anyone.

Paul took Celeste to collect her luggage from the Hotel de Bahia to get her settled into the cute rental he'd found for her. Indeed, this home on the outskirts of town was much more comfortable and quieter than the hotel, as she had heard the elevator go up and down with the opening and closing of its gate many times during her stay. She was grateful for the solace after an exhausting day of detective work. Celeste quickly got ready for bed, read her scriptures, and said her prayers filled with gratitude for the Lord's protection and help.

She lay there listening to the soothing rhythmic pounding of the rain off of the roof and rolling metal shutters; she loved the fresh air and sounds that the rain brought to the area. The mixture of asphalt, earth, plants and water were one of her favorite scents in life. That earthy combination had a way of grounding, calming and relaxing her like no other as she breathed deeply and released the stresses of the day. As she closed the shutters for the evening, she was thankful that they served a dual purpose of keeping out the light and protecting the home. She felt extra safe and warm, even though the tiled floor could be chilly to walk on without a nice gas heater to keep it warm. Celeste fell peacefully asleep to the music of the rain tapping in sync on the rooftop.

CHAPTER 4

Shocking

Celeste awoke refreshed the next morning after it had rained steadily throughout the night and sleepily ambled into the bathroom to wash her face and get ready for the day. As she took hold of the sink's metal handle, it vibrated strangely in her hand. She paused, then tentatively turned on the water and immediately jumped back from the strange vibration she felt again from the handle. Unsure as to what was happening, she delicately touched the water with the tip of her finger, only to be heavily jolted by a painful electric current!

Now fully awake, Celeste was terrified to touch anything. She just wanted to cry out for help, but since she was alone, she quickly decided to get out of the house instead. The only problem was that she wasn't exactly sure how she could get out of the house, as every door and fixture seemed to be made of metal, and the house was entirely electrically charged. She frantically left the bathroom and ran into the bedroom, where she threw on her clothes and grabbed her cell phone to call Paul. She carefully opened the front door with a thick towel, receiving more jolts as she did so. She knew that the only way to save herself was to flee the home immediately.

Finally free from the fully charged house, she sat on the cold, wet concrete retaining wall in the front yard and cried for a few minutes before regaining her composure enough to dial Paul's cell to explain the dire situation.

Paul cheerfully answered on the second ring saying, "Good morning beautiful. What can I do for you today?"

"Paul, It's Celeste, can you come right over? The house appears to be electrically charged and I'm really scared and freaked out."

"I'll be right over. I'm leaving now. Don't move. Stay where you are, Celeste."

"Okay. I think I can do that," she said in relief and hung up her phone.

Sensing her need, a neighborhood dog came over instinctively to comfort her; it just sat quietly right next to her, seeming to say, "Everything's going to be okay. I'm here for you." It was a much-needed tender mercy given to her as she stroked its head methodically and impatiently waited for Paul's arrival. She bowed her head in a silent prayer, giving thanks to God for His protecting hand and for sending the dog to help her during this distressing time.

Paul arrived in record time and wrapped the tearful Celeste snuggly in his arms so that she could cry a bit more after being involved in such a jolting situation. Once she calmed down, he looked at her with smudged leftover makeup, bedhead and dragon breath and optimistically said, "Hey, you look pretty good for just getting the shock of your life. Your hair is still standing on ends, but other than that, you fared well. Let's get some breakfast at a nearby café. I've called my friend, Javier, who is an electrician, to come and find out what is causing the electrical surge on the house."

"I think that would be nice. Thank you Paul for coming right over and taking care of everything. I am very grateful."

"You're more than welcome my dear Celeste," he said as he pulled her up off of the retaining wall and escorted her to the car to head to the bakery for a nice breakfast. "A little *Desayuno* (breakfast) will make everything better," he said, as Celeste nodded her head in agreement.

Celeste felt more like herself after she'd eaten several slices of French bread with *Dulce de Leche,* apple wedges with a sweet potato membrane jelly slice on top, and washed it all down with some calming Chamomile and Vanilla herbal tea. Finally relaxed, she allowed herself to appreciate the beautiful weather and inhaled deeply the refreshing scent of the rain on the streets.

"Just so that you know," said Celeste, "I usually don't react so dramatically to emergencies. I was shocked very badly when I was living here; the light bulb in our apartment's bathroom blew out. I took it upon myself to change it, as I've changed many light bulbs in my life. I thought that I had turned the power switch to the off position but was unable to tell if the 'on' power switch should be pushed left or if the right position was 'off', so I took a 50/50 chance that it was in the 'off' position after switching it back and forth a few times.

"I took out the bulb easily enough, and then as I put the second bulb up to screw it in, I must have slightly touched the metal casing of the socket. The 220-Volt electric jolt lifted my entire body nearly a foot in the air and I was thrown forcefully against the back wall. I've never experienced anything like that, EVER! Amazingly, I didn't go into cardiac arrest from the sudden jolt, but I was miraculously only stunned and grateful that I was all right. Ever since then, I've been very cognizant and cautious about the extreme power of electricity and have remembered to always treat it with extra respect."

Paul gave Celeste another reassuring squeeze. "Whoa, I'd be

Loralee Lago

freaked out too after that experience. I do understand where you're coming from, as I decided not to continue my training as an Electrical Engineer after leaving the Air Force when I saw that there is no room for error when working with electricity. Several buddies of mine that I served with in Misawa were severely shocked and that's when I knew that I didn't want to pursue that line of work any further, so I became an Interpol agent instead. I'm thankful that you are alright," said Paul.

Just as Celeste was feeling at ease, Javier walked into the café to tell them that the wet weather had caused the damage to the electrical panel as several wires were exposed and got wet.

"I was able to ground the electrical wires right away. I'm happy to report that you won't be shocked again," informed Javier.

"Thanks so much for your help. How much do I owe you?" asked Paul.

"No, gracias my friend. I'm just happy to help!" said Javier.

Paul pulled Javier aside and mumbled something in his ear that Celeste could not understand, although she saw Javier nod his head in confirmation to the question.

Both Celeste and Paul graciously thanked Javier and offered to buy him a Croissant and Mate, which he gladly accepted.

As Javier happily ate his breakfast, Paul gave them his tourist digest point of view about *Mate*, saying, "Did you know that another common thread that all Argentinians share, is their obsession with the national drink, *Mate*?"

"That is verdadero (true), my friend," Javier heartily agreed as he slurped at his mate and nodded in favor.

Paul continued, "Mate tea leaves are hand harvested by *herbateros* (cultivators) from a native species of holly tree found deep in the South American Atlantic rainforest on small farms in Paraguay, Argentina and Brazil. The leaves are dried, crushed, and put into a carved cup with a silver straining straw. Hot water and plenty of sugar is added to the drink in the desired amount."

Javier agreed with Paul's analysis and added, "My family drinks Mate morning, noon, and night, and every hour in between. But more importantly, I must know who you're rooting for in the upcoming *futbol* (soccer) playoffs? Inquiring minds must know. Answer very carefully, amigo, as my opinion of you will be greatly affected by your response."

"Of course, I'm rooting for Boca Jr.!" said Paul.

"Boca? Have you lost your mind?" exclaimed Javier as he adamantly disagreed. Then he and Paul got into a heated argument as to which *futbol* team was the best and what political views coincided with each.

"I can confidently say that Boca's team is the best," said Paul.

"No!" declared Javier adamantly. "It's River!"

Celeste knew that although the people of Argentina couldn't decide on who or where they came from originally, there were a couple of topics on which Argentinians had strong opinions: sports (soccer, where at an early age they must decide where their allegiances lay) and politics. After several minutes of loud banter, Celeste attempted to break it up as the two men progressively got louder and louder in their rebuttal as to why their team would prevail, who had the best overall record and who the MVP players were, including memorized stats!

Trying to sway the conversation, Celeste blurted out, "I like the Racing Club *futbol* team the best. I love their blue and white uniforms and especially their very handsome midfield MVP player, Martin Z." Her ploy worked, as both men stopped mid conversation and just stared at her with mouths wide open in total disbelief.

"Is that the only reason why you are rooting for them?" inquired Paul.

Loralee Lago

"Yeah," she said. "Plus, their uniforms remind me of a clear blue sky and include the colors of Argentina's flag, which makes them the most patriotic of all of the teams."

Both men burst out in open disdain at her non-analytically backed comments, bringing further challenges from both men as to why their team and players were statistically the best of the Big 5.

"Hey," Paul said thoughtfully, "maybe she's on to something. There's a gal, Judy, who works in my office that participates in our yearly office Fantasy Football Pool. Every year Peter, Larry and I meticulously research each team with important stats, player injuries, and rankings. We come armed with binders packed full of information, so that we can strategically choose the winning team for the week. But Judy, who only glances briefly at the picks for the week, chooses her winning team in seconds by determining whether or not she likes their mascot, their team colors, and especially whether or not the quarterback is cute."

Javier just stared at him bewildered, saying, "Are you serious amigo?"

"Oh, I know what you're thinking, Javier, but the thing is that Judy almost always wins the grand prize at the end of the season with her non-strategy picks. I think I might have to give it a try this upcoming season; I will secretly consult with Judy each week to save face before I make my picks." Javier only slightly nodded to acknowledge Paul's plan, then went right back into talking about how his team would be winning this week, and Paul immediately shot back as to why his team would win. The debate resumed until Celeste finally had to call a truce between the two men once their argument got so out of control that they were causing a scene.

"You two, stop it! You're embarrassing me," said Celeste.

They both quickly looked over at her sheepishly, having completely forgotten that she was even there, and immediately quieted down momentarily in humility over letting their discussion get so out of hand. Only slightly deterred after being shushed, both Paul and Javier fiercely but quietly continued whispering, "Boca!"

"No, River."

"River," argued Paul.

"Boca!" replied Javier.

"Gotcha!" Laughed Paul. "See, you do agree with me that Boca will win!"

"No fair, Lago! You tricked me!" countered Javier.

"Okay, I've had enough, Paul–please take me home," protested Celeste.

Paul, although reluctant to end their lively debate, agreed to her request and got up to take her home but not before he got in the last jab by loudly yelling Boca's name as he walked out the door. Celeste only rolled her eyes in disappointment. She thought that they really should have been talking adamantly about more important issues, such as how to help feed hungry families, world peace, or how to best serve others in need.

"Men. I may never understand them."

"What's not to understand? We are pretty basic; we like a good meal, the love of a good-hearted woman, and want our favorite sports team to win. Now, women are the true mystery," said Paul, as Celeste shook her head from side to side in disagreement.

With the home electrical system grounded once again, Celeste and Paul cautiously entered the home to get her purse and fresh change of clothes before going out for the day. Paul tested everything inside the home with the voltage indicator pen that Javier had given him to make sure that there were no new unexpected problems and then gave it to Celeste for good measure. Celeste was still very hesitant to touch much of anything, let alone get into the shower, so she just did her best to make herself look presentable and reminded herself that many people only showered a few times a week. She wondered if someone who knew the weather forecast had stripped the wires, once she'd retired for the evening. If so, why would they want to hurt her?

Still a bit humbled by his juvenile behavior at the café, Paul decided that he'd take Celeste on a little shopping trip to make it up to her. After all, he knew how much a shopping trip would do to brighten her outlook on the day. He clearly understood that women loved to shop, especially since his older sisters, Chantel and Caitlyn and mother, Patricia loved to bargain hunt. A little retail therapy was just what Celeste needed to make things right. "How about we go shopping for a new outfit for you and pick up a few souvenirs?"

Celeste's eyes lit up with delight as she said, "Okay, now you're talking *my* language. Let's act like American tourists!"

"But…we *are* American tourists," said, Paul!

"But they don't know that *we know* what they're saying!"

Paul grinned mischievously saying, "This should be interesting!"

They stopped by a popular souvenir shop targeting American tourists. It was fun looking at all of the Mate cups made out of gourds, brass, aluminum, and even hallowed out horns!

"I want to buy this horn Mate Cup. Look, it even has an etching of a Gaucho riding on his horse on the front," said Celeste enthusiastically.

"Cool. He's not taking a bath on it, is he?" Paul said sarcastically. "Did you notice that it has a little spoon that goes with it made from a small horn as well?" They both agreed that the cup would be a great memento of their trip, even though neither one of them had planned on drinking Mate after their return home as the flavor of it reminded them of green hay.

Paul found some *Gaucho boleros* and a riding hat that he just had to buy. Celeste mentioned that if he was going to have the *boleros* and hat that he needed the rest of the gear to complete his look, which included: baggy pants, a white string tied shirt, and a multi-colored poncho to complete the ensemble.

He agreed and said, "If you get one of those knitted shawls and an embroidered lace dress with the matching fan, we could dress up like this for a fall party later on this year!"

She agreed but realized that they had suddenly transitioned into talking in terms of 'we'. They also found a great miniature Gaucho doll to be Paul's mini-me for the party and an ornate hair comb, a beautiful blue gemstone ring, and an incredible handmade knit wool sweater in a Nordic design that Celeste just adored.

Once she got to the check-out area and unloaded all of her treasures, she realized that she had gone overboard and decided to put one item back to show just a little bit of restraint, especially after she'd overheard the cashier talking on the phone excitedly about these two Gringos who were buying a bunch of stuff and how she hoped to get a little bonus from the boss for selling so many items at once. Celeste had a bit of a hard time parting with any of it, but decided that she would put the handcrafted blue gemstone ring back.

Paul purchased a top-quality leather jacket at an amazing price, along with a fridge magnet, ski hat, and fleece-lined leather gloves. At the last moment he quickly added some Alfajores, *chicle* (gum), chips, mints, hot candies, and a fine Andes dark chocolate bar to his pile at checkout.

Celeste looked over at him and said, "By the looks of things, I think that we made the cashier's day!" She quickly said in Spanish as they were leaving, to a surprised cashier, "I hope that your bonus is a very good one, my friend."

He grinned mischievously saying, "*You've* made my day!!

She said to Paul, "I think that you're hungry by the looks of all of the junk food that you added to the pile at the last minute. By the way, what time is it?"

"It's already 5 pm," he said.

"Where did the day go? That was so much fun," Celeste said.

"You call charging up our credit cards fun?" said Paul.

"Indeed, let's do it again soon. But next time I need to show a bit more restraint as all of these bags are getting heavy," she replied.

"Let's go get some pizza and empanadas first," said Paul as he took over carrying her bags. "I know just the place!"

With all of their treasures safely stowed in the trunk of the car, they went to the Pizzeria down the street and ordered some ham and cheese empanadas and a small cheese pizza, Churros and Dulce de Leche flavored ice cream cones for dessert.

As they ate their meal, Celeste said. "You know, the last time I ate pizza here, my companion and I went to this great Pizzeria in Miramar on our bikes and decided to take it back to eat at our *pension* (apartment), but it was a blustery day, and she was having a difficult time keeping the pizza box from blowing off of the bike's handlebars. I proudly took it from her and put it on my handlebars, thinking that I could control the pizza box better. As I rode home, a big gust of wind came out of nowhere, blowing the pizza box off my handlebars and landing open faced down on the asphalt."

"We were both shocked and upset. I took one look at it lying face down on the asphalt and burst out laughing to try and diffuse the situation. It worked, and we quickly decided that the pizza could be salvaged. So, we did what any respectable girls would do in that situation and just picked it up, brushed off the gravel, went home and ate it anyway!"

"I can't believe that you still ate it," said Paul, surprised.

"It was a tad bit crunchy, but hey, when you are on a tight budget, you do what you gotta do. It was still yummy, just with a bit of extra added iron." Celeste winked. "I remember thinking when I had my first pizza here in Argentina how odd it was that the pizza was basically white cheese with a little ham and whole green olives, pits included. I enjoyed it, even if it didn't look or taste anything like my favorite pizza from back home. Good times and with a great companion, Hermana (sister) Cantero," she continued.

Paul nodded his understanding, saying, "We went to a member's house a few times where they made an incredible meat *ragu* (spaghetti type sauce) over *Gnocchis* along with a side of beef empanadas with egg, raisin and green olive filling. It was greatly appreciated, as each recipe was time-intensive and literally a labor of love. I still dream about eating at Maria Celeste's house to this day."

"Hey these empanadas are pretty good too, and the churros filled with Dulce de Leche are fried to crunchy and creamy caramel perfection as well," Celeste declared.

"After all of this food, just roll me home, hon! I can hardly move after all of that food that I scarfed down," he said. They both chuckled as they slowly headed for the car.

"Celeste, would you mind if we could make a quick stop to visit Antonio Gamero's apartment to see if he will answer a few questions? It isn't that far away and is in a secured apartment building."

"Sure, why not? I need to walk off this meal anyways. It will be just the ticket."

They easily found the building close by and noticed that the locked front door had been left slightly ajar, so they just walked in, easily bypassing the security checkpoint. There was no one standing at the front desk, although they could hear someone from a side room cheering on his *futbol* team. "How lucky are we that he didn't hear us?" commented Paul as they walked in. "Sounds like River is playing your team. Shall we peek in to see what the score is and if your favorite *futbol* hunk is playing?" he asked with a wink.

"And have you blow our covert entry with a possible outburst? Not on your life!" said Celeste, as she blushed and lightly punched

Loralee Lago

his arm in jest. "Do you know which apartment he's in?"

"I'm not certain which apartment number Antonio is in, but I think that he is either on the 3rd or 4th floor."

"Alright," she said as they got into the elevator, "floor three it is! It will be like when we were knocking on doors to meet people during our missions."

"Don't worry, we'll find him."

Once they got off the elevator on the 3rd floor, they noticed that there were only four doors to choose from and decided to divide and conquer, each taking a door at opposite ends of the hall.

Paul knocked on the first door, and an angry lady answered, asking how he had gotten in. Paul humbly stated that they were looking for Antonio Gamero and asked whether she knew which apartment he lived in. She simply yelled, "No!" and slammed the door in his face.

"Okay that went well," said Paul sarcastically. "It isn't that door. One down, seven more to go."

Celeste fared much better with the door that she knocked on, when the man, who answered it in his bathrobe, invited her to come in. "No thanks, but do you know Antonio Gamero?" The man pointed his finger up to the ceiling and mentioned that Antonio lived on the 4th floor. "He's the last door on the left. When you get done visiting with Antonio, come back and see me," he said with a wink. She politely thanked him and quickly left to get away from the awkward situation.

Paul and Celeste took the elevator up to the 4th floor, easily finding the last door on the left, and knocked. A woman that looked to be the maid answered it, and Paul asked if they could speak with Señor Gamero. As the woman explained that he had left that morning to go back to his ranch, they could hear the elevator go up a floor and then frantic footsteps running on the concrete floor, as if looking for someone. They heard the elevator door open and close and then slowly begin coming up to their floor.

Paul said, "I think that the door slamming, yelling lady at our first door ratted us out, and we are about to get kicked out of the building." The elevator door opened, and a frantic guard bolted out, demanding, "What are you doing here?"

Paul put his index finger in the air behind him to silence the man, who surprisingly waited for Paul to finish speaking with the woman. "If you could, please have Señor Gamero call the number on the back of this card to speak with Captain Lucas. If he doesn't call back within a day Captain Lucas will be in touch, as it is a matter of urgent police business."

The woman agreed and shut the door. Paul and Celeste were then immediately escorted from the building and asked never to return.

"That was crazy," exclaimed Celeste. "I can't believe that guy just waited for you to finish your business. How did you know that he'd wait the extra few seconds?"

"I didn't," he said, "but it never hurts to act as if you demand respect in these situations. Sometimes it works."

"Amazing! I'm going to try that approach the next time I get chased down by an elevator-riding security guard." Celeste said with a laugh.

On the drive home, Celeste asked Paul point blank, "What did you ask Javier about this morning?"

"You don't wanna know."

"I really do."

"You're not gonna like it."

"Tell me anyway," she said.

"I think someone intentionally stripped the electrical wires last night, but I don't know why someone would target you."

"Hmmm," she said thoughtfully. "I suspected as much. I failed to mention last night that a man was staring right at me outside in the pouring rain as we were getting up to leave the restaurant."

"What? Why didn't you tell me?" asked Paul.

"I didn't say anything because he was gone in an instant, and I thought maybe I had just imagined it and was overly tired."

Paul was not happy that she hadn't mentioned this additional information with him but decided not to make a big deal about it; he didn't want her to be more worried than she already was. "How about I stay on the couch tonight to make sure that you are alright?"

"No, I'm good. Go home and get some rest; I'll be just fine– plus, the storm has passed, and I don't think that there will be a repeat of what occurred last night."

Paul simply said, "As you wish," as he escorted her to the front door, unlocked it, and handed her the keys and bags of items purchased at the souvenir shop. For good measure, he did a quick walk around the inside of the home and the exterior to make sure there was no one lurking in the shadows.

Finally satisfied that there was no one there, he came back to the front door where she was standing, and gave her an official report that all was quiet. He asked again if he might sleep on the couch for the evening to make sure nothing unexpected happened.

"I'm fine," she reassured him, as she playfully turned him around and gave him a little nudge out the door.

He quickly turned back around and said, "I had a great time, and I want to apologize again for humiliating you earlier at the café."

"All has been forgiven," she said as her hand softly touched his sleeve and her fingers slowly walked up his arm to the top of his shoulder. "Maybe you'll let me get a few words in next time we meet up with Javier," she added, as she leaned in close to his face.

She looked deeply into his eyes and then ran her fingers playfully through a stray strand of hair falling over his forehead.

Paul felt a rush of emotions bubble up, but abruptly stamped them out when he said, "Umm, hey, err, no problem. Will do. I'll see you tomorrow."

Alone once again, she was still a bit skittish about touching anything in the home, as she gingerly tested the front door's energy level with the voltage indicator pen that Paul had given her. Eventually, she touched her fingernail on the handle and was relieved that she felt nothing, so she finally let her guard down and pushed open the door. A luxurious bubble bath before going to bed would be just the ticket; a good relaxing soak allowed her to go through her day and decompress from her worries and fears, allowing her to put everything in its place. It was just what she needed for a great night's sleep.

She vividly recalled her days as a missionary when she and Hermana Molinari worked so hard that they plopped into bed fully clothed and fell immediately asleep from exhaustion. Celeste found herself dreaming in Spanish again, something that she hadn't done for many years, and woke up while speaking Spanish in her sleep as she finished the first missionary *Charla* (discussion). She giggled, having remembered that she'd done the very same thing while on her mission, and thought how great it was that her teaching dreams picked up where they'd left off, only this time there wasn't a companion to complete the rest of the discussion with. With that thought, she fell instantly into a sound sleep until the morning.

Celeste awoke to a beautiful, clear and crisp morning. The scent of rain remained in the air. It invigorated her as she prepared to take an early morning stroll around the block for a bit of exercise to enjoy this suburban area. The area was full of busy life with bustling buses, cars and taxis full of people going to work and school.

She noticed a man fast asleep across the street in a car and quickly did a double take, realizing that it was Paul. *Should I wake him or let him sleep?* she debated. He looked like he'd been there all night, and was out cold, hunched over the steering wheel. *If I didn't know better, I would have guessed he looked like someone who'd had one too many drinks and was sleeping it off.*

Wow! I can't believe he stayed watch all night. Why would he do that for me? He looked so peacefully uncomfortable that she decided to let him sleep, as she wouldn't be long. She decided to pick up some items for a nice breakfast to show her gratitude. She knew just what to do.

She would go down the block and take the bus, as taking a taxi was out of the question. Unlike North America, there were very few stoplights or posted signs. Argentina was an exciting place to live, where taking a taxi ride was literally taking your life in your own hands as you traversed the traffic in a speedy and organized chaotic manner. The Argentine people took it all in their stride, as it was always an adventure walking the streets where the cars, buses, and taxis do not stop much. They simply honked their horns and went through each intersection, using it as a yield, as the biggest car earned the right to go first.

The area where Celeste's home was located, although safe to walk in, was also a place where an attractive woman walking down the street would be met with the national male sport of catcalling. This sport of getting the attention of any pretty women on the streets was a cultural art form, with Celeste becoming its next recipient.

As Celeste walked, she heard the construction workers from a nearby building calling out to her. Although embarrassed by the attention, she inwardly smiled at the fact that she was still young enough to pass the test of being their next receiver of unsolicited attention, as the men's *machismo* (macho) ways remained prevalent in the country.

To get her mind off all of the extra attention, she thought about the Cross 7 Mine that Pablo had signaled to her and how it would help in solving Carlos and Graciela's murder. Why would he mention Tierra de Fuego, which was hundreds of miles away, when the mine was just outside of Cordoba on the Pampas? What specifically had they uncovered in the case that made her their target?

CHAPTER 5

Mortadella? Como No?
(Why Not?)

Celeste decided that the best place to go would be downtown to pick up a few items at the corner Deli and Panaderia, as she could get some yummy meats, cheeses, and loaves of bread too. Having arrived at the bus stop, she saw the bus speedily coming down the street in the direction that she wanted to go. She counted her lucky stars for not having to wait long for it to arrive. The bus briefly stopped to pick everyone up. She rapidly jumped onto the standing-room only bus, packed with beautiful people inside, including several men who ended up hanging out of the doors, a common sight within the city limits.

One thing that was very different on these buses from those in the U.S. was that the drivers took great pleasure in personalizing their buses with tassel-like fringes, which hung around the borders of their windshields. Also attached were pictures of the saintly Santa Maria, and other saints were often found on the driver's side visor to protect the driver and riders from harm. There were also stickers of Argentina's flag and other little personal mementos to make their work areas more inviting. Celeste liked their decorating attempts, as the drivers took great pride in their important work.

The bus stopped a few blocks later, and a large number of people got off simultaneously, which allowed her to take a seat for the remainder of her ride. She remembered flagging down rural buses as a missionary, which would be stopped by simply putting out your arm to indicate that you wanted to be picked up. She planned to go to a deli she had seen previously about a mile down the street. She was looking forward to getting some *Mortadella* to make some sandwiches, which was a bologna mixed with cheese chunks. She chuckled inwardly that her favorite bologna was made out of horse (usually donkey) meat, and originated with the Italians who came to the country.

She remembered cringing once she realized what her favorite bologna was made from, and it surprised her even more that the meat's origins didn't deter her from eating it again, because it was so delicious.

An Argentine's diet for breakfast, lunch and dinner consists of beef, *asado* (broiled), or *parrilla* (boiled), along with few fruits and vegetables included in the mix. It was no small wonder that many people she knew complained that their h*igado* (liver) was bothering them. She surmised that it was the price one paid for such an incredible combination of world cuisines. Another one of Argentina's beloved meats is the *Chorizo*, which is a spicy sausage, or the *Salchicha*, a long, thin, less spicy sausage. Lastly, there was the intimidating M*orcilla* blood sausage, which she never had the nerve to eat, it being a mix of kidney, sweetbread, lower intestines, udder, and liver. In addition to her beloved Mortadella, there was a wide variety of Chorizo sausages - *Bife* – (beefsteak), *Bife de Costilla (Beef Rib)*, *Bife de Chorizo* (T-bone) to enjoy. Her favorite was the *Bife de Chorizo* called *Choripan,* eaten as a sandwich with *Chimichurri* vinaigrette.

She planned to get her much-anticipated *Mortadella*, a baguette of *Pan* (fresh bread), and a few condiments (mainly mayonnaise and mustard), eggs, flour, potatoes and apples, plus some *queso fresco* (fresh cheese) to make up some nice vittles for breakfast and lunch.

She knew that there was a little corner *tienda* (store) nearby where she could pick up some premade powdered milk, sold in plastic pouches to add to their *Café Malta*. And she didn't want to forget to buy a bottle of Ivess carbonated seltzer water; orange or pineapple concentrate, which needed to be added to the carbonated water to make a delicious soda. One didn't add the concentrate to the carbonated water, but the concentrate was added to your cup first and then the carbonated seltzer to your cup in grand fashion. The seltzer bottle had a lever handle, and it was always an adventure to get the seltzer ratio just right with the fruit concentrate.

Her favorite hot drinks were *Boldo* (herbal tea made from Chamomile and Peppermint leaves) and C*afé Malta,* which was a natural wheat roasted substitute for coffee. She was certain that Paul would enjoy all of these items for breakfast, lunch or even as a snack later on. She made sure to make one last quick stop to the Panaderia for a freshly baked French Baguette and sweet rolls on the way home, to be eaten with *Dulce de Leche* (caramel spread) slathered over each slice and dipped in *Café Malta.*

Argentina certainly has a National Sweet tooth. *Dulce de Leche* is used similarly to how butter is used in the U.S., as this caramel mixture is a beloved spread found on top of and inside of numerous favorite treats. With several bags full of yummy food and drinks, Celeste found the nearest bus stop heading in the right direction and waited for the bus to arrive. She noticed two American backpackers who looked perplexed as they quietly discussed in English which bus

Loralee Lago

to take. One backpacker was saying that they were at the right stop, and the other, looking at their written instructions, was in disagreement.

The two backpackers looked as out of place as she did in the group of people with their tall frames, light eyes, and blonde hair. She casually walked over to them and said, "Hey, can I help you guys out?"

The two frazzled men quickly turned their attention to her, relieved to hear a native English speaker addressing them. In response, they both simultaneously exhaled in relief, explaining that they needed to take the bus to the *monté barrio* (Mountain neighborhood) as they showed her their directions written in Spanish.

"Okay," said Celeste, "according to these directions, you need to take the bus heading North on the corner of *Derecho*, (Right) street and *Avenida Justo*, (Justice Avenue.) You are almost there, but you just need to cross the street and stand on that corner," she directed with her hand.

"Hey, look," she said. "I see that your bus is coming now. If you leave now, you can catch it just in time!"

The two jumped into action as they smiled in gratitude and yelled their thanks while they sprinted across the busy street to catch the bus. Celeste smiled, grateful that she could be there to help them find their way. She loved helping people; it was her small way of serving her fellow man.

Her bus arrived within a few minutes, and she boarded, happily heading home. This time, the bus wasn't overly packed with people, and she easily found a seat near the front and sat down. The city landscape and its people always intrigued her. A man got on board a several blocks before her stop. He glared at her, then sneered and continued to stare at her as he sat down across the aisle from her.

Celeste kept her gaze focused forward, staring blankly at her cell phone and trying to act as if nothing had disturbed her while deciding what she needed to do next. Someone suddenly yanked her hair back from the crown of her head down to the top of the bus seat, leaving a terrified Celeste at his mercy. He whispered into her ear not to make a sound; his breath reeked of alcohol and decaying teeth. He growled that her boyfriend had better leave things alone or that there would be consequences, then let her go as she sat there frozen in fear.

She noticed that the bus driver and other passengers had witnessed the scene but were too afraid to look at her or help. When her discomfort level was at its peak, she knew that she was close enough to home and quickly got off early at the next stop, just as the doors were closing. She hoped that the men didn't attempt to follow her, but if they did, she'd go inside of one of the stores and call Paul. Fortunately, the men didn't follow her, so she walked the remaining two blocks home to find Paul just waking up in a sleepy, jumbled mess.

He was surprised to see her standing there with bags in hand, especially since he hadn't realized that she'd left. *I'll have to do a much better job with my overnight surveillance skills*, he thought. "Celeste, why didn't you wake me up? I don't feel comfortable with you going into town alone."

"I just wanted to do something nice for you," she said, trying to diffuse his frustration. She flashed him a conciliatory smile, saying, "Are you hungry? Thank you for keeping watch. Did you stay on watch all night? You didn't have to do that, but I am very grateful for your help. You must be famished–do homemade Apple Fritters sound good to you?"

All that Paul could do was nod as he stiffly got out of his car and limped towards the kitchen, where water was heated for *Café Malta*, and Apple Fritters were made and consumed en mass. "Thank you for the tasty breakfast. I need to go home to get showered and shaved," he said, as he rubbed the back of his neck.

"May I get that knot worked out of your neck before you leave?"

Loralee Lago

she asked, as she gently but firmly kneaded the knots on his neck with her agile fingers and thumbs.

"Thanks, that feels so much better," he said. "You're a pro. Have you done this before?"

"Yes! I used to take care of my mother's back frequently when she worked full time as a shuttle driver at the airport. I learned how to properly work out her back knots when she had extra-long shifts." Celeste smiled as she gently placed her hand over his and said, "It is the least that I can do for you keeping watch over me all night."

"No problem," he said. "I don't want anything happening to you. Your safety and well-being are of the utmost importance to me, even more important than any assignment."

Celeste hesitated but knew that she needed to mention the angry men who threatened her on the bus. "About that…umm, there was a scary looking man and another man who threatened me, right before I got off the bus on the way back to the house."

That stopped Paul in his tracks as he stiffened up and looked her square in the eyes. "What? Why did you wait to tell me about this incident until now?" he said heatedly.

"I didn't want you to run off to catch the nearest bus. I wanted you to enjoy your breakfast with me," she said cautiously.

"Can you describe them to me?"

"I only saw one of them, as the other man came up from behind me, and all I could see were his rough, weathered hands. The man sitting across from me was about 5'2, 170 pounds with dark brown eyes and black hair."

Paul hesitated then said, "Well, that's helpful, but there are thousands of men that meet that exact description in this city. Is there anything more specific in his features, clothing, or something else that you can recall?"

Celeste thought for a moment and said; "I saw a gold chain with a lucky horseshoe on it. What made it unique was that there was a large gold nugget nestled inside of the horseshoe."

"Now that's what I'm talking about," he said. "Great observation. Anything else?"

"Yes. They both had grease stained nails and calloused hands like a mechanic's."

"Anything else?"

"Yeah–when the man across from me sneered, his front tooth was gold-capped. There is nothing more that I can recall, but I'll let you know if I remember anything else."

"You did well. Now I need to check that they are not still in this area, so I'm going to take a look outside just to make sure that you aren't being stalked. Please lock the door behind me, close the rolling metal shudders and stay close to your cell, while I'm gone for safety purposes."

Celeste agreed to do all that he asked. Paul came back about five minutes later and said that there was no sign of the men from the bus, but nonetheless, he didn't feel comfortable leaving her again.

"Celeste, I'd feel much better if you'd come with me to my apartment while I get cleaned up, and then we can go down to the Police Station to discuss this newest development with Captain Lucas and get an update on the situation. Do you think you'd recognize that man if you saw him again?"

"Yes, I definitely would–that hate filled sneer on his face is hard to forget. Also, the man that pulled my hair had a voice that seems familiar to me, although I can't put my finger on who he is."

"Okay, mull it over, and maybe it will come to you," suggested Paul.

As she rode in Paul's car towards his apartment, she thought of the man named Paul Ford Lago who seemed to be constantly on her mind. She had learned quite a bit about him in the months that they had called, texted, and emailed each other. He was the youngest child of Manuel and Patricia Lago, and his father was a very handsome, charismatic smooth-talking Spaniard from Madrid. Paul's mother and father met in Illinois while Patricia was working for a college as an executive secretary and his father was teaching an advanced oil painting class there. Paul told her that it was love at first sight.

They soon married and moved to Redondo Beach, California, as it resembled my father's beloved homeland. Manuel had left Spain as a young man, after surviving the Spanish Civil War. He often told his son that you could have a fist full of money but couldn't buy anything to eat, during this time, as many towns had been bombed or raided, and their family was constantly on the run to the next haven until the war ended. Manuel eventually left Spain, then lived in Brazil for a short time with relatives who had also fled Spain before ultimately immigrating to North America. About 9 years ago, after Paul's mother passed away, his father remained in the U.S. until right before his own death, having a strong desire to be buried in his beloved Spain.

Paul's grandfather on the Ford side of the family was a prominent physician in New Jersey, who he was only able to visit a few times as a young child before his grandfather died unexpectedly. Paul's only memories of him were how kind his grandfather was, that he had given him $20 for his 5th birthday, smelled of peppermint, and had a passion for fishing.

Paul grew up as a typical Californian beach kid who loved going to the beach, fishing, swimming in the ocean, and looking for gold in the California hills with his best friend, Tom. Tom's dad often told the boys to let him know if they ever found anything, knowing full well that they would only find fool's gold and dirt. Once Paul graduated from Dos Pueblos High School, he was called to serve a mission in Bahia Blanca, Argentina, for two years, where he improved his Spanish and grew to love the people, food, and culture of the country.

After his mission, he enlisted in the Air Force for six years, where he specialized in Electrical Engineering in Misawa, Japan. He enjoyed the structure and challenges of being in the military but after witnessing several of his friends get shocked and nearly die, he decided that he no longer wanted to pursue that line of work.

Once he completed his time in the Air Force, he applied and trained to become an Interpol agent, where he dreamed that he would travel the world to help solve crimes while serving his country. As an agent, he had indeed traveled the globe helping many people and countries with complex cases. It was exciting, important and demanding work, but he was home for only a few weeks at a time and missed many important family functions.

He told Celeste that although he loved the work, it was hard to see the dark side of life constantly, but thankfully, being a member of the Church helped him balance life and hard things from work. His spiritual life had many happy positives that made him remain less tainted from the harsh realities of his profession. It could certainly be easy to become jaded and critical of life circumstances and humankind if he wasn't careful, but by keeping his life in balance through good living, scripture study, prayer, and service to others, it made his life worthwhile and a happy one. However, he was missing someone to share it with.

As he drove, lost in his thoughts, Paul thought about Celeste and desired that she might be that special someone. He hoped that his budding friendship with Celeste might lead him to his desired destination, where he'd settle down in one city and be there fully for his family. This would mean he'd be home every night and would require a sacrifice on his part to request a desk job, allowing all the younger guys to go out in the field for the investigations, including the notoriety and money that went with it.

He wasn't sure if he was ready to make those changes just yet, but thinking about the possibility made him smile. Yes, he'd miss the thrill of the investigation but not the constant traveling and missing out on birthdays, special occasions, and Sunday dinners with family.

Although his time in Argentina was part vacation, he knew this was an important international investigation, which would affect both Argentina and North America.

He remembered his first experience of getting off of the plane and telling people he was from the great American state of California! The people just smiled and said *WE ARE AMERICANS* too, and they were right! He never forgot that simple lesson of not being too prideful. He could be proud of the country that he was from while allowing others the dignity and pride in their country as well.

Once they arrived at the police station, Lieutenant Sosa took down the information and questioned Celeste further about the incident. He also unsuccessfully attempted to ask her out to dinner as he shamelessly flirted with her between questions by winking and smiling at her, which made her a bit uneasy. Although Lieutenant Sosa was a flirt, he took the time to file a detailed police report, as Captain Lucas would require it to be done properly. Captain Lucas instructed Lieutenant Sosa to have one of their top graphic artists make a sketch of the man that was with Celeste on the bus, including his golden nugget horseshoe necklace and gold-capped front tooth.

After reviewing the report and speaking with Celeste, Captain Lucas said, "Celeste, these men definitely appear to be dangerous– they threatened and assaulted you. I will have my officers be on the lookout for anyone resembling this man. It's the least I can do, as you and Paul have been a tremendous help to our department in this homicide. I will have Lieutenant Sosa check the police data banks for anyone resembling your description and let you know once we find a match."

Both Celeste and Paul were grateful for Captain Lucas' consideration. While they were there, Paul and Captain Lucas discussed the current findings and what course of action should be taken next.

"We must be on the right trail after these threats, but it seems as if these guys are one step ahead of us. There must be a mole," suggested Paul. Captain Lucas solemnly nodded his head in agreement with Paul's suggestion. Paul and Captain Lucas had no concrete proof but suspected that the man with dirty nails and horseshoe nugget necklace might have been a miner or worker at Señor Susaniche's Ranch. "So, we must be getting close to discovering their plans and who they are, if they felt the need to intimidate Celeste."

"I won't be surprised if this sneering man was a thug hired to scare and intimidate us from our current course of action. I think it all stems from the questioning at the mine; somehow it's all connected. Horses, gold, branding irons, seared soles, and horseshoe-nugget necklaces are now key puzzle pieces in this investigation," said Paul.

After scanning the criminal data banks, Lieutenant Sosa reported to Captain Lucas that they didn't get any 'definitive hits' to positively identify the gold-capped tooth, horseshoe necklace-wearing man. He did, however, place before him a few dozen mug shots of various men that were strong possibilities. After Celeste's careful review, it was determined that none of the men were the man that they were looking for.

"Keep looking, Sosa," commanded Captain Lucas. "A man with that much to remember about him certainly has a rap sheet a mile long."

"Will do, Captain."

CHAPTER 6

Our Next Stop Will Be...

As they walked out of the Police Station, Paul attempted to get Celeste's mind off of the case for a few hours by offering her a tour of Buenos Aires, saying, "I found a guy online that will take us on a tour of the city, including seeing the most popular tourist attractions mainly from his car. Do you want to go?"

"Heck YEAH!" said Celeste, a smile spreading over her face.

"Great, I'll text him that we are ready to be picked up now-he will be here within a few minutes. Here's a picture of him next to his car that he texted to me."

"Wow, you can't miss that car driving down the street. It's…vintage."

Loralee Lago

"'Vintage' is a very polite way to say it's a bucket of rust and bolts," said Paul.

"What are you talking about? That car has a ton of personality. Look at that velvet interior with fringed Argentinian Flag on the rear-view mirror, the half dozen bobble head futbol players on his dash and the I Heart *futbol* sticker covering a big dent on the front fender. The rusty florescent green and purple pin stripped custom paint-job is what really catches my eye, though. Do you think that car looks reliable? It looks to be on its last legs, although you would think by the expression on his face that it's brand new, with the way that he stands there with his arm on the hood." she said.

"You're right. I think he does love his car and is proud to be an enterprising business owner, providing for his family. I'll bet you dinner at Café Tortoni that he's named his car," said Paul.

"Deal!" said Celeste. "But it must be an actual name, not the Beast or Señor Frog Legs." Paul shook her hand in agreement to the terms of the bet.

Within minutes, Jose pulled up to the curb and enthusiastically greeted Paul and Celeste in English, saying, "Hi, I'm Jose! I'll be your tour guide for the afternoon. I'm very excited to show you our beautiful city; I hope that you will enjoy the tour."

"Hi Jose!" said Paul. "We'd like your deluxe package please. Go ahead and pull out all of the stops and take us to your favorite stops today."

"Great, you've made the right choice. Let's get going," Jose said as he bowed slightly and opened the car's back door with a rusty creak. "I'm pleased to be of service to you today. Please enter now."

"Your English is very good, Jose," commented Celeste.

"Thank you! I've had lots of practice since I married my wife, Ashley, who is from Riverside, California. We met ten years ago when she visited the city with her friends and went on my tour. I guess the city and I were unforgettable, as she decided to remain here. We married about 9 years ago and have two eight-year-old *gemelos* (twins) named Candice and Cody. I love this city–it has so much history and is noisy and vibrant; like me! You're going to love it too. Here's a quick list of the places that we'll be going," he said as he handed them a well-used binder with "Top Ten Tourist Attractions in Buenos Aires" written on the cover. Inside were ten laminated sheets with the picture and name of each attraction that they would be visiting, including a brief history of each. Each destination was numbered in descending order.

#10 Puerto Madero (Seaport shopping area)

#9 Museo Nacional de Bellas Artes (National Museum of Fine Arts)

#8 Teatro Colon (Colon Theatre)

#7 Carlos Thays Botanical Gardens

#6 El Obelisco (The Monument)

#5 Café Tortoni

#4 Plaza Dorrego

#3 Caminito (Little Street Neighborhood)

#2 Recoleta Cemetery

#1 Plaza Mayo

"I think that you'll want to live in this city and become a Porteño (local of Buenos Aires) indefinitely after the tour. It has a heart of gold, and the people are unforgettable," said Jose.

"You're right, I already do!" said Celeste.

"Jose, from the look of your car's vibrant paint and decor, I'm going to venture to say that she is your pride and joy!" said Paul.

Celeste elbowed Paul and mumbled, "You're not allowed to steer the conversation about the car. This has to come out naturally."

Loralee Lago

"I don't see why not, as I want to win, and I really want to go to Café Tortoni," whispered Paul. "Let's ask him if we can go there last."

"Oh yeah, she's my pride and joy; I painted her myself," said Jose. "We've been through a lot together and taken thousands of tourists around this city through the years. I've put more than 150,000 miles on her and have met many interesting people along the way. Yesterday, I picked up an Italian couple and took them to see Eva Peron's tomb in Recoleta Cemetery. They got into a huge fight about whether or not Napoleon's granddaughters were actually buried there, which artist sculpted the best statuary on the mausoleums, and even bickered over who the other elite people were buried there. I couldn't believe people would fight over dead people. If you're gonna fight, make it worth your time–like about who's going to win the world cup."

Paul gave Celeste a knowing eye and said, "See, he knows what's important too."

"Don't you dare ask him who his favorite team is, as I want to enjoy this tour," said Celeste with glaring eyes laser focused on Paul.

"Enough about my stories for the moment," Jose said, as he pulled out onto the busy street and went into Tour Guide mode. "Please fasten your seat belts. In a few minutes we'll arrive at Puerto Madero in the Rio de la Plata waterfront. This area was originally the main port of Buenos Aires until the late 19th century, when the larger cargo ships made it obsolete. The city decided to make lemonade out of lemons and turned the aging warehouses into homes, businesses and restaurants to add diversity and interest to the aging district. You'll really enjoy everything here he said as they arrived."

"I see what you mean Jose," said Celeste. It's really got a modern vibe here as there are many young people on the docks enjoying the cafés and patronizing the red brick specialty shops."

"There's even a great walking trail that loops around the bay to the wildlife Costanera Sur Ecological Reserve. I like bringing my family here to enjoy the wildlife and to spend time feeding the fish and seagulls. Did you notice the amazing Puente de la Mujer suspension bridge on the bay?" said Jose.

"You can't miss it. That bridge has some sleek architectural lines that engineering enthusiasts could spend days studying," said Paul, in excitement.

Both Paul and Celeste were impressed by Jose's knowledge of the city and history of Puerto Madero. He easily navigated the car through the city at a high rate of speed, weaving in and out of the busy traffic with ease, as if he was driving on a quiet Sunday morning. It was a wild ride, but somehow, they felt at ease with Jose behind the wheel.

"Our next stop will be the Obelisco!" announced Jose.

"Shouldn't it be #9, the Museo Nacional de Bellas Artes, Jose?" asked Celeste. The binder said it was compared to the Louvre in France because of its outstanding collection of European and Argentine artists.

Jose jokingly said, "Hey I'm the tour guide here and get to decide when we'll go to each site. *No te preocupes* (Don't you worry); we'll see each one by the end of the tour, just sit back and enjoy the ride."

"You're the boss," said Paul. "Drive on, Jefe Jose!"

"El Obelisco is a much-loved attraction that stands over 223 feet high over the city and was built to commemorate the city's 160th anniversary in 1936 where 9 de Julio Avenue intersects with Corrientes Avenue. I will drive the roundabout surrounding the monument twice, before leaving the area to give you time to take your pictures. So get ready."

Both Paul and Celeste rolled their windows down and took some great selfies while in the cab, with the Obelisco in the background on their first pass. On the next pass, they each took pictures of the monument and other tourists visiting.

"I have really enjoyed seeing the city in this mode," said Celeste. "I feel like I'm fully part of the city's rhythm and everyday life."

"Are you ready for some unforgettable art collections? We're now headed to the National Museum of Fine Arts. It has an outstanding collection of European and Argentine artists."

"Yes! I can't wait!" exclaimed Celeste.

"I'll drop you off at the front door and will be back in an hour and a half. Will that work for you? Just text me once you're ready to leave, and I'll be waiting for you right where I left you, here by the curb," said Jose.

"That works for us," agreed Paul.

Once Jose dropped Paul and Celeste off at the entrance, they were overwhelmed with vast size of the museum, its seemingly unlimited collections and marveled at the diversity of art that ranged from the Middle Ages to the 20th Century.

"You could spend days here," marveled Celeste. "I'm in heaven!"

"I think an hour and a half is more than enough time, don't you think?" said Paul; not wanting to admit that he wasn't into 'artsy stuff'.

"Let's do a quick review of the layout of the museum and then pinpoint which areas that we will go first, to utilize our time efficiently," suggested Celeste.

"Whatever you decide, sounds great to me," responded Paul.

"I'd like to focus on the museum's highlights, which are here in the brochure. Let's start with Augustine Rodin's sculpture, then go to see Pio Collivadinos's sculpture of 'The Kiss', then see 'The Lunch Break' painting and lastly, my favorite painting of 'Two Dancers in Red and Yellow' by Degas," said Celeste. "It is a real honor for me to experience each work of art in person."

Celeste was like a kid in a candy store as they went from piece to piece and stood quietly soaking it all in, fully appreciating the artistry and beauty of each masterpiece. Paul liked looking at each work of artwork but loved watching the wonder and joy in Celeste's eyes the most, as her face would light up with each new discovery.

"Are you ready to see the last masterpiece before we leave?" said Celeste.

"Sure. Absolutely." Paul said, grateful that their time at the museum was almost at an end.

"I am a big fan of Degas and am so thrilled to see 'Two Dancers in Red and Yellow'," she said as she walked into the room where the painting was displayed and stopping short to catch her breath as she caught the first glimpse of it. "Isn't it incredible? Degas's brushstroke layers and attention to the intricate details of each dancer captivates me. I feel as though I'm a part of the painting, as he has caught the essence of the two ballerinas, their friendship and love of dance. Look how he's managed to even make their tutus appear translucent. Thank you so much for sharing this with me, Paul. We can go now."

"You're welcome, Celeste. I'm glad that we could do this together and that it meant so much to you. I actually enjoyed it more than I thought I would," admitted Paul.

"I think it has been the highlight of our tour thus far!"

"My favorite part of the exhibit was that it was free and especially that you were delighted," said Paul. "I'll text Jose now to pick us up for our next stop."

True to form, Jose was waiting for them outside of the museum with a big smile saying, "Didn't I tell you how incredible it was?"

"You were right; it was more than I could have ever hoped for. Thank you Jose, for bringing us here."

"You're welcome. If you enjoyed that, at our next stop, you will appreciate even more as it is a local favorite called, 'Carlos Thays

Botanical Gardens'."

"Now we're talking *my* language," said Paul enthusiastically.

"You'll be able to get out in nature and just stroll around enjoying the French landscaping done by Carlos Thays. There are more than 5,000 species of plants and it is a great way to enjoy the quieter side of the city. I'll park right here and wait for you; feel free to take as much time as you like to take pictures. It is Ashley's and my favorite place to go for our date nights, especially when we need a break from our active twins," said Jose.

Paul and Celeste immediately became enamored with the masterfully designed gardens, trees, flowers and sculpted bushes. The fall leaves made the Garden seem even more magical with the red, orange and yellow foliage crunching underfoot as they walked along the pathway. There was even a local vendor selling ham and cheese sandwiches with cola sodas, which they promptly purchased and sat down on the park bench to enjoy.

"This is certainly a little piece of paradise," said Celeste. "I can see why the locals love coming here."

"I agree; this place just speaks to my soul. I'm especially cherishing the time watching the various species of birds interacting with each other and all of the cats in the garden basking in the sun."

"Yes, it appears that once the cats detected your pheromones, they've followed after you wherever we've gone. I feel like you're their pied piper–it seems that they each want a bit of your attention."

"That, and I think they want some of my ham sandwich," said Paul with a huge grin, as he relished every moment being in *his* element.

Paul gave the cats each a piece of ham from the last few bites of his sandwich and then looked over at Celeste to see if she had anything left to share. When she didn't, he said, "Hey Celeste, do you happen to have anything in your purse that I can feed to the cats?"

"Umm, I think that all I have are a few peanuts at the bottom of my purse. Do you think that they'll eat them?"

"Let's see... Hey there, little ones. Do you like peanuts?" Each cat cautiously sniffed at the few peanuts that were placed in front of them, then deemed them suitable for eating and happily crunched their treats before licking their paws and chops to show their enjoyment.

"Who knew cats would eat peanuts?" asked Celeste.

As Paul and Celeste walked back towards Jose's car, they noticed a man staring at them intently. Paul put his arm around Celeste protectively and said, "Let's get back to the car now; something's wrong." They quickly got into Jose's car, grateful to be free from an uncomfortable situation. As Jose pulled out onto the street, a man on a motorcycle rode up next to them, pulled a handgun out of his jacket pocket and fired a few shots into the car's window before riding away. Paul quickly pushed Celeste to the floor and ducked for cover as the first shot shattered the back window. The shots sent glass shards everywhere in the car as Jose ducked his head low just above the steering wheel while he drove erratically to escape the scene.

"Estas bien?" (Are you two okay?) he asked, his voice shaking.

"Yes," said Paul. "When I saw the man lift the gun, I pushed Celeste down to the floor and ducked below the window for cover. Miraculously, neither one of us is hurt. It's a good thing your car is built like a tank. How are you, my friend?"

"I'm fine, but my baby has been badly injured! I think that the rider is coming back around the roundabout for another shot. Take cover while I try and exit, right as he drives by. It is our only hope of escaping another direct hit. Hang on...Here he comes!"

The gunman brought the motorcycle near the driver's side of the car and raised his gun for several more shots, but this time, Jose slammed on his brakes as the man shot; as bullets hit the hood of the car and left fender. Jose expertly drove the car off the exit just as the motorcyclist sped past, giving them valuable seconds to flee before another attempt was made. The car groaned from the hits. "I think that one of the bullets hit the radiator hose, as she is spewing something out from the hood. Hang in there, my Maria Angelica," he said as the car sputtered and faltered. They all muttered a quick prayer heavenward that Maria Angelica wouldn't fail them and that they'd escape this volatile situation without harm.

"Okay. Here he comes again! Let him get right up next to us again, but this time, swerve into him so that he loses control of the bike. Can you do that, Jose?" asked Paul. "I'll tell you when to do it."

"Ten-four, good buddy!" responded Jose. "Cut him off on your command. Check!"

Once the shooter got up next to them again, Paul yelled, "*Ahora* (NOW) Jose!"

Jose jerked the steering wheel to the right, causing the car to collide with the motorcyclist, who quickly lost control and crashed into a nearby tree. The car's back passenger tire blew with the hit, causing it to fishtail violently as each person fervently prayed that the car wouldn't flip over as Jose fought to keep Maria Angelica on the road.

"Jose, slow down, but do not stop. Please take us directly to the Police Station. Do you understand?" instructed Paul.

"Si, Señor Lago," he said with a quiver in his voice. "Does this mean that you don't want me to finish the tour? By the way, to your right is Recoleta Cemetery," he offered. "I'm glad that we won't be going there today."

"Correct, my friend. Let's get you, Maria Angelica, Celeste and I to safety."

Jose drove the car like a bat out of H-E double hockey sticks, hardly acknowledging the blown tire, directly to the police station and came to a screeching stop, blowing out the front passenger side tire with a loud pop as it slammed into the curb. Jose placed his forehead on the steering wheel in utter relief then lifted it from its resting spot and exclaimed, "That was the most terrifying experience of my life, yet exhilarating. No one is ever going to believe this story!"

"Yes, it is an epic tour tale for the books," said Paul. "I don't think you'll ever top that one. Jose, please come inside with us so that we can report the incident. Plus, it will give us all time to recover from the trauma."

"Yes. I'll be talking about this one for years to come although I'm not sure if Maria Angelica survived," he said sadly. "Why would someone want to shoot at us–at my baby? What am I going to do? What will I tell my wife?"

"Let's get inside and talk with the police first, and then you can call Ashley to tell her that you are okay," recommended Paul assuredly.

"Yes. You are right. Good call," agreed Jose.

After dispatching the police to the scene of the crash, they found little evidence of the biker, except for a large scar on the tree that he'd hit. It was as if nothing had ever occurred, leaving the police the arduous task of knocking on all of the neighbors' doors to look for eyewitnesses of the crash.

After several hours at the police station, they were finally released to go home. Paul called a cab for Jose and a tow truck for Maria Angelica, saying, "Jose, I'm very sorry for Maria Angelica's injuries. I will personally cover the cost to get her repaired, so you can be back in business pronto. Here is the money that I owe you for the tour plus a 500% tip. I'd give you more, except that is all of the money that I have on me. You went far beyond the call of duty to save us from a dire situation–we owe you our lives."

"Thank you, Paul. I don't know why someone has done this, but I hope that you are able to get the people involved arrested for all of our sakes. Yes, I think that I earned your tip today. *Mucho Gusto*! (Thank you)."

After Jose had left for home, Paul hailed another taxi to take them back to Celeste's Air B&B.

"Celeste, may I please sleep on the couch tonight? Scout's honor, you will hardly know that I'm here. I would feel better knowing that you are okay after all of this."

"Yes, please," she said as she gave him a big hug in gratitude and just held him for a few minutes, then lifted her head and said, "Don't forget that I owe you dinner at Café Tortoni's."

"You're right, you do! Although he actually referred to his beloved car as both baby and Maria Angelica, so I call it a draw on the bet," said Paul.

"Do you think they'll deliver?" said Celeste. "I think I'd like to dine in for the rest of the evening."

Paul nodded in agreement. "Consider it done."

CHAPTER 7

I Heart Bariloche

Paul felt that now was a good day to take a little trip to a place that he and Celeste had always wanted to visit, the magnificent Andes Mountains. The timing couldn't be better to get away from all of the madness for a few days, and he knew just the place: the Swiss Village of San Carlos de Bariloche or Bariloche for short. The chocolate of Bariloche was world-renowned in this quaint town known as Little Switzerland, surrounded by the 21,780' Andes Mountains, and home of the highest peak in the world – Aconcagua. Bariloche was also famous for its own German Oktoberfest (chocolate fest) and Welsh Eisteddfods (competitions that involve testing individuals in singing, dancing and musicianship).

Celeste happily agreed to a day of driving and visiting this beautiful town, as she was particularly enthusiastic to ingest as much gourmet chocolate as humanly possible. She didn't want to miss an opportunity to see the majestic Andes Mountains first-hand, try her hand at yodeling and indulge in as many varieties of fine Swiss and German foods available. They drove for part of the day through the golden Pampa grasslands with vibrant wild sunflowers lining the roadside, which gradually gave way to the lush pine greenery, colorful autumn leaves ablaze in full fall glory and finally arrive at the snow-covered mountains of Bariloche.

"Back home, I can't wait to go on my yearly color ride." said Celeste.

"What's a color ride?" he said.

It's my favorite time of year to take a drive up the mountains to see the vivid reds, yellows and oranges of the trees as they prepare to drop their leaves before winter begins. I look forward to witnessing nature's masterpiece every fall and call it the color ride." said Celeste.

"That's pretty neat. I think we have fulfilled your color ride hopes today as I've never seen a better variety of leaf colors." said Paul.

"We have. I'll try and take a mental picture of this season's splendor to keep in my memory banks until we experience it again in the U.S. in October. This time of year gives me such gratitude for the magnificent creations of God."

"Yeah. You're right. It feels good to be a part of such incredible vistas. It's truly amazing. I'm glad that we could enjoy the color ride together this year." said Paul.

"Me too," she said as she held his hand. The wild sunflowers and daises along the road seem to be calling to me to get out and run through them singing "The Sound of Music" like Julie Andrews."

"Your wish is my command," he said, as he promptly pulled over the car for a mini photo shoot of Celeste peaking up over the flower tops with a crown of daisies in her hair that she'd made. Paul also got some candid selfie shots of both of them walking hand in hand in the field of yellow sunflowers.

Celeste couldn't help herself and sang a snippet of the song with gusto, "The hills are alive, with the sound of music!" as she twirled amongst the flowers.

Suddenly stopping mid twirl, she said, "Hey, look at that waterfall coming off the side of the mountain. Do we have time to walk closer to get a few pictures of us in front of it?"

"Yes! Let's do it!" he said as he took her hand and they ran through the field to the base of the mountain for a couple's photo op. It was clear by their sense of awe that both Paul and Celeste were in their happy place out in nature.

Rejuvenated, they returned to the car after a half an hour and began their journey once again towards Bariloche.

As they drove, Celeste couldn't resist asking Paul, "Who do you really think is behind all of these murders?"

"I think it is a small band of robbers whose sole purpose is to gain riches, power and notoriety. This type of band will stop at nothing to reach their objective, which is to rob, steal and kill anyone who gets in their way as well as form strategic secret alliances with other people of influence. That is why it what makes them so difficult to track as they help one another in times of trouble, but are also known to take out any member who reveals information about their illegal activities."

"So, do you think that Carlos, Graciela and Rafael were killed because they betrayed the band and that the group's calling card is the O.N. searing of their soles?" said Celeste.

"Yes I do. These kinds of groups can be very successful and more than likely have several branches throughout the country. They are usually very close knit and are similar to the mafia, but are smaller and more secretive in their movements. The few suspected members that we've interviewed haven't given us anything significant; just a piece here and there is extracted from them, which allows us to slowly put the puzzle pieces together before we can see the full picture."

"This group seems to be relatively well organized. I believe that if we can detain either the informant or ringleader, everything will come together to get this case resolved. Patience is the key and paying close attention to every minute detail helps us in solving the case. That is why Captain Lucas is putting so much time and effort into interviewing each person of interest and then having us follow up on each piece of information from those interviews."

"Crime circuits like this group are all over the world and many times involve high-ranking officers and officials. I treat everyone I meet on each case as a person of interest; even someone like Captain Lucas, a Judge or a District attorney are included. Being cognizant of all persons involved in the case is imperative, especially when you suspect a mole." said Paul.

"Do you really think our mole is Captain Lucas? He seems so unlikely."

"I won't count him out, but I do know that by following each person of interest along with both their verbal and physical cues, we'll have our question answered soon enough." said Paul.

"Wow! I've never even considered how complicated an investigation could be before now. It gives me plenty to think about. How about I lighten the mood and ask you a not so important personal question?" said Celeste.

"What do you want to know?" asked Paul.

"By any chance, do you have a name for your car back home?" asked Celeste.

"No...Do you?"

"Yeah I do! I have an emerald green Toyota, Venza, which I

lovingly named 'Vanessa'."

"Why Vanessa?" he asked.

"Because it rhymes with Venza. Get it? Vanessa Venza," she said.

"Do all women really name their cars?" Paul asked curiously.

"Not all, but many do. Would you tell me what kind of car that you drive, and maybe I can come up with a name for your baby?"

"Sure. Umm…Make it a manly name though. Nothing wimpy."

"Okay, manly it is. Color, make and model please?"

"It's a Red Nissan Altima."

"Okay. I think I have an idea, and it will be Oriental in theme, since you were stationed overseas in Japan. I think you're gonna to like it."

"Okay. I like that theme," he said.

"How does…'Red Dragon' sound to you?"

"Hey, I like it! Red Dragon it is. Thanks, Celeste. Now my life is complete, but don't ever mention his name in front of any guys, as I'll get a lot of flak for it."

"You got it!" she said as they drove into Bariloche.

"I feel like I've been transported to another time and country." said Celeste looking at the European designed businesses and quaint chalets in wonder.

"This city was designed by European immigrates who wanted a reminder of their beloved Swiss homeland. You certainly get the feeling that you are in Switzerland," Paul informed her.

"I think they've accomplished their objective. It's absolutely magical, like fairytale magical!" said Celeste. "I want to move here immediately! Maybe one day I could have a little ski chalet right there on the mountain," she said pointing at the mountaintop.

Loralee Lago

As they drove down Main Street, it truly felt like they were riding through a Swiss Bavarian Village in the Alps. The architecture was breathtaking and the scenery was the finest that God offered on earth. It was just what they both had envisioned it to be and more.

For lunch, they dined at a fine restaurant, named Rastros, enjoying culinary delights such as *Matambre* (stuffed rolled steak*)*, Potato Pie and a dessert of crepes with *Dulce de Leche,* topped with sliced bananas and strawberries slathered in fresh whipped cream and chocolate sauce, not to mention that they sipped on the best hot chocolate of their lives. Paul asked the waiter if he wouldn't mind asking the chef to come out to speak with them, so that they could properly thank him for such an exquisite meal.

Within minutes, a petite, spunky, red headed chef came out to greet them. "Hello, I am Denia, your chef. I understand that you've enjoyed my cuisine."

"Yes, thank you for your time. We wish to express our deep appreciation for your superb culinary skills. We especially wanted to thank you for making our time here so memorable."

"It's not often that I get such praise. Thank you–you've made my day. Your desserts will be on the house!" she said.

"Thank you for your generosity. We are much obliged!"

After their gourmet lunch and decadent dessert, they spent much of their time strolling around the quaint city and enjoyed watching the locals walking their dogs along the beautiful cobblestone streets. The architecture of all of the churches and city buildings as they strolled hand in hand were of particular interest to Paul, as he got caught up in the construction process of each building that they passed. It was if they'd been transported back to the 1940s, enjoying the slower pace and simple pleasures that the locals so kindly offered to them.

"Look! There's the world-famous Havanna Chocolate

Museum!" said Celeste. "Let's take the tour and buy some Alfajores! You can never have enough chocolate on hand. My sister's father-in-law, Frank is proof, as he has chocolate stashes in every room and drawer of his home. My grandmother Ora also has a big sweet tooth. That might explain where I get my sweet tooth from?" she said.

"Frank is a chocoholic without a doubt. I think we should buy a few boxes to bring home to share with your grandma Ora and Lynda, plus one extra box to add to Frank's chocolate stash. We don't want his chocolate supply to run low," said Paul.

"I hope that the chocolates actually make it all the way home, as I might accidentally eat many of them before they get there." chuckled Celeste.

"Okay, how about we keep one box of chocolate to eat on and mail the others home for good measure?" said Paul.

"Great call," she replied.

They relished in the time that they spent talking with one another and being a couple, even though they didn't know if they considered themselves as officially dating just yet. Celeste's face flushed beet red when the waiter referred to her as his esposa (wife) in his strong German-Spanish accent, when he'd asked what they would like for lunch as he took their orders. She did, however, love the moment when Paul placed his hand over hers and just let it rest there as they perused the menu together. They held hands throughout the day and relished walking throughout the town, looking for just the perfect special memento to remember their time there.

"I hope that we find a gift shop that sells Cuckoo clocks!" expressed Celeste. "It's my dream to own an extra-large one that has a couple kissing in front of a chalet, with people dancing around the cuckoo bird when it comes out to usher in the new hour."

"I think I see just the shop right over there. It even looks like a Cuckoo clock from the outside." Paul observed.

Loralee Lago

"I think I've died and gone to heaven!" Celeste exclaimed in excitement. "Quick, let's go before they close for the day."

To her amazement, every square inch of interior wall-space of the shop was covered in Cuckoo clocks of various sizes, shapes and themes. After meticulously examining every clock, she was able to find an extra-large Black Forest cuckoo clock with a couple kissing on the front next to a barn with a cow, sheep and dog, including dancing couples that came out at the stroke of each hour. Celeste squealed in delight as she gingerly pushed the large hand to the twelve position, as the couple kissed, music played, couples danced and the small bird cuckooed twelve times. "This is music to my ears. It's truly a dream come true!" cooed Celeste contentedly.

"It's incredible to watch your infatuation each time that it cuckoos. I love how you are so passionate about the little things in life and how much happiness that it has brought you to have finally found your heart's desire," said Paul.

At Paul's insistence, he promptly paid for the treasured memento, then had it wrapped up and shipped home to Nevada so that it wouldn't get crushed in her luggage on its way home. Celeste was amazed at his generosity, foresight and thoughtfulness, as each day she grew to cherish him more and more.

That evening they dined at Antojos Restaurant on an unforgettable meal of *Churrasco Rebosado* (Filet Mignon in Egg Batter) with Chimichurri Vinaigrette, Au-gratin potatoes, Fire-Roasted Asparagus, Orange Salad and French bread to sop it all up.

They ended their meal with Celeste choosing a delectable Mango Pudding topped with fresh strawberries and Paul ordering the Orange and Chocolate Flan with extra chocolate syrup, whipped cream and a cherry on top!

Celeste mentioned, "I've never had so many decadent foods and treats in one place! After all this chocolate I've eaten today, I may not sleep for days. I think that I've officially got chocolate coursing through my veins now. Maybe the people here will consider me an honorary Bariloche citizen since I've got both Swiss and German blood in my family heritage and want to live here indefinitely."

Paul winked, smiled, and said, "You never know; I think that they just might. Hey, I see on the travel brochure that they have night skiing here. Want to go?"

"Yes! But only if I can have a bite of your Orange and Chocolate Flan. But, I must warn you that my skiing is pretty basic. All that I know is how to put my skies together like a pizza slice to stop and keep them parallel like French fries to go," said Celeste.

"Sure, here's a bite," he said as he lifted his spoon full of flan to her mouth and then followed up with a chocolate and whipped cream laden smooch on her cheek to top it off. "No problem about only having basic ski skills, as that's about all I know too," Paul said as he licked his lips in pure bliss! "May I have a bite of your Mango Pudding too?"

"Only if I can give you an amazing chocolate cheek smooch too," said Celeste in delight.

"You got it, babe!" he said.

Later they were able to rent their snow gear and took the lift up the mountain that was literally only a few blocks away from their hotel. "Now this is how you live up close and personal to everything," said Celeste. As they rode the lift, they held hands as they looked down over the mesmerizing candlelit ski slope. "It looks like the winter wonderland of my dreams," said Celeste. Suddenly, she couldn't help herself as she sang.... "Yodel-ay-dee-ohhhh!" Then waited for the echo to return from the mountainside.

The echo reverberating off of the mountain was magical, and Paul also tried his hand at yodeling, singing 'yodel-ay-dee-ooooohhhh,' which quickly turned sour as he sputtered and coughed, trying to save face in his yodel fail.

Loralee Lago

"I think I may have to leave the yodeling to you–I sounded more like a cat coughing up a fur ball," grimaced Paul. They both laughed as they continued yodeling, with the other skiers joining in on the yodeling fun until they got to the top of the mountain.

Celeste beamed and said, "I've always wanted to do that!"

"You've been practicing, haven't you?" said Paul. "That was an amazing experience that I won't ever forget!"

"Yeah, I have to admit that I have, as it is the 2nd thing today that I've checked off of my bucket list," responded Celeste.

"You have a bucket list?"

"Uh, yeah. I thought everyone did. Don't you?" she asked.

"No. I don't, but I'm curious to hear what's on your list."

"Do you really want to know?"

He nodded sincerely in the affirmative.

"Okay, here are a few, and in no particular order of importance. Write a mystery novel, write a song, yodel in the Andes, travel to Switzerland, buy a Cuckoo clock, travel to England, Spain, France, and Italy to experience the culture, and especially to enjoy the people and their foods. I also want to become a voice-over artist for TV and radio spots, publish a children's book made from the bedtime stories that I made up with my niece and nephew, save enough money so that I can help others in need, retire comfortably, marry, have two children, raise them in the church and to be productive and honest citizens. Additionally, I want to be a service missionary with my husband. How's that for a few?"

"Wow! You really want to do all of THAT?"

"Yep," said Celeste.

"I'm impressed; you've inspired me. I think I need to rethink this bucket list stuff and make one of my own. First on my list is to ski down this romantic, glowing slope with the most beautiful woman I've ever met," he said, as he grabbed her hand and kissed it!

She blushed at his compliment and hand kiss but tried to recover from her embarrassment by saying, "Is there anything that you want to do that you haven't done yet?"

"I want to write a screenplay about many of my experiences as an Interpol agent —where the names, places and top-secret stuff will be altered and classify it as fiction —work normal hours in one city, go deep sea fishing and swim with a great white shark! How's that for a start?"

"Awesome! You already have your bucket list ready to go. I think I can help you with the writing portion of that script for your screenplay, but I'm not too sure about swimming with a great white shark," she said with trepidation.

"Hey, I didn't realize that I actually have a number of things that I still want to do. Thanks for helping me think it through. I'm anxious to begin checking off each item, especially if you're with me," said Paul.

They helped each other off the ski lift and attempted to ski hand in hand, but they found it too problematic, so they just enjoyed staying close by one another.

Skiing down the slopes with glow sticks in hand was more magical than they could have imagined. They reveled in the midnight star-filled sky, in one another and the majestic scenery. Celeste was proud of herself, as she only fell once during the run, and Paul was right there, helping her get back up on her skis. She was grateful for his attentive ways. The air was crisp; the snow was like powder and glistened like diamonds in the moonlight.

As they skied, Paul suddenly blurted out. "How did your parents meet, and how did your dad propose to your mom?"

Shocked but encouraged that he wanted to know about her parents, Celeste said, "My parents were high school sweethearts.

They wisely realized that they weren't ready to get married at that point and decided to attend different colleges first to make sure that they didn't miss out on being single. Then, after three years of studying and dating other people, that they would return home and get married, if they were unattached and interested in one another."

"I guess it worked out for them," said Paul.

"Yes, it did. The time on their own proved to be very beneficial, which allowed them to be free of ties, while going to college. It gave each of them the time to grow into who they were, before settling down. Once they got home after graduation, my father didn't wait another moment and proposed to her that evening at the Venetian Hotel in an Italian gondola, and included a singing gondolier. It was truly magical! Every year they celebrate their anniversary at their favorite Italian restaurant, Maggiano's, where they had their first date. It was so romantic, overlooking the bright lights of the Las Vegas Strip. Mom said yes right away, but with one important caveat; he needed to formally ask permission from her father for her hand in marriage, and it needed to include a ham and bag of flour."

"What? Why a ham and bag of flour? I've never heard of such a thing," said Paul.

Celeste smiled and explained; "During the days when most people worked the land and finances were tight, when a bride-to-be prepared to get married, the groom-to-be would officially ask for permission from the parents. This would include formally asking for their daughter's hand in marriage, and the giving of a ham and bag of flour to replace the work lost from their daughter's absence. This allowed the family a bit of help during that time so that they had a little something extra to get them through to the next season. And so, this family tradition was born and the giving of the bag of flour and a ham. It started with my great, great grandparents, Brigham and Mary Hardy."

"How did it go when your dad asked for your mom's hand with the ham and flour?"

"It went well, as my grandfather happily gave his permission. This year, they'll have been married for 36 years!"

"There must be some merit in this ham and flour proposal tradition then," said Paul.

She laughed and said, "There certainly is."

Before they knew it, they had reached the bottom of the mountain and just stood longingly staring into one another's eyes. Paul wrapped his arms around her waist and leaned in for a kiss but was sidelined by a bunch of rowdy teens coming off of the mountain not far behind them as they walked by laughing, yodeling and making loud kissing noises.

Paul and Celeste decided to enjoy the energized group's fun by quickly taking off their skis and joining in their antics and nonstop yodeling as everyone tromped down the street. A local Bernese mountain dog, which also had come down from the ski slope happily tagged along, barking along with the ruckus. Paul was determined to give yodeling one last try and was pleased that he finally got in a decent yodel before they made it to the hotel.

One teen, acting as judge, said, "That yodel was rated four out of five stars, Señor. Not bad for an old man."

"Old man? When did I become an old man?" asked Paul.

"We both became old once we turned thirty, Señor Lago," Celeste teased.

"Good to know, although it's a sobering reality check indeed." Regardless, they had a great time enjoying the fun banter between the teens and reminiscing about how it was for them, when they were the same age.

Out of nowhere Paul mentioned, "I think I have an idea who tried to kill us on the motorcycle the other day."

"Who is it?" she said earnestly.

"I'm almost certain that is was either Felipe or Marcelo. I'll put in a call tonight to the station and ask detective Molina if she could see if either one of them owns a Harley Davidson Limited Edition motorcycle and verify it with the DMV."

"If my suspicions are correct, we'll have yet another major player identified in this case." Paul said.

"That would certainly explain why we've suddenly become their target." Celeste said.

"In the meantime, let's enjoy our last evening in this magical place." he said.

Paul had thoughtfully booked two separate rooms down the hall from one another so that he would be close enough should she needed anything. However, they were not too close, so that when she called her family that evening, she could speak freely, knowing that they would be pleased he was a man of his word. She would alleviate any remaining concerns regarding their vacation with her latest report of their travels.

"Hey, does 7 a.m. work for you to leave in the morning? I want to take you to one last place before we head back to Buenos Aires."

"Sure! Sounds great," agreed Celeste.

He wrapped his arms around her and leaned in to kiss her as she stroked his cheek softly with her fingertips, each leaning forward in anticipation for their long awaited first kiss but were thwarted once again as a young family walked out of the room next door with two rowdy kids, who would have surely been grossed out witnessing a kiss between them.

Paul and Celeste just smiled and acknowledged the family with an "Hola" as Paul walked towards his room, saying, "I'm in room 214 if you need anything." Once Celeste settled into her room, she called down to the front desk to inquire if there was a phone that she could use for an international call. She was delighted when they told her that there was, and she promptly walked downstairs to buy the necessary tokens for the all-important reporting call home about *all things Paul.*

The lobby's old-fashioned, dark wood phone booth was so quaint, with its hinged glass-closing door for privacy. She only needed a few minutes to speak with the operator and was instructed to insert the tokens for the call. First on her list was to talk with her twin sister, Lynda, to give her the 411 on their trip and how things were progressing with Paul.

"Hi Sister-pooh! I'm having a great time–"but before Celeste could utter another word, Lynda said, "So... how is it going with you and Paul? Inquiring minds need to know!"

"It's been incredible," said Celeste. "So much has happened. You'll never believe it, but I've been helping Paul with an investigation! It's been an eye-opening experience to see that side of him and how he handles each situation that comes up."

"Give me the scoop, sissy! Is he marriage material?"

"Indeed!"

"Has he kissed you yet?"

"Not yet, but it will happen soon. Each time the opportunity has come up for a kiss, we've been sidelined by one thing or another," said Celeste.

"What have you done today?"

"We've just walked all day through my dream town of Bariloche! I can honestly say that I adore this town and its people. You're never gonna believe it, but Paul bought me my dream Cuckoo clock! You know, the one that I've wanted for the last 15 years!"

"Wowza, if he did that and at that hefty price tag, he's really serious about you! Aren't those things around a few thousand dollars?" said Lynda.

"Yeah...I've been saving for one for a while and was blown away that he insisted on buying it, and he even had it shipped to the house. It will be home about the same time that I will be. I can just picture now where I'm going to put it on my wall, next to the fireplace in the family room. I'm so excited, that I can hardly see straight about finally getting it and especially about how well things are progressing with Paul," exclaimed Celeste.

"Where else did you go today?" said Lynda

"We went on a chocolate tour! It was very educational to see how they painstakingly make the gourmet chocolate on site, pour it into molds and put it into the boxes for sale. We got to go on a walking tour, which ended with each person getting a free piece of chocolate. I was drooling the whole time and the Alfajores that they sell here were outstanding with so many different varieties. I had no idea what an extensive process it is to make the chocolate and the variety of delicious treats that they sell. The gift store at the end ensured that we didn't leave empty handed; I got boxes for you, mom, grandma Ora and Frank too! Paul had them shipped out, so I wouldn't be tempted to eat them before they made it home."

"Oh yum! That was very insightful of him. Please tell him I'm grateful that my chocolates have been saved, as I know you would have delved into them before they made it home. I think that I like him already, especially since he saved my chocolates!" replied Lynda

"He also took me night skiing tonight! I've never done anything so romantic in my life! I don't think I'll ever forget us skiing down the slope together with light sticks in our hands. The yodeling and tromping down the street with some local teens afterwards was pure bliss as well. It was so magical!" said Celeste.

"Dang. That does sound amazing. He's impressed me and has really pulled out all of the stops in courting you during this trip. If I weren't already married, I'd marry him for sure! What has been your favorite food that you've eaten so far?" said Lynda

"Oh, definitely the gourmet Filet Minion in Egg Batter with Chimichurri Vinaigrette over the top, and the *Dulce de Leche* filled Crepes have been my favorite dessert so far, but how do you choose one favorite food with so many incredible things to eat here?"

"Wow. Those foods do sound super yummy. Okay, now the important stuff...what are your overall impressions of Paul and how the relationship is progressing? Do you think that he'd fit in with our zany family? Don't leave out any details; your sister's gotta know."

"He's a true gem for sure. There have been several times that he's put my needs before his own and is easy to be around. I love his integrity and work ethic and that he's just fun to be with too. He'd make a great addition to the family. I think you'll totally fall in love with him once you get to know him!" said Celeste.

"I'm glad to hear such a positive report about him. Do you believe that he's been true to the faith and solid in his covenants with God?" she asked earnestly.

"Yes. He is a man who has remained stalwart and true, even though his work circumstances have been challenging to keep it all in balance," replied Celeste.

"That's very good to hear. Now for the $100,000 question of the day... Do you think that he'll get along well with my dear hubby? You know this is an important one, since he may not realize that we'll be together often for family dinners and activities."

"I think that they will like each other, as they have several of the same traits of loyalty to God and country and are men of integrity. Not to mention that they both have a love for the outdoors. I'm confident that he'll do well," said Celeste.

"Great news sis! You know as your older sister by five minutes, he's gonna have to understand the twin bond thing and the importance of our daily calls and sister time together. Do you think he'll be okay with that?"

"Yes. I think that he will," confirmed Celeste.

Before she knew it, her time was up, and the operator interrupted the conversation to tell her that she had 30 seconds remaining or to please add additional tokens to extend the call. She had purchased 40 minutes worth of tokens, which she realized wasn't nearly enough time. Celeste quickly told her sister right before the line went dead, "I love you sissy. Please give mom my love too. I'll be home next Friday. We can all go out to lunch and dish on all of the fine details about the oh-so-handsome Paul Lago."

"Sounds great. I love you too sister-pooh! See you soon and safe travels," said Lynda.

Celeste hung up the phone with a contented sigh, grateful to have been able to speak with her better half. *Life is so much better with your twin and partner in crime*, she thought. *Now, I can sleep.*

Paul was up bright and early the next morning and raring to go. He lightly tapped on Celeste's door; he could hardly wait to take one last drive around the lake before they returned to Buenos Aires. He knew that Celeste would be as thrilled he was to take in every last bit of beautiful scenery in the Nahual Huapi National Park before they returned home.

"Good morning, handsome! How did you sleep? I'm ready to go!" said Celeste.

"Great! Whenever we come back again, let's take the train up here," said Paul. "I wonder if they offer a chocolate train like they do in Switzerland, where you get treated with unlimited amounts of hot chocolate and chocolate-filled croissants en route!"

"Oh, you had me at chocolate," said Celeste. "Now I'm dying to have some."

The drive through the park was all that they had hoped it would be with the beautiful vistas of the snowcapped majestic Andes Mountains and calm, clear lake. Paul pulled the car over and parked at the scenic overlook.

"I think that we've officially arrived at the pearly gates," said Celeste in awe of the view.

"I've got a little surprise for you," said Paul as he pulled out a box full of assorted sweetbreads and chocolate filled croissants for her to choose from behind the back seat, along with two large cups of hot chocolate with extra whipped cream that she'd been wishing for. As she looked over the treats, her eyes grew wide in anticipation at the chocolate lover's overload!

"I don't think I could be happier than I am at this moment," said Celeste.

Paul teased, "That might still be the chocolate talking from last night. See, I remembered to feed you this time."

She sheepishly grinned and enthusiastically enjoyed all of the treats that he had thoughtfully purchased for their morning excursion. "This is living life to the fullest!" she exclaimed as she and Paul lightly bumped their gourmet hot chocolate cups together in cheers.

"I think that you're right," he said, as he peered out of the corner of his eye–only he wasn't looking at the food or scenery, but at the beautiful woman sitting next to him.

As they reluctantly headed back down the mountain to return home, Paul said, "I have one more surprise for you back in Buenos Aires that you're going to flip over! I'll give you a clue; it is the one thing that we absolutely must do before we leave the country."

"What? Tell me!" Celeste said excitedly.

"Drum roll please," he said, as Celeste pounded her hands on the dashboard anxiously complying with his request. "Captain Lucas has invited us to his home, along with a few work comrades, for *Carne Asada*!"

Celeste squealed in delight at the thought of an Argentine cookout. "What's on the menu? I hope it includes steaks, ribs and chorizos!"

"It does, as no one knows how to BBQ quite like the Argentinians," said Paul enthusiastically. "They have truly perfected the art. I'm not sure if the 'master of the grill' gene is passed down from father to son through the generations, or if it is from the years spent cooking over an open fire that makes it superior."

"I've never had better food in my life than the open flamed grilled meats and sausages. Don't forget about the other foods of Gnocchis, Empanadas, Russian Potato Salad, and Milanesas too." said Celeste. "Or the decadent desserts of Caramel Flan and Jam Pie that makes my mouth water uncontrollably," she added. "Are we there yet?" she asked in anticipation.

Paul laughingly said, "We just left Bariloche. It's going to take us most of the day to get back to Buenos Aires."

"We are in immediate need of a Sci-Fi transporter beam stat! It's going to be hard to wait that long to eat that glorious feast. 'Beam me up Scotty!'" she commanded, but, to her disappointment, it was futile. "Are we there yet?"

During their drive back to Buenos Aires, Paul took the opportunity to ask Celeste additional questions about her interests saying, "What is one of your favorite things to do, Celeste?"

"I love to read! I am especially drawn to historical fiction novels. I just love to learn about historical facts, people and cultures while I'm reading a great book!"

"Did you always love reading?" Said Paul.

"No, it took me longer than most kids to learn to read well, but my grandma Humphries, who is a librarian, would send books to all five of us children each year for our birthdays. I looked forward to reading the books that she sent to us. Soon I began reading the books that she mailed to my brothers as well, and before I knew it, I loved to read.

"My favorites were the teen classics like the Hardy Boys, Nancy Drew and Little House on the Prairie book series. Because of my grandmother, I learned to love reading. She is also our family genealogy specialist, scriptorian and a gospel scholar as well. I always look forward to calling her on Sundays to pick her brain about various gospel related questions that I have, knowing that she will accurately tell me her thoughts and impressions. She lovingly calls Lynda and I her 'Chickadees.'"

"She sounds like one amazing woman!" said Paul, admiring Celeste for showing so much passion.

"Oh, she is, and with attitude! I hope that you'll be able to meet her someday! She is our family's rock-solid foundation, without a doubt."

"I would enjoy meeting her very much," said Paul.

"What about you? Is there something that you have a passion for?" inquired Celeste.

"Yes, I love the sea. I love being on the sea, in the sea and near the sea. One of my favorite things to do is go to the Birch Aquarium at Scripps Institution of Oceanography to enjoy the sea life and just sit there watching the fish, sharks and stingrays swim by out in the open sea. They have floor to ceiling Plexiglass wall observation areas to enjoy them in their natural environment. It is so peaceful that it renews my soul and really fills me with wonder and happiness," said Paul. "Once we return to the states, would you be interested in coming to California so that I can introduce you to my home turf?" he asked. "I'd be honored to take you there. You'll quickly see why I am drawn to it. If I hadn't become an Interpol agent, I think I would have become a Marine Conservationist."

"Yes, I'd enjoy that very much. I appreciate learning more about you. Do you have a favorite fish of the sea?" inquired Celeste.

"Yes, it is the stingray. They're a member of the shark family and are majestic, graceful and fascinating to watch. When we go to the beach, I'll even teach you how to do the stingray shuffle."

"What's the stingray shuffle?" asked Celeste, her eyes widening.

"It is how you shuffle your feet in the sand when walking on the beach's shoreline. If you shuffle your feet and come upon a stingray, they just swim away. If you walk normally on the shoreline, the stingray gets stepped on and can sting you. Believe me, you don't want to be stung by a stingray. It's very painful," explained Paul.

"I agree! I'd appreciate your tutelage on sea protocol for certain," said Celeste.

"What's your favorite fish or sea animal?" asked Paul.

"Hands down, it is the sea otter!" replied Celeste. "They are just plain adorable. I'm enamored with how the mother otters float on their backs, keeping their babies safely on their bellies. I find it endearing that the sea otters hold hands while they are sleeping and tie themselves to kelp to keep from floating out to sea."

"Yes, the sea otters are one of the favorite exhibits at the Monterrey Bay Aquarium. Now that I know that you love otters, I want to take you to the Elk Horn Slough Reserve near Monterrey. We can even take a kayak tour to see them first hand. It is an experience not to be missed. It's really cute how the mothers wrap their babies in seaweed to keep them safe and in one place, while they go hunting."

"Oh, that sounds divine! Let's do it!" expressed Celeste.

Once they arrived back in the city, they drove directly to Captain Lucas' house so that they didn't delay in getting to the BBQ. Celeste helped Julia Lucas and Mia Molina prep the Steaks, Ribs and Chorizos for the BBQ and then they made the Gnocchis, Empanadas and Jam Pie together. Celeste noticed that Captain Lucas looked to be in his happy place as he whistled a lively tune while he flame-grilled the meats. He had on his 'When I cook, I wear my cape backwards' BBQ apron as he attentively cooked all of the meats to perfection. Celeste mentioned to Julia that she was certain that no other place on earth would have all of these incredible heavenly foods and more. Julia and Mia agreed with Celeste's food assessment.

As she spread the sweet potato jam over the bottom layer of the piecrust, a hand touched the top of hers and began helping her spread the jam, and said, "I don't think heaven could be complete without an angel like you in it!"

She froze, looking up in shock to see Lieutenant Sosa standing so close to her and jumped back in bewilderment.

Nearly everyone there snickered knowingly, being fully aware of Lieutenant Sosa's advances towards any beautiful woman that he met.

Paul immediately walked up next to him and said, "Hey, leave my beautiful angel alone, Sosa!" Although his voice was joking, his eyes clearly conveyed that he was not happy with what he had just witnessed.

Lieutenant Sosa immediately held up his hands in surrender but proclaimed loudly, "There's no ring on her finger, muchacho. All's fair in love and war."

Celeste felt ill at ease with both men vying for her attention. *That's never happened to me before*, she thought. She remained close to Paul's side for the remainder of the evening, in case Lieutenant Sosa decided to try and woo her again–especially since he'd been drinking non-stop since his arrival.

After eating a scrumptious feast fit for a king, everyone sat down to calm their stomachs with some Mate and Boldo herbal tea, while Captain Lucas and officer Jaime took turns skillfully playing their guitars, with many joining in singing along with their favorite tunes. Captain Lucas' beagle bayed along with the singers, having found and claimed Paul as her own early on in the evening. Chalupa was clearly in doggy heaven with plenty of ear scratches and belly rubs as they swayed back and forth to the music together. Celeste noticed that Chalupa had the cutest way of expressing her contentedness with her belly rubs by rubbing her ears with both of her paws.

"She's adorable," said Celeste. Paul nodded in agreement and looked as though he had never been happier in his life; Celeste felt equally contented to enjoy such a perfect day.

After a fun-filled few days of being a tourist and ending with the best BBQ feast in all of Argentina, they were officially exhausted. It was after 1 a.m., well past Celeste's usual 10 p.m. 'pumpkin hour.' They graciously thanked the Lucas' and sleepily lumbered towards the car to go home. The drive to Celeste's was quiet as she dreamily gazed out at the starry night, then back at the good man that she was snuggled up next to in the car.

Once they pulled up to the front of the house, she thanked Paul for an unforgettable trip as he opened her car door, retrieved her luggage, and escorted her to the front door. He kept hold of her hand; somehow never wanting to let go of her in case it was only just a dream.

This time, before returning to the car, he faced her, holding both of her hands snuggly up to his chest and said, "Thank you for the best day of my life." He leaned in, softly kissed her lips, and then just lingered there for a few extra seconds, enjoying her scent and the special experience of a first kiss. Without another word, he softly kissed her hand and turned around to go, leaving a star-struck Celeste waving goodbye as he drove away.

It was a perfect moment in time. He practically floated back to his apartment in a daze, not realizing how he'd already gotten home without causing an accident, as he'd been lost in thought and the growing hope that he now had for this blossoming relationship.

So this is love, Celeste thought as she softly hummed a beloved Cinderella song. "Wow, it's amazing!" she whispered to herself as she prepared to get into bed. She said a prayer of gratitude for all that she'd received and immediately fell blissfully asleep, as their first kiss and her favorite song floated through her dreams. *So this is love. So this is love. So this is love!*

After a blissful night's sleep, Celeste awoke with vigor, determined to go on a refreshing nature walk in the nearby meadow before Paul came to pick her up for the day. Paul had called earlier and mentioned that new leads had come in from the interviews that Captain Lucas had conducted, and he'd asked Paul to follow up on back at the Cross 7 Mine.

Captain Lucas called once again after Paul had spoken to Celeste and requested, "Paul, I would like to ask a personal favor of you."

"Sure. What can I do for you Captain?" said Paul.

"I was going to fly out today myself to take care of this, but the station has been overwhelmed with new witnesses coming forward. Would you be willing to go to Tierra de Fuego later this afternoon to interview a few persons of great interest? It would mean a lot to me, and you could even include a bit of sightseeing by showing Celeste the glacier and penguins."

"Okay. You can tentatively count me in, Captain, as I want to okay it with Celeste first," said Paul.

"You're a wise man Lago," responded Captain Lucas knowingly.

Celeste's morning walk was just what she needed to align her soul and refresh her senses. As she walked down the dirt path, all around her were chirping birds welcoming the day, butterflies flitting every which way and a colorful variety of wildflowers, adding an exhilarating fragrance in the air. The sun was just coming up over the horizon, creating a brilliant orange-yellow sunrise. She found herself singing to the birds a favorite tune, "Good morning, Good morning, it's time to start the day. Good morning. Good morning to you!" To Celeste's delight, the early birds seemed to sing their replies to her as they flew by in search of their worms.

Simple country homes made of brick and mortar were scattered throughout the area. A calico cat, which she decided to name Daisy Blossom, passed by with a sweet meow and request for a little scratch on its head and back, as it headed out for an early morning stroll. This was the side of Argentina that Celeste loved the most: rural, unpretentious country people, who were kind, generous, and loved the simple pleasures of life.

She inhaled deeply to try and savor the moment fully as she relished in this quiet time before heading back to the paved streets of the busy city with its nonstop honking horns and commuters crowding into the buses to get to their jobs for the day. For a few minutes, she lay down in the field and closed her eyes to soak in the morning rays and recharge.

She remembered to say a morning prayer for safety and was filled with happiness for the unique and incredible experiences that she was having in her beloved Argentina. Mostly, she said prayers of *Thanks* for Paul. He was the utmost priority in her thoughts and prayers, and she already knew that he was someone that she'd like to spend the rest of her life with into the eternities, but didn't know if he was on the same page. Right now, that kind of thinking was premature–but she couldn't help herself, as that first kiss was truly magical, and they seemed to have a very natural friendship with plenty of chemistry between them. Hopefully, answers to all of those questions would come to both of them during the remaining time that they had in the country.

Before she knew it, she'd dozed off in the field but was awakened by a slight thump on her stomach. She opened her eyes to see Daisy Blossom purring and looking at her as if she was pleased with herself. Celeste put one hand on her stomach and felt something furry there. Bolting up, she realized that Daisy had brought her a freshly caught mouse for breakfast.

She squealed in fright, scaring her newfound guardian away, which left the gift mouse lying on the grass to be reclaimed later.

Now fully awake, Celeste decided that it was time to return home after the cat and mouse adventure, reminding herself that her new friend was only trying to show approval and claim her as her own. She hoped that a little bit of the gift with the animals that Paul enjoyed had rubbed off on her.

Celeste walked towards home, with joy in her heart as she strolled down the dusty path. People were beginning to come outside to sweep their dirt porches, as they always took great care of their surroundings whether they lived in the city or the country. She waved and said hello to several women riding by on their bikes to get fresh Pan (Bread) for the day's meals.

Without warning, an oversized hog began chasing after her down the dirt road. She sprinted as quickly as she could, but was no match for the fast hog, who must have weighed over 600 pounds. Celeste felt certain that she was going to be overtaken and trampled by the mean beast when it was suddenly yanked back, stopping instantly in its tracks. Once she realized that it had stopped chasing her, she wondered how she'd escaped certain injury and looked back to see that it was chained up to a huge post. No doubt this angry hog was very near to becoming this family's food storage for the upcoming winter months.

Being chased by the pig reminded Celeste of the time that she and her companion were served a pig head gelatin by Sister Kubala, who was German, having immigrated to Argentina with her husband years earlier. Celeste cringed at the thought of the pig head gelatin appetizer, pig hairs included. She could never quite get the nerve to try it. She especially loved Sister Kabala's heavy German-Spanish accent whenever she offered them *Café Malta* each time they visited her home. Her heavy accent helped Celeste feel more at ease with her American-Spanish accent, as she learned that it was okay to speak a bit differently than everyone else.

Those were times, never to be forgotten. As she walked, she suddenly felt compelled to take another route home. The thought came with urgency, so she immediately changed her direction and walked the long way around the outskirts of the city and then back to the multiplex home. She knew never to question such thoughts.

It reminded her of a time when she and Hermana Gomez, were simultaneously prompted to stop instantly in front of a family's home that they were visiting one dark moonless night. The feeling was so strong that they both immediately turned around and rode their bikes home without saying a word to one another. They just knew that they were in grave danger and must immediately do as instructed.

The next day, when they returned to the family's home, they found out the reason. The father had dug a 10-foot by 10-foot hole in front of the home to add a septic tank. In the darkness, when they'd arrived the night before, they would have fallen in and hurt themselves severely or worse. They were grateful for the saving grace of the Lord that evening and many other days after that. That night they learned that listening to spiritual promptings, or the still small voice within, was very important and should always be heeded promptly.

Finally arriving back at the little multiplex house, grateful to be unscathed by her piggy adventure, Celeste quietly chuckled that something like that would never have occurred back home in Vegas. She would never know why she needed to take the other route home but was grateful that she didn't find out.

She quickly got ready for the day, as she had spent more time on her walk than she'd anticipated. Paul would be there shortly to pick her up, as he'd texted her that he was on his way, and that they had lots to do. He'd received word from Captain Lucas that there had been an 'incident' at the mine with a person who had attended the tango contest, that Captain Lucas had recently interviewed extensively, knowing that they were on the cusp of an important breakthrough in the case. Paul felt honored that he was trusted to go and find out why, to see if they could uncover a definitive motive for this incident. From what Celeste could figure out, it appeared that the mine was a key factor in the case.

As they drove, Paul's cell rang. Celeste answered it for him. It was Detective Molina with the information that he had requested.

"Paul, I verified that Marcelo owns a Harley Davidson Limited Edition motorcycle. How do you want us to proceed?" she said

"With great caution. I'll give you a call a bit later to let you know what course of action to take after I get there." he said.

"Got it. I'll talk with you later Lago." she said.

"Goodbye." He said

They drove back to the mine with several unanswered questions, as the victim had received a bullet to the back of his neck, which would have instantly paralyzed him. Whoever shot him had made quick work of it, as they followed up with a second shot between his eyes. No doubt the killer used a silencer, so as not to alert anyone in the vicinity. The victim's shoes were off, and his feet had also been freehand engraved in acid with the initials O.N. It appeared from the shell casings and blood trail found on the ground that the victim had been dragged and thrown into an adjoining cavern 200 feet below and was only discovered by the other miners because their mules began braying nonstop.

Once they arrived, Paul asked Celeste to stay in the car with the doors locked until he returned, as much because it was going to be a disturbing sight as well as for her safety. She readily agreed, as she had once seen pictures of a dead man with gunshot wounds as a juror in a Coroner's Inquest. Those haunting images still came to mind, even though it had been several years since her jury duty as the indelible images of the perpetrator lying in a pool of his blood never left her memory.

Celeste took advantage of the quiet time and laid the passenger's side bucket seat all the way back, allowing her to look up into the beautiful clear blue sky. Within minutes she closed her eyes and thought that she'd take a powernap before Paul returned.

She overheard a familiar sounding voice talking rapidly on his cell phone. She was too far away to hear his conversation at first, but as he walked closer his conversation became crystal clear.

"I told you, I took care of the problem. He's sitting at the bottom of the cavern with a few holes in his head to clear his mind."

Celeste's eyes flew open at what she'd just heard. The man was standing at the front hood of their car now and then leaned back on the hood as he spoke. She fervently thought, *Don't turn around. Don't turn around!* If he did and saw her, he would surely be clearing her mind with a few bullets as well.

"No, the woman's not with him this time. I don't think she knows who roughed her up on the bus, Señor V."

Celeste took a quick breath in surprise at this newest revelation and tried not to move a muscle or even look at him in case he could sense her stare.

"Yeah, the American is here talking to everyone. No, he knows nothing; I slipped out before he got to me. No one else is gonna say anything, if they know what's good for them."

With that, he began walking forward again and soon was out of hearing range.

Celeste exhaled in relief, but she didn't dare move a muscle for several minutes in case he returned the same way that he had come. Finally, she put her seat back into the upright position but remained hunched down so that she couldn't easily be seen in the front seat.

The fellow miners were rattled, nervous, and refused to speak to Paul. Not one of them would even look him in the eye. Everyone was on edge; fear hung thick in the air. Even the mine supervisor was tight-lipped as to who, what, why, and how the 'unfortunate incident' occurred.

Fortunately, Paul was able to extract a bit of information out of the supervisor: the victim was heavily in debt and had to be checked with a metal detector carefully after each shift to make sure that he wasn't carrying extra baggage (gold) on him, as there had been a string of gold nuggets mysteriously disappearing without definite proof that of who had done it.

The owner of the mine trusted very few people and required that all employees be scanned each time they came out of the mine to keep the gold from being carried out one nugget at a time. It was a costly endeavor to do this, but paid great dividends once he realized how prevalent it had become and how much they were actually losing, as their inventory suddenly began decreasing steadily without pinpointing the reason.

Once they determined the cause, each employee was scanned daily on their way out and if they were found with anything, even a small pebble on their clothing, they would be fired on the spot and blacklisted from ever working at any mine again. It appeared that Marcelo was in charge of the body-scanning machine, and made certain that it wouldn't go off whenever a member of the group walked through.

The mine supervisor allowed Paul to examine the victim's body, and he immediately recognized him as Rafael, Señor Susaniche's stable hand, and the very person who had threatened Celeste in the stables. Rafael's body was hoisted up by pulley to ground level, then loaded into a van and sent to the morgue; an autopsy would be necessary to verify his cause of death for the police reports. Paul now knew exactly who and what direction they needed to go: the Susaniche Ranch.

Celeste heard rapid footsteps crunching through the gravel headed in her direction. She crouched fully to the floor of the car and listened as the feet walked closer and closer and stopped as the car door opened. She nearly screamed but was relieved when she saw Paul's concerned face.

"Why are you on the floor?" he asked.

"You'll never guess what happened while you were gone," she said.

"Feel free to enlighten me," he replied.

Celeste told him in detail about the man's phone call and how he just stood in front of the car and reported to someone, who she supposed to be the ringleader of the group.

"Did he say the leader's name?" said Paul.

"He mentioned a Señor V and said that he didn't think you suspected him and that no one else was going to say anything."

"I only interviewed Marcelo today. I think the man on the phone may have been Felipe."

"If it was Felipe, then he was probably the man behind me on the bus, as he flat out said that we didn't suspect it was him on the bus," deduced Celeste.

"Let's keep it that way. We won't reveal this information to anyone, not even to Captain Lucas for good measure for a few more hours to see how things play out." said, Paul. "I wouldn't be surprised if Felipe was responsible for a little electrical work on your house as well," he added. "I'll make certain that both Filipe and Marcelo are taken in for questioning before the end of their shift today and that Filipe is charged in the death of Rafael and Marcelo is charged with attempted murder, now that detective Molina confirmed that he is the owner of the Special Edition motorcycle. We'll also need your eyewitness account about what you heard Felipe say on his cell phone," he said.

They drove in silence to the Susaniche Ranch as Paul mentally prepared the direction of the questions that he needed to ask Señor Susaniche and Pablo.

Señor Susaniche was very generous in responding to any questions that Paul had; he asked his entire staff to help them with anything that they needed. Paul was grateful to have his full assistance after receiving very little help at the mine. Paul asked Señor Susaniche if he knew of Rafael's extra activities outside of his work at the ranch. Señor Susaniche mentioned that he had heard that Rafael owed a large sum of money to some unsavory men, due to betting losses on the horse races.

He mentioned that occasionally Rafael would win at the races, but mostly lost on his bets and also worked at the Cross 7 Mine, since he only worked at the Ranch part-time. "There were rumors that he'd discovered a rather large gold vein in the mine and may have paid other workers hush-money to keep it under wraps. I thought that was just hearsay, until I heard of his untimely passing this morning."

Paul asked him if he knew of anyone else that he might speak with that knew Rafael well. Señor Susaniche said that Rafael rarely spoke to anyone and kept to himself, but that maybe Pablo might know a bit more.

Paul thanked Señor Susaniche, and he and Celeste went to the stable to speak with Pablo. Celeste recalled her previous meeting with Pablo, as a serious, quiet teen with hopeful eyes. He was distressed that Rafael had been killed but not surprised, as he spoke of men occasionally showing up and threatening Rafael if he didn't pay up. "When Rafael gave them his sporadic winnings from the horse races, it didn't stop them from visiting frequently to remind him of his 'Obligations', said Pablo.

Celeste asked, "What does O.N. stand for, Pablo? Now that Rafael is gone, are you free to tell me what you know?"

"It stands for the gold found in 'Tierra de Fuego', although I don't know of any active gold mining going on there. Rafael had plans to leave here soon, as he'd smuggled out enough gold to pay for the trip to Tierra de Fuego and planned to rent a place there."

Paul asked, "Why would anyone want to live there? It's so cold that even the marching Magellan penguins don't want to hang around a place where the wind never stops howling. Talk about the literal end of the earth and as far south of the pole as you can get."

Pablo said, "Rafael planned on going there as soon as he won his next horse race and had no plans of ever returning."

"Do you know of anyone that he was going to meet up with there?"

"I think there was one man that works at the Refinery, but I do not remember his name. I think his name started with a 'B', or maybe it was a 'V'. I heard Rafael making plans with him a few days ago, so I knew that he was about to leave here for good," said Pablo.

"Pablo, would you allow me to check Rafael's work area?" said Paul.

"Sure, follow me."

Paul opened Rafael's multi-drawer freestanding toolbox and began looking for any evidence. He quickly found foam sole insert 2-packs opened in sizes small, large, and an unopened extra-large package. Paul took out his handkerchief and placed the evidence into a sealed plastic bag, careful not to touch anything with his fingers. Next, he found another pair of inserts that appeared to be Rafael's practice pieces, with the O.N. initials hand lettered inside with a piece of brown paper over the top. Paul thought that he must not have been happy with the finished lettering and made a custom branding iron to make the application more neutral looking.

Paul placed each item carefully in its bag and sealed them to be taken to the station for careful analysis. In the last drawer, buried under a number tools, Paul found a single online receipt for airfare purchased the day before, to Tierra de Fuego, alongside a note that simply said, "**Come Now or Else! V.**" In a separate envelope was a picture of Celeste and Paul sitting at their table at Rosita's.

"Pablo, may I see the area where you keep the branding irons?"

Paul asked.

"Rafael always kept those carefully locked up in his storage closet," said Pablo.

"Do you know where the key is?"

"Yes. I know where it is, as I've seen him put it away many times when he didn't know that I was looking. Here it is," offered Pablo.

Paul carefully opened the closet and found a half dozen custom made branding irons with various O.S. fonts with numbers on them, no doubt to help them to identify the age of each cow. Paul spotted one miniature branding iron that looked out of place next to the others and carefully looked at its lettering. As he'd hoped, it read, 'O.N.' Paul was relieved that he'd finally found the concrete proof that they needed in the case as he carefully wrapped up the evidence to take back to the station.

"Thank you, Pablo, you've been a great help to me," said Paul. "I hope that you will prove to Señor Susaniche what an excellent choice that he's made in having you as an employee, so serve him with honor. You are now free from Rafael's influence, so take this opportunity that you've been given to show Señor Susaniche what you can do to make this ranch an even better place. Be innovative and think outside of the box to improve your work, and it will take you far. You are a good young man, and I'm proud of you."

Pablo lifted his chest in pride, having never realized what an asset that he was to Señor Susaniche and knowing that he'd played a pivotal role in helping to solve the murders. "I will work hard and become the man that you and Señor Susaniche believe me to be."

Paul and Celeste waved goodbye to Pablo as they were leaving, promising to return soon to ride Oso. Pablo was pleased with the idea of seeing the two American's again and gave them a huge smile and thumbs up, promising that he would do all that was asked of him.

CHAPTER 8

Tierra de Fuego

Back in Buenos Aires, Paul reported what they'd uncovered in the Pampas to Captain Lucas. Captain Lucas confirmed that both Marcelo and Felipe had been arrested near the end of their shift without incident by a group of specially trained officers over violent criminals and were now being escorted back to the police station to be questioned about the death of Rafael. Officer Jaime and Detective Molina, who eavesdropped on the conversation, mentioned the fact that there were also rough men that Rafael was beholding to, due to a mountain of gambling debts, that may have done it.

"The manner in which he was murdered is a possible calling card for the Argentine Mafia," said Officer Jaime.

"While they are commonly tied together with the Sicilian Mafia, they operate independently from them. They are known for drug trafficking, racketeering, weapons trafficking, extortion, murder, political corruption, robbery, and conspiracy," added Detective Molina.

"They have allies in Sicily, America, Russian and Latin America with the drug cartel operators, including Los Zetos! Rafael was clearly in way over his head if he was involved with them," said Captain Lucas.

If he were involved, why would they kill him now? wondered Paul. *It would mean that they wouldn't get the rest of the money that he owed them.*

Although Officer Jaime was adamant about Rafael's involvement with the Mafia, Paul wasn't fully convinced that they were responsible; he felt that this was a copycat crime done by a smaller group saying, "The Mafia would have claimed responsibility by now, as they like the press coverage, prestige, and fear that it produces. I think these O.N. crimes are the act of only a few trying to appear to be Los Zetos to keep us off of their trail. There was something else that Rafael knew; I think that the answer lies in Tierra de Fuego," said Paul.

Officer Jaime commented, "I highly doubt that the answers that you seek are there. I think it would be a huge waste of your time," he said as he walked out of the room.

Captain Lucas agreed with Paul and mentioned that he'd found a connection between Carlos and Rafael.

"What is it?" said Paul.

"They are cousins, and both have past encounters with the law. Carlos was probably murdered for the same reason that Rafael was murdered–for being unable to pay back the money owed, or they double crossed whoever it is in Tierra de Fuego."

"But there is something else. Why did they murder Carlos in such a public way, other than to leave a clear message for Rafael that he was next?" asked Paul.

Captain Lucas said, "There has been a string of coin store robberies throughout the city in the past few months. They took in total about $50,000.00 USD gold coins and small PAMP Suisse gold bars targeting this side of the city. Whoever did this had extensive knowledge of each store's security cameras, alarm system, motion sensors, and locks, to be able to get in and out within a matter of a few minutes before we arrived. Each store's live camera footage feature was overridden, and upon review they showed no footage of the robberies. These gold burglars always seem to be one step ahead of us, as the crime scene was always cleared of fingerprints and sanitized before we even stepped foot in them. I'm confident that Carlos, Felipe and Rafael were part of that operation. There appears to be another person cluing them into our actions."

"Looks like a modern-day 'Mission Impossible' job," said Celeste as Paul and Captain Lucas nodded solemnly in agreement.

Captain Lucas asked, "Can you be ready to go to Ushuaia in less than two hours to find out what was so important to Rafael and cost Carlos, Graciela, and Rafael their lives? I've asked Detective Molina to take care of the flight arrangements for you. She initially was going to accompany you, but I need her here to wrap up this side of the investigation."

Celeste just looked at Paul and said, "I'm ready to go when you are."

"We'll need to go to the store first and get some fishing supplies and gear, as well as buying you an extra warm parka, hat, mitts, scarf and gloves first. Then we'll head over to my apartment to get my winter essentials, so we won't become frozen popsicles the second we step off the plane. After we conclude with our interviews there, I'd love to get a bit of fishing in before we return to Buenos Aires," said Paul. "It's the chance of a lifetime to fish at the southernmost tip of the world for some world-renowned Chilean Sea Bass. With any luck, we can have a little fish fry of our own once we return."

"Oh, now that's a deal! Who can pass up fresh Sea Bass?" agreed Celeste.

At the sporting goods store, Celeste modeled several parka options that looked best for Paul's consideration.

"You know, a man would quickly choose the one that is the best deal and has the most warmth, then buy it and be out in a matter of minutes," observed Paul. "Women add a whole new element to shopping, in that they enjoy the process as they consider the price, color, fit and whether or not the item coordinates with their hat, scarf, and mittens. It's incredible that you have already put that much thought into these purchases. You're amazing, and I would never have thought about any such thing before I met you. It helps me think outside the box for the investigation, and I think I now know why Rafael wanted to go to Tierra de Fuego."

"You're welcome," she said, blushing. Why?"

"I'll tell you when we get there. You're gonna have to wait just a bit, so that I can prove my theory is correct before revealing it to you."

Celeste playfully punched his arm and said, "Don't keep me waiting too long, Sherlock." She gave him a quick peck on the cheek and lightly whispered into his ear, "Even Sherlock shared his theories with Watson. So, spill it!"

"Nope. You're going to have to wait and see."

As they boarded the seaplane headed to Ushuaia, Celeste was glad that it was the early fall instead of winter, as the cold and unrelenting 40 mph winds went right through to your bones. She had served in Comodoro Rivadavia, 100 miles North of Ushuaia, so she knew exactly what to expect for this trip.

Thankfully when she was a missionary, she had served in Comodoro Rivadavia during the summer months with Hermana Molinari, but even the summers there consisted of unrelenting, fierce

Patagonia winds, which were referred to as *Cada de Milanesa* (Sand face) by the missionaries. This was because the dirt-riddled winds constantly blew with fierceness all year long but were especially brutal during the winter months. *Cold as ice is an understatement*, she thought.

While living in Comodoro Rivadavia, she often wondered why she ever washed and styled her hair, as it was utterly useless. The moment that she walked outside, she was dirt assaulted from head to toe. She remembered trying to get a brush through her hair at the end of each day but was never successful, at least not without taking out significant chunks of hair in the process.

At the executive airport, they met up with their highly recommended pilot Lanzo, who promptly introduced himself and then helped to load them and their gear into his Cessna Caravan Amphibious Aircraft. Within minutes, they were headed towards Ushuaia in Tierra de Fuego.

After they'd been up in the air for about half an hour, Lanzo mentioned, "My wife, Abril, is an excellent cook and has made Sopapillas, Empanadas and Mate for us to enjoy as she knows that we won't have an opportunity to stop and eat."

"Wow, a woman after my own heart," said Celeste! "Please thank her for her foresight and generosity. We are deeply appreciative."

Paul took one bite of his Sopapillas and exclaimed... "Oh yummy, yum, yum, get in my tummy!"

Celeste said, "Well that about sums up my thoughts exactly! This Empanada is so *rico (*rich)! I think I'll eat another one. Do you think she'll give me the recipe? Is that nutmeg I taste in the meat mixture?"

"Yes, it is, Celeste," said, Lanzo. "You obviously know a great deal about cooking to identify the nutmeg. The Empanadas are a special family recipe and if you need to know the key to making fantastic Empanadas, is an extra thin crust made with lard. The ingredients in the filling are green olives, eggs, whole raisins and quality beef seasoned well with a pinch of nutmeg. Abril will be most happy to hear that you loved her cooking and will gladly share our family's recipe for the Empanadas," he said, as he slurped his Mate.

"You are very generous Lanzo. I'm very excited to speak with Abril about this recipe and any other special family recipes that she's willing to share." said Celeste.

"If you like that, my Kreutzer side of the family has a delicious family recipe for our famous German Potato Salad that you will really enjoy! And you'll never guess what the secret ingredient in it is either. I won't tell it to you yet, just to keep you guessing," said Lanzo with a wink.

"Well I look forward to trying it and getting that recipe too. Thank you very much, Lanzo!" exclaimed Celeste.

"My pleasure, Celeste! I love talking with people who enjoy eating and making food as much as Abril and I do!" said Lanzo.

As they flew, Celeste played the Tour Guide, saying, "Here's what the travel app says about Argentina and Ushuaia in Tierra de Fuego. Argentina covers 1.1 million square miles of a mixture of tropical terrain, mountains, plains, and the South Pole named Tierra de Fuego. Here, one could be at the end of the world in Ushuaia, which is the end of the earth and as cold and windy as H-E-double toothpicks!"

"Does the app really say H-E-double toothpicks?" Paul asked sarcastically.

"No, I ad-libbed that part," said Celeste wryly. "But it does say that Tierra del Fuego is known for its sheep farming and the oil wells that dot the grasslands and hills along the coast."

"Did you know that Ushuaia is the home of a large naval base, government offices and stores for imported goods? It is a center for assembly plants, sawmills, crab fisheries and is most famous for its octopus-shaped prison," informed Paul. "I've also asked Lanzo if he wouldn't mind circling the world famous Perito Moreno Glacier. It is named after the Argentinian explorer Francisco Moreno, and is the 3rd largest reserve of fresh water on the planet, covering 100 square miles by three miles wide," he continued.

As they flew over the glacier, they marveled at its beautiful marbled deep blue and white color and sheer massive size.

Lanzo said, "At certain times of the year, the front part of the glacier forms an ice bridge, blocking off Lago (Lake) Argentina until spring, when the glacier begins calving."

"I've heard that it sheds enormous ice shards every thirty minutes year-round. Is this true, Lanzo?" said Paul.

"Yes. Keep your eyes peeled as we fly over it, as we have a really good chance of witnessing super-sized chunks of ice cracking off its face."

"Look! It's cracking," noticed Celeste. "Quick, may I borrow your camera? This scenery is so majestic. I'm unsure if the camera can even do this breathtaking glacier any justice."

The impact of the enormous slab of frozen ice falling into the water caused massive tidal wave swells in the water and onto the shoreline below them.

"I can't believe how loud the cracking is, even from up here. It's a good thing we're not in a boat, otherwise we'd be in real danger of capsizing," said Celeste.

"This frozen tundra is amazing. I didn't realize how incredible it is to witness it first hand," mentioned Paul.

As Lanzo turned the plane towards their destination he mentioned, "The final ten minutes of the flight coming into Ushuaia are going to be a bit treacherous, as the winds will provide plenty of

Loralee Lago

turbulence. I recommend that you double-check that your seat belts are fastened securely and then hold on tight, as the landing is going to be pretty crazy as the choppy waves will give us an additional bull ride experience."

"The view of this amazing frozen country is indescribable," said Paul as they got their first glimpse of Ushuaia. "Did you know that Ushuaia is Argentina's top tourist destination? It is the southernmost city in the world, if you don't count Puerto Williams, Chile, which technically doesn't qualify as a city with only 500 people. Ushuaia is considered the portal to Antarctica."

"At one time, there was even a penal colony here back in 1883," said Lanzo.

"Is that a golf course I see?" asked Celeste

"Yes," said Lanzo. "They even have a ski resort, too."

"What? Who knew?" said Celeste. "Are we about ready to land? I'm getting really green around the gills, and I'm not sure how much longer that I can hold my cookies in at this point."

"Landing now," he said as he dipped the plane's right wing down towards the bay. Try not to barf in my plane please, Celeste."

She could only nod, not daring to open her mouth in response; for fear that she might not be able to comply with his request. Celeste nearly threw up several times from all of the turbulence, but somehow managed to hold it in until they landed. The moment that Celeste got clear of the plane she promptly lost any food remaining in her stomach and added a few extra dry heaves for good measure.

Paul put a comforting hand on her back and then gave her a fresh handkerchief he'd taken from his pocket, saying, "Are you feeling any better?"

Celeste nodded, "Yes, I believe I am. Wait, here comes another wave of dry heaves!"

Lanzo reminded them that he'd return tomorrow to take them

home later in the evening, stressing that the weather report forecasted that the winds would be significantly lighter for a much smoother ride home.

As Paul rowed the short distance to the dock in their dingy, he said, "I can tell this place never gets over 50 degrees, and it appears that it is never hot as the name implies. I would bet that the fire part of its name could be compared to hell, as I consider it to be a very cold and dark place rather than fiery like most people believe. Indeed, the extreme temperatures feel hellish here in this southernmost town in the world and home of the Magellan penguins!"

"I wonder if it was named that way for the same reason that they called Greenland and Iceland by their opposite names; to deter people from coming in search of the oil found here," Celeste said.

Celeste admired Paul's strong arms and gave him a wink of appreciation as he rowed steadily making for a speedy arrival at the dock. Paul easily jumped out onto the dock, and then held out his hand to help her out of the dingy. As Celeste was pulled up safely onto the dock, Paul raised her hand to his lips and kissed the top of it, saying, "Now, let's get to the business of finding out why Rafael wanted to live here. I won't be surprised if we find another 'cousin' or two of his here as well."

Celeste agreed as she wrapped her coat and scarf snugly around her neck as the frigid wind fiercely bit at her face. "It must be about 40 degrees right now, but with the wind-chill, it feels like 30, and it is only going to get colder as night falls," she said. "Why anyone would want to live in these subzero temps is beyond me. Although, come to think of it, people say the same thing about living in Las Vegas with its del Scorcho (flaming hot) 115-degree summers. I definitely consider myself a desert tortoise rather than a artic penguin."

As she lifted her arm to adjust her scarf to cover her nose and mouth, Paul reached over and softly kissed her on the cheek, saying,

Loralee Lago

"I'm glad that you are with me for this final leg of the investigation. I thought that you would say *no* to coming to this ice cube town, but you didn't even hesitate. You're amazing, Blue Eyes."

Wow! Did he just call me Blue Eyes? she thought. All she could do was nod and gave him a shaky extra cold-nosed Eskimo kiss in loving reply. "Here," she said. "Put on my scarf. You need it more than I do."

"I'm fine," he said. But she insisted, saying, "I've got a faux fur lined hood with a drawstring on my jacket that will work just as well."

"Thank you very much," he said gratefully as they walked towards the taxi, which had awaited their arrival.

Celeste whispered, "I'm grateful to be on land again. Hey, are you hungry? Here are a few granola bars."

Paul took them and put them into his pocket to appease Celeste. "Lanzo has asked a trusted friend of his who lives here, to unload and take care of our carry-on bags and gear until we return hopefully in about an hour, so that we don't lose any time before the day shift ends. I've got his number, and will call him to tell him that we've arrived and will coordinate with him where we'll be staying once we come back into town." As they got into the taxi, Paul asked the driver if they could be taken directly to the Refinery on Oro drive.

Celeste blurted out, "Wait! What did you just say?"

Paul said, "Driver, take us to the Refinery on Oro Drive. Yeah, what about it?"

"O-R-O Drive," she repeated slowly, looking excitedly into his brown eyes. When he didn't understand, she said, "What is oil referred to, especially in the old west days when it was just becoming valuable?"

In unison, they said, "Black Gold!"

"But in Spanish, it doesn't translate as Black gold, but...Oro

Negro! O.N!" she said triumphantly.

"Fantastic detective skills, Watson," said Paul. "I think this assessment is correct, and now with a positive ID of what O.N. means, I know we are getting close to finding out the remaining answers in this case. I feel if it would have been the Mafia, they would have claimed it by now, but I wouldn't be surprised if my suspected group is at the heart of our murders and have a stake in all of this. We're getting into dangerous territory. If at any time I feel like we are at risk, I'll ask to speak with Señor Susaniche. Please be sure that I need you to immediately leave the facility and head to the nearest hotel for safety, and then I will meet up with you as soon as possible. Do you understand?"

"Yes. You don't think it will come to that, do you?" asked Celeste.

"It doesn't hurt to be prepared, just in case," he said. "There are a number of unruly people who work at the Refinery. Your safety is of the utmost concern to me."

Celeste nodded in agreement. "Do you know I have a little experience with the Mafia?" This peeked Paul's interest as he looked over with a raised eyebrow for an explanation. "Do you remember when we were serving here and were asked to take off our name badges for several months when the mafia was targeting North Americans?"

Paul nodded and said, "It was both weird and scary being their target, but with or without our name badges on, we stuck out like a sore thumb. Our height, fair features and suits especially made us stand out. We'd be walking and suddenly people going past us would just stop and stare at us; it was intense."

"Yeah, I remember when that happened! I was grateful once everything calmed down, and we could put our badges back on without being in constant fear of being assaulted," said Celeste.

The taxi pulled up to the Refinery near the end of the 6 o'clock shift, as many workers were coming and others were going. There was a group of men taking a few minutes to drink Mate before they began their shift who were socializing with those preparing to leave for the day. Celeste was immediately spotted by many of the men as she walked by. She did her best to ignore them, but began to question her choice of wearing such a vibrant, blue coat. She should have thought more carefully about her need to blend in with their dark black and brown coats, although she was pretty sure that it would not have made much of a difference.

Paul returned the men's stares with a protective glare, which helped some, especially as he put his arm in hers and carefully escorted her to the cafeteria where more men were congregating. Paul was able to converse with many of the workers, who said that the day shift had been a difficult one with many mechanical problems as the main pipeline was clogged with debris again, causing the pumps to malfunction. "If we don't get it cleared and fixed soon, we'll be here all night until the problem is solved." they lamented.

Paul and Captain Lucas's research had verified that indeed, Rafael had a cousin named Thomas, who was an employee at the refinery. Paul inquired with the front desk about his whereabouts, stating that they were on official business on behalf of the B.A. Police Department. The worker nervously pointed them in the right direction. As they walked out of the office, Paul noticed that the receptionist made a discrete call to someone, no doubt giving the boss a heads up about their arrival. As they walked towards the designated area, it looked to be where all of the oil was collected before being refined and distributed via various lines that would fill the barrels and load them onto awaiting oil tankers to be transported up the coast for distribution.

Paul and Celeste were shown where the manager of the oil pit and pumping area was and set out to get there quickly. They were introduced to Señor Luna and identified themselves as part of an ongoing investigation and asked to see Thomas.

"Thomas hasn't been seen for a few hours and will be reprimanded the minute that he's located for not completing the mandatory repair work on the debris in the pipeline by our end of shift deadline. No doubt he's gone off drinking again," Señor Luna mumbled unhappily. "To make matters more severe, we're dealing with several malfunctioning pump lines. I don't think this day could get much worse," he said glumly. "I just want to go home and have a nice dinner. Is that too much to ask?"

"Excuse me, boss," said a breathless worker who had quickly approached. "We've found the cause of the blockage, and your assistance is needed." As Señor Luna rapidly walked away with the employee, Paul asked, "May we tag along?" Señor Luna stopped and hesitated momentarily but then nodded in agreement as he continued walking towards the area of concern.

Once they arrived at the pumping area, there was quite a bit of commotion with several men yelling over the loud machinery and others pacing nervously as the boss arrived to evaluate the situation. The foreman informed him that they had found the cause of the pump malfunction and were in the process of fixing it, as well as extracting the debris.

The foreman said, "It appears to be another unfortunate animal and vegetation that got through the protective barrier again, as they are the usual culprits. Wait, look–it is much larger and longer than the usual debris. It looks like a tree branch. No, it can't be a tree limb; there aren't many trees this close to the shore," pondered the foreman. Suddenly the true culprit of the clogged line became crystal clear. Celeste put her hands to her mouth in horror, trying to keep herself from making a sound as they hoisted a lifeless body onto the cement. The foreman made a positive ID by cleaning off the plastic lanyard ID card hanging around the victim's neck.

"It's...*Thomas!*" he said in astonishment.

Loralee Lago

Paul quickly looked around to see the expressions on all of the faces of the men in the area. Most had genuine expressions of surprise and horror, but one man had a slight smirk on his face as if to say, "You had it coming!"

As Señor Luna and the other workers rushed to pull Thomas's lifeless body completely onto the concrete to rest, Paul told Celeste, "Stay here. I'm going to walk over there, he pointed, to speak with someone about his reaction to finding Thomas." As Paul got closer, he saw that the man's ID card said Vicente.

Vicente just glared, and he then growled, "Gringo, why are you here? You had better leave now, if you know what's good for you."

Paul asked, "Why?"

Vicente said, "You don't want to meet the same fate as that good for nothing, Thomas, do you? Don't ask another question and leave now."

Paul just returned his stare in defiance. Vicente lifted his jacket, revealing a concealed gun in his waistband as he pulled it out and pointed it directly at Paul. Paul said loudly without looking at Celeste, "I just need to speak with Señor Susaniche."

Vicente yelled, "Shut up!" and ordered Paul to walk with his hands up to the far end of the oil pit away from the commotion. Both the boss and foreman tried to stop the situation from getting out of hand, but were shot and wounded by Vicente before they could utter another word.

Celeste, upon hearing the safety phrase, quickly realized that Paul was in grave danger, recognizing with certainty that it was the same man that had sneered at her on the bus days earlier. She immediately ran out of the facility, not daring to look back for fear that she might be chased down by the other workers. It was now dark outside, and the dirt road to the city was a lonely, windy and frigid 30-minute walk.

It must be in the 20s, she thought, although it felt so much colder now that the sun had gone down. She was scared and didn't even know where the nearest hotel in town was. *Is Paul okay? Did he diffuse the situation? Has he been shot and killed?* Her mind went wild with all of the terrifying scenarios. She was crazy with worry and scared stiff as she walked towards town.

Men on bikes soon followed behind her, who taunted, pushed and threatened her to "Say nothing, if you don't want to end up like Thomas and your boyfriend." Their scare tactics worked well on her until they finally tired of their harassment and passed by her with one last shove onto the frozen ground. Thankfully, the only thing that they had seriously hurt was her pride. As she brushed away the gravel and dirt that had embedded into her hands and knees, she could feel warm blood oozing from them. In her flight, she had not stopped to put on her gloves. She was overwhelmed and prayed fervently for her safety as well as Paul's.

After about a half an hour of walking in darkness with only a half-moon to light her way, she made it to a paved street with lights. She walked several more blocks before reaching Main Street and saw a blinking 'vacancy' hotel sign. She was so relieved that she exhaled loudly, as she had been nearly paralyzed with fear. Being a well-prepared woman, she was able to pay with the 'mad' money she'd brought with her, just in case she needed it. Good thing that her mother, Mary had always taught her to have a little extra cash on hand at all times for anything unexpected. She made a mental note to call and thank her mother for her timely advice as soon as they could both get out of this dire situation.

Once she was checked into the hotel, she asked the hotel clerk where the nearest payphone was and if she could buy a few phone tokens from her. After paying for the hotel room, she had just enough money to buy only one token, which would give her only a minute to speak with Captain Lucas before the phone went dead.

Back outside, she practically sprinted towards the payphone on the corner and reached Captain Lucas within a few rings. She rapidly mentioned that she had only a minute's worth of phone time before telling him all that had occurred, especially the description of the man that pulled the gun on Paul and that she was sure it was the same man that had sneered at her on the bus.

He told her, "Stay put! What is the name and room number of your hotel? Don't leave the hotel under any circumstances, until I come to get you. Do you understand?"

"I do," she said. "My room number is 333 at the Heaven Sent Hotel.

"Thanks. Got it. It is obvious that we've found a key player in this investigation, and it's highly probable that he means to silence both of you now that he knows you are on to him. Have you heard from Paul at all?"

"No, I haven't, but I will continue to try and text him to see if he responds, but there is nothing but silence. No bubbles…nothing!" She realized that her cell phone was now dead, and with no charger on her and little to no Internet access in the area, it would be of no use.

Captain Lucas said that he'd come right away, but that he wouldn't be there until morning as no further flights were going out until then. "There are a handful of police volunteers there, but it's more like the wild, wild, west. Before you do anything, please…"

The phone went dead with only the sound of a dial tone ringing in her ears. "Please what?" Celeste frantically spoke into the receiver, knowing that there wouldn't be a reply. As she hung up, a few trucks drove by and she quickly took cover inside the phone booth shell so as not to be identified. As soon as the vehicles passed, she sprinted back to the hotel like a hungry cat hearing the dinner bell. She was insane with worry, so she did the only thing that she could do: pray.

What did Captain Lucas need me to do? She prayed as she'd

never prayed in her life, for knowledge to know what to do, for Paul's safety, for comfort, peace, and heavenly help. She prayed for a miracle. She prayed throughout the night, too afraid to move or sleep or even make a noise, for she was paralyzed with fear that the men would locate her, kick in the door and kill her. After all, there couldn't be more than a few dozen hotels in this town. *I'm a sitting duck,* she thought. *It's just a matter of time before they find me!*

At the Refinery, Vicente had taken Paul at gunpoint to a remote area of the oil pit away from any eyewitnesses. He had Paul stand in front of the pit with his hands above his head. His plan was to kill Paul in the same manner as Thomas. He lifted his gun, pointed and fired, but nothing happened, as he heard it click–the gun had miraculously jammed.

As Vicente briefly looked down to free it, Paul took that split second to grab Vicente's arm and try to force the gun from his hand before it went off. The gun wrestle was fierce, as each fought like lions for their lives. Trying to keep the gun pointed away from his body proved to be difficult, and for a brief second, he was able to push it up above Vicente's head as a wild shot rang through the air, alerting the other workers of the struggle. At this critical moment, Paul managed to punch Vicente in his stomach with his free left hand, but that only angered him more as Vicente head-butted him, nearly causing Paul to black out.

Still, Paul persevered and fought, praying as he never had prayed in his life for the strength to break free and escape. Soon others were coming to see what had happened, but once they realized there was a gun involved, they slowly backed away, not wanting to risk their lives.

For a brief second, Vicente, who Paul noticed wore a gold horseshoe chain with a nugget, lost his balance after he attempted to head-butt Paul a second time. Paul quickly slid his right leg around and under Vicente's leg to trip him, which gave him just enough time to make a run for it. It worked, and Paul sprinted for cover to the nearby machinery. He wanted to get as far away as he could before Vicente could get back on his feet and fire. It was only a matter of a few seconds as Paul ran for his life before he heard the gun shoot again and again and then it clicked, having run out of bullets. He knew he had mere seconds before Vicente reloaded his gun.

Paul prayed as he ran that the bullets would miraculously miss him or at the very least, miss all his vital organs. Something had hit him on his back shoulder as he sprinted before hearing the clicking noise. He could feel his energy slowly diminishing, as the realization that he'd been shot was understood. He would not be stopping to verify the extent of his injuries and was running on pure adrenaline. Paul, seizing the opportunity to unlatch the cover of his concealed gun under his pant leg and began returning fire behind some barrels he noted were marked with O.N. The added gun power allowed him to run from one piece of machinery to the next until he could get out of the area. He was careful to keep count of all the shots he'd taken, so as not to use all his bullets in case he needed one urgently later.

Now far enough away to run without being an easy target, he ran out of the refinery into the frozen night. He was grateful that there was very little moonlight, to keep him undetected as he ran. After quickly surveying the area, he identified the employee parking lot full of vehicles and quickly found refuge from the frigid wind under a tarp in the back of a worker's truck at the far end of the parking lot. He was determined to stay there until the end of the shift, hoping that the driver would return to town soon, so that he could get some help and make sure that Celeste was safe from harm. As he lay there, trying to slow his breathing while listening to the running footsteps and the voices nearby, he could feel the blood oozing from his head as he'd gotten a bloody nose, and a big gash on his forehead from the head butts, not to mention the blood oozing from his shoulder wound.

He knew that he was in shock, but he fervently prayed to be able to have the strength to remain conscious and make it safely back to town. He could hear Vicente outside shouting orders to "Find him!" as they searched the trucks and cars. He heard lots of cursing and footprints in the gravel all around the truck that he was hiding in as they continued the search. It appeared that the man with the Gold Chain had many like-minded *campañeros* (friends) who did not want him to survive, and he fervently prayed that they would somehow overlook the truck that he was hiding in.

His only saving grace was that the parking lot was full and he estimated that it had over 200 vehicles. He'd run to the outermost area of the parking lot, hoping that they'd tire of checking all of the trucks and cars after starting with the ones nearest to the facility. After several hours, he heard footsteps walking directly toward the truck again where he was hiding. Paul mentally prepared for the tarp to be lifted, revealing his hiding place.

Paul held up his gun in preparation for one final shot, but instead of lifting the tarp, the man opened the truck door, got in, and started the engine. Relieved, Paul figured that he was going to head back into town, obviously tired of the search and wanting to go home after a long shift. Paul exhaled in relief, as he didn't realize that he had been holding his breath. It was long after midnight, and he had hoped to escape with the cloak of darkness. He knew that he couldn't go to the medical facility, as they would look there first for another opportunity to finish him off.

As the man drove towards town, Paul could hear him energetically singing a lively tune about a crazy chicken on the radio, drumming in time on his steering wheel with his fingers as he drove. Paul was grateful for a way out of this dire situation. He remembered that it was only about a 10-minute drive down the bumpy dirt road to get back to town as he could barely make out a single traffic light as they pulled into town. The man stopped, then turned into a parking lot and got out of the truck, continuing to hum off-key as he walked. Paul wondered, *Where am I?*

He cautiously peered out of the tarp again to see if there was anyone around. He listened carefully as the man's feet faded in the gravel. Paul heard a door open and close before peering out of the tarp again. He was surprised to see that he was surrounded by other trucks and looking up, realized that the man had stopped at a diner on the outskirts of town.

Grateful for this chance, Paul gingerly got out of the truck and hobbled towards the lights of downtown. He recognized the Panaderia that he and Celeste had seen on their way through town earlier in the day. He knew that if he made it to Main Street, he'd find a place to stay until help came. Paul hoped that Celeste had also found a safe place to stay and that she'd been able to contact Captain Lucas. The texts that he'd sent to Celeste while hiding in the truck had been undeliverable.

He took heart that she was okay, since he hadn't heard anything from the men talking as they searched for him. He prayed to be guided as to where she was so that they could be reunited and come up with an escape plan. He desperately needed to inform Captain Lucas of the situation, as backup was urgently needed. Captain Lucas had given him his friend Sancho's name and phone number, who he could contact once they arrived, but the paper must have gotten lost during the battle with Vicente. Paul hoped that Sancho didn't become a target due to his negligence.

He was grateful that the bullet appeared to have missed any major organs, although his wound caused sharp shooting pains up and down his shoulder and arm. As he slowly and cautiously walked towards the middle of town, several pairs of headlights were seen coming down the street, no doubt coming home from the Refinery. Paul quickly jumped into a large bush for cover and instantly regretted the decision. He'd come so far in his escape, but he realized too late that the bush was full of thorns, which tore at his skin and clothing. After all that he'd been through, a few more scratches mattered very little and he was grateful for the prickly cover.

Once the line of trucks coming from the Refinery subsided, he resumed his slow and sticker-laden walk towards Main Street. He had stickers in his hair, coat, pants, socks and shoes. He stopped and wondered how a lone sticker had made its way to his armpit, as his attempts at removing it proved to be useless. He remembered seeing a few hotels on their way into town that Celeste might have gone to for the evening. He mentally prayed that he'd be guided which way to go, and especially which hotel and room she was in. He needed to take cover before the sun came up, not to mention that he was completely exhausted from the events of the day.

Paul uttered a desperate, heartfelt prayer for immediate divine assistance. The moment that he uttered "amen" and opened his eyes, a black hound dog appeared out of nowhere and began walking beside him. "Hey sweet girl, what are you doing out on such a freezing night?" he said, as he patted her head. "I think I'll name you Destiny." The dog jumped up on his coat, seeming to love the added attention and name, and began sniffing at Paul's pockets.

Paul chuckled and said, "I think you must smell the granola bars that Celeste gave to me. You know what, that girl can't stand the thought of anyone going hungry. Hey, it does sound good to eat about now." Paul opened one of the granola bars, took a bite, and then broke off a piece for Destiny, who happily devoured it in one gulp and looked back at him, expecting more.

Destiny seemed to come at the exact moment that Paul needed her most, and he felt that she was also serving as his guardian. He took solace in the fact that despite everything, the animals were always there to comfort him.

Suddenly a thought that was not his own told him *Take off your scarf, and give it to Destiny.* As he wondered about why Destiny would need his scarf, the thought came urgently a second time. *Take off your scarf, and give it to Destiny.*

Paul did not hesitate and quickly took off the scarf and wrapped it around Destiny's neck.

"Now what?" He was next instructed, *Let Destiny smell* it. A light bulb suddenly went off inside of him as he quickly pushed the scarf onto Destiny's nose and said. "Go find Celeste. Come on, Destiny! Vamos!" (Let's go!) Destiny immediately went into tracking mode as the vanilla sandalwood perfume scented scarf made her jump into action. She immediately began methodically going back and forth on the street until she located Celeste's scent and then was off on a happy trot to find Celeste.

Paul followed as quickly as he could and watched with great hope as Destiny occasionally stopped to recalibrate Celeste's whereabouts, and then bayed with delight as she picked up the scent again and continued in her quest for Celeste. Paul immediately offered a prayer of thanks heavenward for the miracle of Destiny.

After walking for another 10 minutes, he saw the neon lights of a hotel sign blinking 'vacancy' and prayed that Celeste would be there. Destiny suddenly let out a few bays, marking her success that she had indeed found what she was looking for and then promptly and quietly sat down in front of one particular door at the hotel, somehow knowing that she needed to be quiet.

He went up to Destiny in gratitude, saying, "Good girl," then gave her the entire second granola bar in payment for a job well done. It seems that Destiny chose the logical room, which was in plain sight of the road, and just out of view of the front desk. He knew that he'd trusted in Destiny so far and that with God, all things were possible.

Paul's energy was spent and he needed to rest to rebuild his strength and to get his body temperature back to normal as hypothermia was taking its toll on him. Even though he had on an extra warm coat, it did little to keep the cold out with the wind chill, which seemed to go all the way through to his bones.

The only thing that was keeping Celeste sane was her constant prayer to God for help, comfort and protection for Paul. She recalled her favorite hymn; "Be Still My Soul" which calmed her troubled heart and allowed her to place all of her fears in the Lord's hands. Now that she'd placed it entirely in His hands, Celeste was able to snooze until around 2 a.m., when there was a movement outside of her door.

The door handle wiggled; she heard a voice whisper something. She nearly fainted from fear, but remained quiet as she looked around for something that she could use to protect herself. There was a light knock on the door and a soft voice on the other side of the door said, "Celeste, are you in there? It's me, Paul!" She dropped the lamp that she'd been holding like a baseball bat to the ground and opened the door in shaky relief to see him covered in blood, oil, and stickers. She quickly pulled him inside the room and bolted the door behind them.

"Wait," said Paul, "I need to bring in my dog, Destiny. She led me to you." Celeste quickly reopened the door, but saw nothing but her scarf on the ground, which she quickly grabbed as she closed the door.

Paul also opened the door to check, but Destiny had vanished, almost into thin air. "Where could Destiny have gone? She was just at my heels!"

Celeste assured Paul that she'd keep a lookout for Destiny, which allowed him to relax, even though he mumbled that she just had to be there. After a long hug and quick inspection, Celeste could tell that Paul also had a black eye, a bloody nose, and bleeding hands as well as a hole in his jacket.

"Have you been shot?" she asked, concerned.

"I think so, but I'm still standing."

She nearly fainted once she got a glimpse of the gunshot wound. She gingerly guided him to the bed and laid him down to rest from all of his distress.

"Were you able to contact Captain Lucas?" he said urgently.

"Yes, he is on his way here."

With that information, Paul could finally relax and was instantly nearly unconscious to the world.

Once she got him situated comfortably on the bed, she got up the nerve to take his jacket and shirt off, to assess what treatment was needed and the extent of the damage caused by the bullet. Celeste only had her Girl's Camp first aid training to rely on for this trauma; she hoped that she'd remember the steps needed to stabilize him, as he appeared to be in shock. She elevated his upper body to relieve the pressure on the wound. She prayed for recollection about what to do and was quickly instructed to get every towel and rag possible so that she could clean his wound.

As she cleaned the wound, she extracted several splinters of fragmented bone. The bullet must have grazed a bone–she'd need to try and flood the wound with water to help get the remaining splinters out. After that was accomplished, there was nothing to sterilize the wound with, so she did her best to clean it up with the towels and rags then remembered that she had a travel-size bottle of hand sanitizer in her purse. That would work, but it would be a painful application.

By this time, Paul was semi-conscious from the shock of the wounds, which were bleeding moderately, as it appeared his clothing had acted as a scab, having dried over the wound. Once she cleaned him up she would need to apply direct pressure on the wound to stop the bleeding. She was now ready to pour the hand sanitizer into his wound and then keep the pressure on the wound until the bleeding subsided.

She decided just to tell him quickly that she needed to sterilize the wound, that it would hurt, and to hold onto the bedpost to deal with the pain that was sure to come. He was barely coherent as she placed a rolled-up hand towel into his mouth to act as a noise muffler before she poured the entire contents of the hand sanitizer bottle onto his wound. Paul immediately yelped in agony! She took the sheets from the bed and ripped them into large strips to make a sling for his arm and shoulder so that when he was well enough to stand, it could support his ailing shoulder and arm.

He was coherent enough to tell her that he had barely escaped with his life and that he'd stowed away under a tarp in the back of one of the worker's truck, which brought him to town.

"I just knew that I'd find you at the first door that Destiny led me too, as I prayed to be led to where you were. Thankfully you were at the first door! Celeste, here, take my gun, it's got one bullet left in case we need it."

"Okay," she said as she squeamishly took the gun out of his hand. *Miracles never cease,* thought Celeste as she said a silent prayer of gratitude for his providential escape and protection. She wanted to hear all of the details of his flight, but knew that would need to happen later and just snuggled up beside him. She softly stroked his forehead and hair to soothe and lull him to sleep. Soon, they both slept for several hours until they heard a loud knock and an urgent voice at the door. Celeste gripped the gun, ready to fire if the door was kicked in.

"Celeste, Lago! Are you in there?" asked Captain Lucas. Celeste leapt up, trying not to disturb Paul, as she quickly answered the door, grateful that the cavalry had arrived.

All that she could say was, "I'm relieved that you made it here so quickly. Paul is right inside and pretty banged up, but will be able to speak to you about everything."

"Whoa, Lago," said Officer Jaime. It looks like you had a rough night."

Paul faintly smiled through his black eye and banged up face as he immediately went into police mode, giving Captain Lucas and

Loralee Lago

Officer Jaime all of the details up to that point. Captain Lucas just shook his head and said, "Lago, you sure know how to choose the right guy to talk with first. I'm glad that you are okay."

Paul nodded, stating, "If you consider being shot 'okay', then yes, I'm fantastic."

They both snickered at his attempt to try and lighten the mood. Captain Lucas said, "Celeste, did you call my friend Sancho? I wasn't sure if you got his name and number in time before the phone went dead."

"No, unfortunately I didn't."

"Okay, I'll call him now, and we'll start making plans."

CHAPTER 9

Operation Lighthouse

In addition to providing backup relief for Paul and Celeste, Captain Lucas was there to investigate the death of Thomas. Paul was glad that Captain Lucas had come as he had vital information to share, but first and foremost, Captain Lucas was told that Señor V (Vicente) was still at large.

Paul told Captain Lucas, "It is truly amazing that I escaped with my life." Paul then described how Thomas died and how the group that Carlos, Thomas and Rafael belonged to and lead by Vicente, was responsible for his death.

"I made the connection between all of the killings, including the attempt on the American couple, which I investigated earlier in the month. It is most likely that they seared O.N. on their soles as a calling card to warn the others members who were faltering in their allegiance.

"This group is responsible not only for stealing the gold from the mine and coin-stores, but also for smuggling gold inside of barrels full of oil. I notated the location of the marked barrels at the refinery as I was escaping the facility last night. It appears that this operation begins in Buenos Aires and the Pampas, where the gold is brought here to the refinery to be put in specially marked O.N. barrels and shipped out via sea barge. The gold is then smuggled out of the country easily via the barges into North America and throughout Europe."

"I concluded that the American couple were also operatives who became greedy once they realized that the operation included not only gold and oil, but the rigging of horse races. They tried getting a much larger cut for their contributions, but were rejected by Vicente. Vicente realized that he could get additional money from the U.S. by holding the couple for ransom.

"The transporting of race horses from the O.S. Ranch through an unsuspecting Señor Susaniche was just a ruse to cover up the transportation of the gold nuggets, coins, and bars in the horse carriers. These were put into the horses' feed bags with easy access to buyers as they traveled from racetrack to racetrack. It offered Carlos a perfect opportunity to make extra money quickly and with little notice from the others in the group, until Vicente figured out that he was tapping into his bottom-line," continued Paul.

"The gold coins and bars were sent via Seaplane to the refinery, where Thomas made sure that the specially marked O.N. barrels included the carefully wrapped gold within the shipment before they were loaded onto the barge for transport to the U.S. and other European countries where black market buyers awaited their arrival. It was the perfect set up, until a few of the group members decided that they wanted more money and threatened to leak the group's activities to the authorities if they were not given their fair share. Carlos, Felipe, Marcelo and Rafael were the main players in Buenos Aires and the Pampas, who stole the gold and nuggets of gold from the Cross 7 mine."

"The nuggets were then taken to the Susaniche Ranch on the day of each race in which their stallions would be racing. The plan worked well until Carlos started delivering only a portion of the gold he'd taken from the Cross 7 Mine and coin stores, keeping the rest for himself. Graciela was just an innocent victim and was killed through her association with Carlos. Their O.N. calling card was a way to give a warning to the other group members wanting to take advantage of their situation. This calling card gave other members that veered from the group's plan notice that they were next, and would emblazon their feet with O.N. to send a clear message that a similar fate awaited those who deviated from their assignment."

"Lucky for you, I brought a medical kit with me, as I was a medic in the military years ago," said Captain Lucas. He was able to properly diagnose and treat Paul's condition after taking his vitals, and determined that Paul was in much better condition than he looked.

Once Paul was cleaned up and bandaged, Captain Lucas concluded that Paul had fractured his collarbone and verified that the bullet had gone clean through his shoulder. "The sterilization that Celeste administered kept the infection at bay until I could more fully cleanse, suture and bandage the gunshot wound," he said.

Captain Lucas praised Celeste for her ingenuity and makeshift sling to stabilize Paul's shoulder and arm until they could get him to a hospital for treatment. Once he was done and the goose egg bruise on his forehead and black eye were attended to, he pronounced, "These treatments are as good as it is going to get. Try to take it easy for as few hours before we go after Vicente tonight, Lago."

Paul smirked, saying, "NOT on your life! We have a killer to catch," as they immediately began making plans to snare Vicente. Paul, Officer Jaime and Captain Lucas then carefully planned each detail of the sting operation.

"We have Officer Jaime, Sancho, me, you and of course, Celeste! After your description of what you saw at the Refinery. I'd say that Vicente has approximately four to ten thugs with him at all times," clarified Captain Lucas.

"One thing that we've got on him this time is the element of surprise," said Paul. "He is not expecting to see me again. I think I should send him a little note to meet me at the far end of the shore tonight." Paul immediately wrote out a message that could be delivered via courier to Vicente at the Refinery. "Let's see what he does with my little invite," said Paul.

Captain Lucas agreed that meeting up at the Refinery was too dangerous, as there were many like-minded friends of Vicente there that could gang up on them. "Neutral ground is a plus, and the lighthouse just might work."

The men continued their plan of action as Celeste took detailed notes, offered additional input, and then ordered food before she got too ravenous. She noticed with amazement that the men never seemed to be hungry, especially when they were in planning mode. She took food matters into her own hands and ran nervously to the nearby bakery and butcher shop to make sandwiches to keep everyone fueled.

"First things first," said Paul. "Here's the note, which reads, **Meet me alone tonight at eight at Les Eclaireurs Lighthouse.** Short and sweet is best," said Paul. "Of course, I know he's not going to come alone, but neither are we. This is going to get very interesting."

"We need to record as much of the conversation as possible, for evidence," said Captain Lucas. Celeste offered to do the audio recording, as she had an app on her phone that she used when she wrote down ideas for stories and songs. She could easily use this app to record the conversation now that Sancho had brought their gear and belongings to them and helped in the planning portion of the operation.

"That's good, as long as you can be far enough away to be out of danger," said Paul. "Now let's begin 'Operation Lighthouse'!" They sent the note to Vicente via Officer Jaime, who impersonated a courier at the Refinery during the lunch break. Officer Jaime was able to easily deliver it to Vicente and then remained close by after the delivery for a brief moment to observe his reaction after he read the note.

Vicente did not disappoint in his livid response and quickly rounded up 5 of his thugs to discuss it. Officer Jaime took mental notes of each man, whether Vicente mentioned their names, and if they had any identifiable features that were easily distinguishable for the Lighthouse sting operation.

As Officer Jaime slipped out, he came face to face with a big, burly man who tried to block his way out of the facility wielding a bat in his hand. As Officer Jamie was much younger and agile, he was able to easily get past the man due to his many years playing *futbol*, easily outmaneuvering the big man with his fancy footwork and spinning action. The man didn't even have a chance to take a good swing at him. Once past the man trying to block him, Officer Jaime sprinted out of the place and was immediately picked up by Sancho who drove them out of sight before any others could follow them.

For Celeste, it was hard to tell who was reveling in the planning phase of this operation more–Captain Lucas or Paul. They both talked so quickly over each other in coordinated chaos. You could tell their years of police work were a huge benefit in comparison to the thugs that Vicente would be bringing. Celeste found herself standing back in awe as she observed their efforts and hoped that all would go as planned.

Each person had a specific duty to fulfill, and all were of the utmost importance and must be executed properly to be able to successfully apprehend the ruthless criminals in such a remote part of the country. They usually had dozens of backup officers, electronics,

Loralee Lago

GPS, tracking devices, an arsenal of weapons to choose from and computers to coordinate each move. In comparison, they only had the few items that they had with them, their experience and good old fashion paper and pencil to carefully orchestrate each phase of the operation. The group prepared themselves with a few extra backup contingencies for various possible outcomes to be ready for whatever might come their way.

"What do we have here as far as equipment, ammo, and transportation?" asked Paul.

Officer Jaime listed the items, "We've got Celeste's cell phone with a recording app, five pairs of handcuffs, three 9 mm handguns, three vests, one standard-issue Police First aid kit, a flashlight, one therapeutic red light, one bait box, eight fishing lures, fish weights, two spools of fishing line, two fishing poles, one fishing net, eight ammo clips and Sancho's car.

I've arranged for the transportation of the detainees via seaplane tonight. I've dispatched Lieutenant Sosa to meet us around midnight to have Officer Jaime bring the prisoners back in one plane and the rest of us in another, which will fly directly into to Buenos Aires, where the police will be awaiting their arrival." said Captain Lucas.

"That's great, but why do we need the fishing gear?" said Celeste.

Captain Lucas shrugged, saying, "Because you never know if you'll have time to fish." Both Captain Lucas and Paul smiled and nodded their heads in approval at such a possibility.

"Fishing is always a great idea," said Captain Lucas and Paul in unison; Celeste just rolled her eyes at the thought of them wanting to fish in such stressful circumstances. Once they fully planned and rehearsed a dozen times various scenarios at the lighthouse earlier in the afternoon, everyone felt like they were as ready as they were ever going to be. Captain Lucas assigned Officer Jaime and Sancho to be on look out over the area and to update him regularly, in event that

Vicente made an early entrance.

"Looks like we just might have a few hours to cast a line or two over there on the rocks," said Paul. "It looks like we'll have an easy task of getting a lot of bites quickly since this area hasn't been overly fished, and the fish are not wise to our strategies. Do you want to come with us, Celeste?" offered Paul.

"No thanks, I'm happy to sit here while you two fish. I'm going to seriously ponder one of my favorite Bible scriptures from James, Chapter 1:5-6, which says, *If any of you lack wisdom, let him ask of God, that giveth to all men liberally, and upbraideth not; and it shall be given him. But let them ask in faith, nothing wavering.* After I ponder the intricacies of these verses and ask for the Lord's aid and added wisdom in our efforts today, I'm going to personally conduct a deep analysis of the inside of my eyelids, so I'll be on total alert once our infamous guest arrives."

"Suit yourself and enjoy your cat nap," said Paul. "We won't be long."

Paul and Captain Lucas eagerly cast their fishing lines near the rocks on top of the jetty, with hopes of a big catch. Within an hour and a half, both men were walking back to the lighthouse with a Sea Bass each and big smiles on their faces.

"Can you believe I got this 20-pound beauty?" said Paul proudly as he showed off his Sea Bass. "He sure put up a fight, but I persevered for the last hour and reeled him in for the win!"

"Holy Sea Bass, Batman! Wow! I can't believe that you got such a huge fish that quickly!

"I spent the bulk of my time fighting him. A times, he seemed to have the upper hand, but ultimately I wore him down and was victorious!" said Paul.

"Looks like you did quite of bit of wading in the water and mud, judging by the looks of your clothes. You're covered in mud from head to toe," remarked Celeste.

"Huggy?" Paul said as he stretched out his wet, muddy arms and came in for a hug, which sent Celeste squealing and running for cover.

"Not on your life! I don't want to smell like fish all night," refused Celeste. "It's quite the catch though, I can't wait to fry it up. What bait did you use, the ham and cheese that I suggested or the sardines?" she asked.

"I used the ham and cheese that you recommended from the leftovers from lunch," said Paul. "It worked like a charm."

"Who knew that ham and cheese would be a favorite last meal," said Celeste.

"Great call," said Captain Lucas. "My mackerel bait was good, but his was so much better. Still, I'm very pleased with my 10-pound beauty."

"Okay, let's take a few pictures to commemorate your glorious catches for posterity. Okay boys, now get back to work." said Celeste with a smile. They both saluted her in earnest and began marching gleefully in sync back to the lighthouse to pack their fish in ice.

"Wait, before we get back to work, let's start with a word of prayer, asking for divine intervention and our safety," said Paul.

"Good call," said Captain Lucas. "I'll say it, as we're going to need every bit of assistance for this plan to actually succeed with very few hitches."

At 7:45 p.m., Sancho signaled to Captain Lucas & Paul that Vicente and four men were coming down the road towards them. Vicente and his thugs pulled up to the lighthouse in his truck a few minutes later, leaving the headlights on for additional illumination; they immediately noticed the silhouette of a man nearby fishing off of the jetty in the rocks. Vicente and his men took advantage of the situation, rapidly taking out their semi automatic guns and opening fire, using several rounds of ammo before realizing that it was a decoy.

During their firing frenzy, Captain Lucas had carefully aimed and shot out the truck's headlights to protect them from detection. Maddened by this trickery and loss of ammunition, Vicente ordered his men to begin canvassing the area for Paul, with strict instructions to take no prisoners.

Once inside of the lighthouse, his men opened fire upon another stuffed dummy wearing Paul's bullet scarred shirt. Celeste had nicely set up the table with a Mate cup and baguette, as a teakettle whistled in the background on the coal burning stove–yet another clever distraction successfully completed as planned by the team. The men immediately came back to report in frustration that it was another trick. By this time, Vicente was fully enraged and yelled, "Find him now! I'll give any man that can kill him an extra 4,000 Pesos! ($1,000 UDS) I'm tired of his games."

A voice from behind Vicente said, "Why are you trying to kill me? What have I ever done to you?"

Vicente spun around and shot blindly into the night. He yelled in rage, "Come out so that I can kill you properly, Lago! I'm in no mood for your little mind games."

Paul asked again, "Tell me why you want to kill me first? I need to know why you want to murder me in cold blood."

Vicente spouted, "Because of you and your investigation, you have threatened my livelihood at the Mine and my operative at the O.S. Ranch has been terminated, not to mention that every police officer in the country is now looking for me! You and your family are going to pay dearly for delving into my business. We'll start with killing your girlfriend and then you!"

Celeste inhaled quickly at the mention of her and began fervently praying that no such thing would happen to any of them. Vicente heard footsteps to his right and shot blindly into the blackness. He heard more footsteps to the left of him and shot in that direction and then in front and behind him, each time taking a blind shot into the dark.

Hearing a groan and someone falling to the ground he said, "Hah! I finally got you! Guido, Franco, come help me now!" Vicente ordered, but with no response to his command, he said, "What's going on? Get over here NOW!"

Little did Vicente know that Captain Lucas and Officer Jaime had already apprehended them and tied them to the bolted-down wood-burning stove within the Lighthouse. Vicente again commanded his other two henchmen to help, but with no response! He yelled at Paul, "What have you done with my men?"

"Oh, that. They're out cold, with the help of my friends and a little added chloroform. They are already in handcuffs and are being guarded during their siesta, but they couldn't help you anyway as they used up all their ammo in the bullet frenzy within the first few minutes of your arrival. Guido and Franco were easily apprehended, having been temporarily blinded by the red laser light after they kicked in the side room door inside of the lighthouse. The other two were easily overtaken from behind."

As Paul spoke, Vicente slowly walked towards him. Paul was aware of his movements and was buying a bit of time for Captain Lucas to get to safety, saying, "Stop right there, or I'll shoot you."

Vicente shot at the dark immediately, going right through the pile of wood as wood chips pelted Paul's body. Despite the splintered attack, Paul was able to throw a well-placed punch right into Vicente's nose, which began spouting blood like a fountain. Paul quickly retreated further back into the darkened safety barrier with his gun aimed and ready for the next course of action. Paul ducked as Vicente threw a massive blind punch in his direction. He ended up striking the woodpile with his fist as Paul returned the punch with a large piece of wood onto Vicente's burly back. This caused both men to fall to the ground, each having dropped their guns in the fight. Soon they were wrestling in the dark as each man tried to locate their gun in the darkness.

Vicente, in a blood and pain induced rage, blindly swung towards Paul's face and made contact, momentarily dazing Paul. With the extra few seconds, Vicente felt for and located his gun on the ground and shot Paul point-blank in the chest. The force of the shot knocked Paul completely to the ground in agony as he battled for his breath, although he quickly bolted back up despite the gunshot, acting on pure adrenaline.

"Now, Lucas! Now!" Paul screamed, as he fought to breathe.

Celeste, realizing that everything was not going according to plan, left the safety of her shelter, threw her flashlight towards Paul, and jumped onto Vicente's back to keep him from taking another shot. She was immediately thrown onto the ground, and before she knew it, became Vicente's hostage.

"Now you will pay with her life, Lago!" growled Vicente, panting and pointing the gun at her head. He dragged her towards his truck, as Celeste ended up as the pawn in this deadly game of chess. As he opened the door and pushed her inside the truck, she heard a loud thud; it was Captain Lucas hitting Vicente on the head. Having been momentarily stunned, it allowed Celeste to shut the truck door and lock it.

She knew it would do little good, but just knowing that it might give Paul and Captain Lucas an extra few seconds to regroup was good enough for her. As she did, Paul struck Vicente's arm with a large rock, knocking the gun out of Vicente's hand and into the dirt. This only added fuel to his rage as they began punching one another relentlessly. As they fought, Paul carefully maneuvered Vicente away from Celeste for both her and Captain Lucas' protection. He knew if he could get Vicente far enough away, he might have one last chance to get the upper hand.

Loralee Lago

The battle between Vicente and Paul continued down by the rocky Jetty near the Lighthouse, with Vicente having been blinded by Paul's flashlight and a well-placed punch to his jaw, causing him to lose his balance and fall off of the cliff. Paul reached out to pull him back, but Vicente defiantly refused the helping hand as he fell off the edge. Paul focused his flashlight down the cliffside to see if Vicente had somehow survived the fall. He quickly got his answer when he located Vicente's lifeless body more than 50 feet below, as the arctic high tide waves slammed against his lifeless body relentlessly upon the jagged rocks.

Paul signaled with his flashlight and then yelled as he returned, "It's over! Vicente is dead at the bottom of the cliff."

He found Celeste, who had safely hidden behind a large pile of coal near the door to the lighthouse and asked, "Did you get the recording?" Celeste could only nod her head up and down as she ran crying towards him, fearing that his life was ebbing away from the gunshot wounds he'd received, when she realized that Paul was wearing a bulletproof vest. Although he'd been badly bruised from the hits to his side and stomach, he had been spared.

They embraced, giving each other fervent kisses in rapid-fire, as they spoke each other's name, saying, "*Te Amo, mi Amor*," (I love you, my love) over and over in gratitude. As they held and comforted one another, Celeste looked into Paul's eyes in gratitude and exhaled with a huge sigh of relief that everything was finally over. They spoke to each other in hushed tones of their love and how grateful that they were to be alive.

Suddenly they heard a movement close by and a voice weakly say, "That was so touching you two, but could you come over here and help me? I've been shot in the leg and am unable to walk more than a few steps at a time." said Captain Lucas. Embarrassed, they immediately ran to his aid. As Captain Lucas weakly emerged from his hiding place, he said, "I think it's time to retire after this investigation concludes! I'm getting too old for all of this 'life and death' nonsense."

Now with Vicente dead and his thugs in custody, they hoped the additional evidence would convict the others and that they could put the case to rest. Paul attended to Captain Lucas's leg wound, which, although serious, was not life threatening, having missed his femoral artery.

Paul said, "That hit to Vicente's side couldn't have been timed any better, Captain! Thank you! You saved Celeste's life."

Captain Lucas said, "It is the least I could do, since you managed everything after I'd been hit. I'm grateful that you are both okay. Don't worry–I'll attend to Vicente's body, with Sancho's help in the morning. Officer Jaime will make sure that these thugs are personally escorted back to Buenos Aires tonight. I'll stay an extra day to be treated at the local clinic and then file my report once I return. Lieutenant Sosa will be here soon to help us tie up any loose ends and then fly back with you, as there isn't enough room for me to go with you anyway. I'll catch the next seaplane out tomorrow."

An hour later, Paul and Celeste gratefully boarded the seaplane with Lanzo and Lieutenant Sosa to return to Buenos Aires.

After discussing the events of the evening with Lieutenant Sosa and Lanzo, very little was said during the flight home as exhaustion set in. Lanzo expertly flew them through a calm, clear and starry sky.

The moon seemed to light their way home. It was more beautiful than ever at that altitude as the stars seemed to light their way home.

"Look!" said Paul. "It's the magnificent Southern Lights of the Aurora Australis!"

"The beautiful ribbon-like threads of blue, green, red and yellow are mesmerizing!" Celeste said.

"You know, there is a science behind the Auroras, whether it's the Northern Lights, which is the Aurora Borealis or the Southern

Lights of the Aurora Australis. In a nutshell, the sun blasts bursts of charged particles into space. This solar wind is attracted to the earth's magnetic fields, with the poles having the strongest pull. The result is an incredible display of curtain like beams that radiate from a central point. Sometimes they even become sudden beams of light that rapidly switch on and off. Auroras are one of the largest natural phenomena," said Paul.

"Wow! I feel like we're flying through heaven's gates. It has always been a dream of mine to see these lights in person. I never dreamed that I would have a front row seat, this up close and personal," said Celeste.

Once the celestial light show ended, Celeste and Paul closed their eyes and cuddled as they tried to get a little sleep to decompress from the extreme events of the evening, as Lieutenant Sosa and Lanzo quietly discussed the latest *futbol* scores.

An hour into the flight, they were jolted awake as the plane's hatch door was flung open and cold hurricane force winds pulled at them. They were shocked to see that Lieutenant Sosa had put a parachute pack on his back and was in position to jump out.

In horror, she saw that he had completely knocked out Lanzo as he slumped forward like a rag doll in his seat, and the plane nose-dived towards the sea!

She jumped up at the same time as Paul did, as he grabbed at Lieutenant Sosa's leg, causing him to fall to the floor while they violently fought, giving each other blows to the eyes, jaws, and ears, all while Paul tried to keep Lieutenant Sosa from leaping out of the plane.

Celeste somehow made it to Lanzo and unbuckled his seatbelt, pushed him out of the seat and sat down at the controls as she fought her way to upright the plummeting plane as the two men fought behind her. Celeste tried to level the plane out of the dive without success.

A Tango To Die For

All that she knew about planes was from watching movies. Celeste knew that she needed to pull the yoke back to level it off. With the plane steadily losing altitude, it was no easy task; even after all that they'd done to survive, she wasn't so sure that they'd make it out this time.

Not one to give up easily, she fought even harder to get the plane leveled by putting her whole body into pulling the yoke back. It wasn't until she uttered aloud a desperate prayer requesting heavenly help, that she was given the strength to perform the lifesaving task. At last, the plane responded accordingly and began recovering from its dive and gradually began regaining the lost altitude. She was grateful for the plane's recovery, as she could tell that the sea was quickly approaching.

Had the plane not recovered at that pivotal moment, it wouldn't have mattered who won the fistfight in the back seat! As the men's fight intensified, they began trying to strangle one another, and in the process, they each came close to falling out of the airplane. This was not a problem for Lieutenant Sosa, since he had a parachute on. Celeste tried a drastic move and pulled the yoke forward to plummet the plane just enough in Paul's favor. It worked, and Paul was able to wrap his arm in a vice-like hold on Sosa's neck from behind to try to keep him from jumping out. With this hold, Paul pulled the parachute strap off with his free hand from Lieutenant Sosa's left arm, as he pulled him back into the airplane.

Paul then used the fishing line from the fishing rod and reel nearby to get Sosa's wrists securely tied before he could begin the difficult task of closing the door, but it resisted because of the outside pressure that the wind placed on it. Paul had no choice but to let go of Lieutenant Sosa to secure the door. As he did so, Lieutenant Sosa took advantage of the sudden liberty and plowed past Paul, jumping out of the airplane. Having forgotten in the struggle, that he no longer had the use of his hands and that the parachute backpack was only partially on one of his arms until after he jumped!

Lieutenant Sosa's face showed a conceited victory for one brief instant, before realizing his fate as his face registered his plight. They witnessed in slow motion Lieutenant Sosa's defiant jump and deadly free fall as the parachute pack blew violently on his arm in the wind. Paul lunged for the fishing pole as it zipped past him with Lieutenant Sosa attached as he jumped from the plane.

Paul grabbed the fishing pole's handle just as it flew past him and desperately began reeling in the catch of his life! He seemed to be making progress as he methodically reeled Sosa in. His efforts proved to be futile once the line was fully spent, causing the pole to bend forcefully downward over the plane's doorframe until it snapped and flipped out of Paul's hands, leaving him standing there with only the bottom half of the fishing rod in stunned disbelief.

Celeste barely acknowledged Sosa's deadly jump; she had to remain focused on the most important task of keeping the airplane level. As she finally accomplished her duty, she looked over in relief, as Lanzo regained consciousness and immediately took control of the plane.

After struggling for several minutes, Paul was able to get the cockpit door closed. He plopped down to rest, saying, "It appears that Lieutenant Sosa planned to have all of us killed and parachute to safety. We now have pretty good idea who the informant was in this whole operation. That would explain why we didn't find Vicente and the others in the police data banks, or identify them during the gold robberies, and how they slipped through the screening process at the Tango contest. Captain Lucas is going to be very distressed to hear this news about one of his own officers, as he treated him like his own son. Dang–that was an expensive fishing pole. I hated losing it. At least we still have our Sea Bass safely in the cooler. I'll need to replace the pole for Captain Lucas before we leave for the U.S."

Celeste just looked at him in utter astonishment. "How can you talk about a lost fishing pole and the Sea Bass at a time like this?"

"Don't judge," Paul said. "It's a coping mechanism; it helps to keep my thoughts compartmentalized, so I don't lose it. Don't read too much into it, Celeste."

Celeste raised her eyebrows and slowly nodded her head in understanding.

"Regardless, I would wager any amount of money that Sosa was related to Rafael and Thomas. I'm certain he was our mole in this investigation, which kept Vicente one step ahead of us."

Lanzo interrupted, "I need to make an emergency landing in the nearest town to make sure everything is in proper working order and report the incident to the police so that a search and rescue team can begin to look for Lieutenant Sosa's body. I have the basic coordinates of where he jumped, and they can start from that point and begin their recovery efforts. If Sosa miraculously survived the free fall, he would not have survived long in these subzero waters."

Paul asked, "Where is the nearest city where we can land?"

"The nearest city is Miramar; we will be there in about 40 minutes. There is an executive airport there."

Celeste immediately lit up, saying, "Did you say Miramar? I love Miramar!"

"We should be there for just a few hours, but it will give me time to file a search and rescue report, have the plane serviced, and decompress from these extreme circumstances," said Lanzo.

"How does one go about reporting something like this to the authorities?" asked Celeste.

Paul and Lanzo both looked at each other knowingly, as Paul said, "You can leave that up to us. Let's just say it's going to take a while."

Five hours later, after filling out their eyewitness reports and signing affidavits, both Paul and Celeste left the police station, starving. "Hey, there's a pizza place called La Astral right across the street. Let's get a pizza to go," suggested Celeste.

"Okay," he said, "but don't drop it in the street this time. My teeth can't handle biting into gravel toppings–I'm already banged up enough as it is."

"You got it," she said, chuckling. "Let's dine in, just to be sure, as it's pretty windy outside right now." As they ate their favorite comfort food of pizza topped with mozzarella slices, ham, and whole green olives, it helped ease their minds a bit from the trauma of the last 24-hours.

"It's been so long since I've been here, I'm unsure if I could even show you the way to our little apartment, the chapel, and homes of the families that we taught. It is highly unlikely, but wouldn't it be great if I saw someone I knew?"

As she said those very words, a tall, handsome man walked in with a woman. Celeste immediately recognized him as the young 12-year-old she once knew. "Gonza, is that *you*, and Alejandra too?"

"Hermana Humphries! You have changed very little since the last time we saw you," he said as he gave her a hug and kiss on the cheek.

"The same almost goes for you two, except that you're much taller and older. I'm so happy to see you! We are here for an unanticipated layover."

They spent several minutes talking about their family and getting caught up on the happenings in each other's lives. It was a tender mercy for her to be able to see this faithful brother and sister who meant so much to her, as nearly their entire family had been baptized.

"Celeste, would you mind if I send out a group text to a few friends that you know to see if they can stop by for a few minutes?"

said Gonza.

"I would be honored if you would, as long as it is okay with Paul?"

"Sure, go for it," said Paul.

Before they knew it, they were joined by the Milan-Susaniche, Battaglia, Roman, Lurachi, Vega, Sosa, Imhoff, Vargas, Fernandez, and Paralta families in a joyful reunion, packing the small pizzeria to capacity, like a can of sardines. No one seemed to mind the tight quarters as the pizzeria was filled with great conversation and laughter. Even the owner of La Astral joined in the jubilation, offering free sodas and fries to everyone.

"Talk about answered prayers. Thank you for coming to eat pizza today, Gonza, Alejandra, Pablo, Nadia, Manuel and Martha. And thank you all for coming to see us on such short notice–it means more than you'll ever know," she said as she hugged each one in a tearful farewell.

As they walked towards the airstrip, Celeste said, "Did you know this was my favorite area of service? We had a number of baptisms, and I was fortunate enough to be here when the city celebrated its 100th anniversary. The city spared no expense to commemorate its first century. I particularly remember that the local Panaderia made a replica of the city out of cake and cookies! It was an incredible work of art to behold. The city ate the cake creation during the final day of the celebration. They had a Centennial parade that represented many of the countries of the world. I was honored when our apartment landlord, who was on the planning committee, asked my companion and I to march in the parade holding the American flag. It is something that I'll never forget. I've never felt so much pride for my own country than when I was far, far away in another part of the world, marching with Old Glory."

"What a great memory," said Paul. "I bet you were the talk of the town."

"We were. We were recognized throughout the town afterwards and were always treated very kindly. I love these people as much today as I did back then." She said, then stopped dead in her tracks and said, "Let's go back in and order another pizza to take to Lanzo. I doubt that he's been as lucky as we have been in finding something to eat at the executive airport while the plane is undergoing its repairs and final inspection. It's the least we can do after his unexpected change in flight plans."

"Good idea," said Paul. "Let's get him one with Chorizo on top! I'll carry it, in case a wind gust comes up out of nowhere," he winked.

"Smart move, but hold on to it tightly with both hands, as the wind gusts are pretty fierce," Celeste advised.

CHAPTER 10

O-so Joyful!

Once they arrived back in Buenos Aires, Paul and Lanzo were taken to the hospital for evaluation and treatment of their injuries. Both Lanzo and Paul had concussions, and the hospital required that they be kept overnight for observation. Paul had burst all of the stitches that Captain Lucas had so painstakingly sewn in for him during his Sea Bass fishing battle and fights with Vicente and Lieutenant Sosa that also needed immediate attention.

By early afternoon, Celeste and Captain Lucas were summoned to the hospital to pick them up after they had given the eyewitness reports that were required for the investigation's completion. Paul had to file additional reports with his Interpol employer to complete the investigation for the U.S. portion of the case as well.

Upon their return to the Air B&B, Celeste treated Paul, Captain Lucas and Lanzo to homemade *Milanesas, Empanadas, Chorizos* with *Chimichurri Vinaigrette*, *Chimichurri* Bread, *Kreutzer Potato Salad and BBQ'd Sea Bass*. For dessert, she made the delicious *Postre de Mansana*! (Apple dessert!) It was a feast fit for a king! "Did you make all of this yourself?" asked Paul appreciatively.

"No! I had considerable help from Captain Lucas' wife Julia, Lanzo's wife Abril, and her sister Isabel, so that I could get it all done in time before you were released. Hey Lanzo, Abril spilled the beans and told me the secret ingredient in your family's Kreutzer Potato Salad.

"Did she now?" he said with a wink as he hugged Abril in greeting.

"I would not have guessed the secret ingredient is cream cheese," said Celeste. "Thank you for generously sharing your family recipes."

Paul said, "Wow, this looks and smells amazing! Is that the Sea Bass that I caught that I see?"

"It sure is!" said Celeste.

"I can't wait to sink my teeth into that. Thank you!" he said.

Paul's mouth watered from the buffet of foods spread before them that delighted their senses as they socialized with the group of special people around the table. "All that I can say is 'Yum!' I'm so hungry; I think that I could eat for two days, nonstop! *Con Provecho y Salud*! (To your benefit and health!) Who's saying the prayer on the food?"

*****

Once the investigation had been marked completed, Paul and Celeste took one last trip to Señor Susaniche's O.S. Ranch on the Pampas to go horseback riding for the afternoon. Señor Susaniche was more than pleased to have them come for an informal visit. Paul and Celeste carefully prepared and packed a basket lunch of *Mortadella* sandwiches, apples, grapes, and various sliced *Queso frescos* (fresh cheeses), crackers, and *Alfajores*. After preparing and packing everything into the car, Paul said, "We make a great team!"

"We sure do," said Celeste. "But don't forget the Ivess carbonated waters, orange concentrate, sweet rolls and a blanket to sit on, hon."

"Yes, dear. And so, it begins," said Paul as he winked and acknowledged her list of reminders.

The car was also fully stocked with every snack and drink that Celeste could ever need. "Sorry for being so uptight when we went to Señor Susaniche's before," said Celeste. "I see that you didn't forget a thing; it appears that you've anticipated my every snacking need. You're a true gem."

"It is my pleasure, my love," said Paul.

The car ride to the ranch was tranquil as they enjoyed the scenic countryside and then joined in singing along with a few of the more lively tunes on the radio. As they passed bovine after bovine grazing along the Pampas during their journey, Paul started counting out loud. "One steak, two steaks, three steaks, four! Now that's some great looking BBQ in front of me."

"How can you say that about those poor, sweet, gentle cows?"

"Wasn't it YOU who told me about your mischievous grandpa Humphries who put you on the back of your favorite cow, Rusty in the pasture, behind his home in Hurricane, Utah? If I recall correctly, good old Rusty promptly ran and bucked you off into a cow-pie, and you barely missed hitting a tree by inches. I beg to differ that they are always gentle, plus I've recently had a scuffle with an oversized cousin of one of these cows and can solemnly swear that he was neither sweet nor gentle and have a large hole in my favorite pants to prove it. Carnivores unite!" boasted Paul in victory!

"Touché," she said. "You've got a point–this country is no place where vegetarians can thrive. Moooooo!" she bellowed in reply.

"No, no, no! That's not how a cow sounds. You've got to put

your heart into it, and it needs to come from deep within your chest cavity from the back of your throat and through your nose," he said as he *moo*ed both low, long and loud. Paul took the extra time to prolong the *moo* for ultimate lung output. Celeste tried once more as instructed and then Paul *moo*ed again, each trying to outdo the other until they both laughed until they cried from their silliness. "The cows don't appear to be impressed with our impressions of them," laughed Paul as he wiped tears from the sides of his eyes.

"What? How can you say that? I think we sounded Mooooo-velous," Celeste said, cackling.

A big, juicy bug splattered all over the driver's side windshield. Paul had to turn on the windshield wipers and apply the washing fluid spray multiple times just to be able to see out of it properly, and then said, "I bet that he doesn't have the guts to do that again." Celeste just rolled her eyes at his corny humor, but internally she loved that he could let his hair down and *be* corny.

Celeste and Paul relished just being together as a couple. They held hands throughout the ride, and Paul frequently raised the hand that he was holding, and tenderly kissed the back of it. Celeste turned up the car's radio and they both sang with gusto to the chorus of a rock love ballad.

As they pulled into the Susaniche Ranch, the afternoon sun shone brilliantly over the amber Pampas; everything appeared to be a vibrant amber gold. The weather was perfect for riding, and Señor Susaniche had Pablo saddle up Oso for the ride. Oso whinnied in anticipation as Paul and Celeste approached. Both the saddle and Oso's beautiful black hide glistened in the afternoon sun. Celeste quickly snuggled up next to Oso, who whinnied in delight at her return. She was amazed at how Paul effortlessly put his foot into the stirrup and lifted himself easily onto the saddle, while she needed a lot of help just getting her foot up and into the stirrup.

"Here, let me help you," Paul offered, as he leaned over, put his right hand down, grabbed her hand and easily lifted her up behind him onto Oso's back in one swoop saying, "Ally-oop!" Oso jumped slightly in anticipation of a nice ride.

"Let's go! Daylight is burning,'" said Paul.

"Yee-Haw!" yelped Celeste. "Hey, you could have had worn your Gaucho chaps for this ride," she suggested.

"I'm really glad that you didn't think of that until just now; I don't think I'm prepared to live up to that epic Gaucho gear anytime soon," said Paul, with a smirk. "Are you ready? Give Oso the command, and we'll be off."

"*Vamanos (Let's Go!)* Oso!" said Celeste as she wrapped one arm around Paul's stomach with the other looped around the picnic basket full of goodies, which sat nicely on Oso's back with little effort on her part. Celeste nestled her chin over Paul's broad shoulders for the ride.

As they rode Oso through the golden prairie, Celeste frequently kissed the back of Paul's neck and whispered sweet nothings into his ear. Oso pranced like a true champion as they picked up the pace a bit going through a small steam. Paul turned his head towards her, making a guppy fish face, which made her laugh as she clung to him tightly until they were across safely. After few minutes later, they found a shady tree to rest under to share their picnic. Paul got out of the saddle first, grabbed the picnic basket, and carefully placed it under the tree, then helped Celeste get off of the saddle and safely to the ground.

"Thank you for your help." she said.

"I think that forgot something." he said.

"What," she said looking around.

"A kiss is needed to complete your *Thank you* transaction. So pucker up buttercup!" he said with a grin.

"My pleasure!" she said as she leaned up on her toes, wrapped her arms around his neck and gave him a nice long, *Thank you* kiss

Loralee Lago

in gratitude. "Here's a bonus tip for your excellent equestrian skills too," Celeste exclaimed as she leaned in for a nice long 2nd round smooch. "How's that for a *thank you*?"

"Now that's my kind of *thank you*!" he said and then kissed her again and then took Oso's reigns and tied them to the tree. Okay now, first things first," said Paul as he gave Oso a nice drink of water and then gave him a few apples in appreciation for his services. Oso whinnied a thank you and quickly slurped up the water and politely bit into one of the apples and then ate the other apple in one bite from Paul's hand. He then shook his head in gratitude for the delicious treat. Celeste just put her face against his head cooing, "Good boy, Oso!" Oso nodded twice in appreciation of the extra attention.

Paul and Celeste made quick work of getting the blanket set out and everything ready for their picnic. "Tengo mucho hambre!" (I'm really hungry!), exclaimed Paul. He took a big bite out of his sandwich and whole heartedly agreed, "I'm with you, Celeste. Mortadella is my now my favorite bologna to eat. It's really delicious, or as my little nephew Brad would say, "La-licious!"

"Please pass the *jugo de naranja* (orange flavored concentrate) and carbonated water," he asked. Paul expertly added the orange concentrate into each of their cups, then began squeezing the extinguisher-style handle on the carbonated water into the first cup, but squeezed the handle too hard and water spewed all over the place.

After laughing at the unexpected water assault, he tried again, pressing ever so slightly, resulting in a perfect amount of liquid going into each cup for a refreshing drink. He then tried his concoction to make sure the amounts were sufficient and declared, "Now that's what I'm talking about," as he quickly finished his first cup, made another and began drinking it. "I think I've got the concentrate and carbonated ratios perfecccc..." he said as a loud carbonated burp spontaneously erupted from his lips. "Umm, Ha ha...I apologize, as I think that I may have added a bit too much carbonation," he said in embarrassment.

To cover his burping blunder, Celeste let out 4 melodic short carbonated burps, saying, "Name that Tune in 4 burps."

Recovering from his mishap, he quickly said, "Mary Had a Little Lamb!"

"Correct. Your turn!" she said.

Paul let out 3 burps in quick bursts, saying, "Can you Name that Tune in 3 burps?"

"Please repeat the tune for added clarity," Celeste said with a wink.

Paul repeated it, "Can you Name that Tune in 3 burps?" and then said, "Well?"

Celeste just shrugged her shoulders and said, "Paul, Name that Tune, as I have no idea!"

"What? You couldn't tell that it was *Choose the Right*? Or as Garrett in my primary class refers to it as *Choose the Sprite*!"

"There's no way that could have been *Choose the Right*. I need to hear it one more time." Celeste laughed.

"You're fooling with me, aren't you?" he said.

"Yeah, I totally knew it was *Choose the Right*, but loved hearing you play up your pro burping skills," she giggled.

"Why YOU!" he exclaimed, acting upset. Somehow, Paul sprayed a large burst of carbonated water at her, resulting in carbonated water wars, with each grabbing their own bottle for ultimate aiming power and douse-ability. After a minute of complete water war frenzies, Celeste raised her limp white, water-soaked napkin in a ceasefire, as Paul was ruthless in his fizzy water assault.

Having won the coveted Fizzy Water Award, Paul jumped up and began clucking and strutting, as he flapped his elbows in a crazy chicken victory dance.

After their picnic, Paul laid his head on Celeste's lap as she fed grapes to him, while appreciating the light breeze and soothing sounds of nature. Oso snorted in protest. "Oh, I see! It appears that someone would like a few grapes as well," she said. The stallion simply draped his head her way, as she fed a few grapes to Paul and then a bunch to Oso. Both boys munched happily, grateful for all the extra attention.

Celeste cherished having Paul on her lap as she caressed his face and outlined his lips with her fingers. Paul playfully shark-attack snapped at her fingers in response as she giggled in delight. She ran her fingers through his hair until he became so relaxed that he fell asleep–until Oso snorted loudly in complaint that he wasn't getting the same treatment, jolting Paul awake.

"Wow, I can't believe I fell asleep. That was so relaxing. Thank you! I think maybe we both better give Oso a bit of attention now if we know what's good for us," he said. Both Paul and Celeste quickly got up and showered Oso in pats and scratches behind his ears. Celeste even gave Oso the last bunch of grapes and another apple as the horse whinnied in utter delight. Paul pulled out a Swiss Army knife from his pocket and carefully etched a heart on the tree trunk, with a P+C in the middle, and included the date.

"Now, everyone will know that we were here and that this is our tree forever," said Celeste.

"This will give us an extra reason to return to visit. I think that we need to seal this tree heart creation with a kiss and selfie to commemorate the occasion," suggested Paul.

"I agree," said Celeste, as she stood on her tippy toes and wrapped her arms around his neck adding an abundance of hugs and kisses then posed for the couple selfie.

Oso snorted again now that all the attention wasn't heaped upon him, but since Celeste gave him the rest of her sweet roll, he decided that it was a fair enough compromise.

After she sat back down, Paul said, "You know what? It just dawned on me that we never got to dance our Tango that first night after you arrived. Señorita Celeste, would you Tango with Me-go?" he said, as he bowed and then grabbed her hand to pull her up quickly from the blanket. They began to Tango down the grassy plain, cheek to cheek, then abruptly turned and came back the same way that they had come. Celeste squealed in delight as he dipped her down low and then went in for a passionate kiss. Oso whinnied as he slowly brought her back up, Paul said, "Sounds like Oso approves of our tango and gave it a solid 2!"

"Two? I think that we deserve at least a 4 or even a 5!" Contested Celeste. "That dip and kiss was worth a few more points at the very least."

"Agreed," said Paul as he gave her one more kiss to verify the points earned. "We mustn't disappoint our judge." Oso nodded his head up and down, appearing to concur with Paul's assessment.

Paul walked over to Oso and said. "Celeste, come over here. What's this in Oso's mouth?"

Celeste walked over, to see that Oso had a small black satchel hanging by its drawstring in his mouth. "What do you have there, my handsome boy?" She took the pouch from Oso's front teeth and untied the drawstring to reveal a small black velvet box.

"What's going on here, Oso?" she asked.

"Go ahead and open it," said Paul.

Celeste looked down in wide-eyed wonder and slowly opened the box, but it was empty. She looked up in confusion and then gasped as she saw Paul kneeling down on one knee, with a beautiful ring shaking in his outstretched hands.

"Celeste, love of my life, partner in crime, and better half. Will you marry me?"

"Yes, yes, and yes!" exclaimed Celeste as she shouted for glee!

As he placed the beautiful blue gemstone ring on her ring finger, Paul said, "Celeste, I will forever be faithful to you and promise to daily kiss you abundantly, pray with you morning and night and tell you that I love you every day! Whenever you doubt and ask me if I still love you, my answer will forever be... ALWAYS!"

"You bought the ring that I adored from the souvenir store! When did you buy it? How could I have missed it? I can't believe you got the ring; I love this ring! Thank you!" she said as she hugged and kissed him repeatedly.

"It wasn't hard to plop it in the middle of all of the treats that I bought that day. Plus, I gave the sales clerk the cue with a wink and finger over my mouth to keep it low profile as she rang it up. I've kept it in my pocket for the few days waiting for the perfect moment to propose to you. I was going to propose to you over a nice dinner under the stars, but this day seemed to be all that I'd hoped for. I hope that it will do, until I can get you an official engagement ring."

"Yes! I love it! It's perfect; I don't need another engagement ring!" she said. "But I will only accept it on one condition; that you formally ask for my hand in marriage in person with my father. My mom will have a say too, but traditionally the father gives the final approval."

"And it entails the family's requirement of giving a ham and bag of flour as part of asking for permission to marry you," he interrupted.

She giggled and nodded in agreement to his remarks. "You remembered!"

"I wholeheartedly agree to these conditions," he said as he grabbed her in a bear hug, spinning her around and around in euphoric bliss.

Oso whinnied in congratulations as they embraced and kissed each other in pure joy, as only two newly engaged star-struck lovers would do.

A Tango To Die For

"I didn't dare put the ring in the box, as I was certain that Oso might eat it," said Paul. "I think he understands more than he leads us to believe. I never thought that I'd ever marry; I felt that it was too late to find someone to love in my life. Then you walked into my life, and I knew immediately that you were the one!"

"You did? I knew the instant that we locked eyes at the airport!" said Celeste. "Do you think that we can call my family tonight to tell them the fantastic news? My father will want you to sit down with him to officially ask for my hand in marriage and talk with him about our future plans together. Are you up to all of that?"

"Yes, I am."

"There's one last, very urgent matter that is of utmost importance to the family. Your answer could have significant consequences."

"For heaven's sake Celeste, tell me, what is it?" said Paul.

"Do you or do you not like playing cards and other board games, mainly Mexican Train Dominos, Fibbage, Cover Your Assets and Joker board games? Answer very carefully, as it will determine who your family allies will be."

"Umm, I like to play games sometimes, but don't know most of these games you're referencing. Is there any hope for me?" he asked.

"Yes, but we'll have to train you extensively BEFORE the meeting with my parents, as this Intel will be required of you before making their final decision. Are you up for the task?"

"Yes. For you, I'll do whatever you ask, *mi amor!*" said Paul. "By the way, what are your feelings about playing these games, Celeste?"

"I personally can take them or leave them, so I play most of the time, but like to have an out whenever I don't feel like it, unlike some diehards in the family who will play every day, all day whenever we get together."

Loralee Lago

"Do you think my response should be a truthful maybe or definite YES?"

"Definitely go with the YES for now, and then we can ease them into your preference of opting out sometimes after a few years," Celeste recommended.

"Roger that, Mi Amor! Let's pack up our picnic and start for home, my beautiful fiancé," said Paul.

"I like the sound of that, my *guapo* (handsome) fiancé!" replied Celeste.

In record time, everything was packed up, and they were riding Oso back to the Ranch. Time seemed to stand still as if they were in a dream as they rode. Life never looked so bright and beautiful than at that moment, as they relished in the aura of the special occasion. Oso practically pranced all the way home, knowing that he had played an important part in their special day.

Celeste couldn't stop smiling and repeatedly looked at the beautiful blue gemstone ring on her ring finger to make sure that it all really happened; especially that it actually happened to her. Tears of gratitude welled up inside of her heart for the blessing of finding a true love to go through life life's ups and downs together.

Back at the Ranch, they thanked Señor Susaniche and excitedly shared their engagement news with him and Señora Susaniche, who were delighted. Señor Susaniche said, "Now you will have a reason to come back often to visit us at our beautiful *Ranchero*. I think Oso has adopted you as his own and will be expecting you back."

Paul said, "You bet we'll be back! Thank you for the generous invitation."

Señora Susaniche quickly went back into the house and returned with a beautiful crocheted ring pattern afghan, giving it to Celeste and saying, "This is to remember your beautiful engagement day. I hope that you'll remember us and your special day each time that you see it in your home."

Celeste kissed Señora Susaniche on the cheek in gratitude, saying, "I will remember your loving hands crocheting each stitch every time that I see it. Thank you so much. It will always be treasured in our home."

"*Denada* (You're welcome) *bonita* (beautiful) Celeste!"

Before they left, Paul pulled Señor Susaniche to the side and asked him something. Señor Susaniche nodded, and then shook Paul's hand in agreement.

As they walked towards their car, Paul summoned Pablo over to him as he was taking Oso back to the stable and quietly whispered something into the teen's ear. Pablo eagerly nodded his head in approval, and then Paul handed him a white envelope. His eyes went wild with excitement as he looked inside and then thanked Paul again and again, saying, "*Muchas Gracias Señor* Lago! (Thank you very much, Mr. Lago!) I won't let you down!"

"Pablo, I'm counting on you to be a force for much good in your life and would like for you to *pay it forward* to another person one day. Will you promise me that you'll do this?" said Paul.

"*Lo Prometo, Señor Lago!*" (I promise Mr. Lago)

"I'll check back with you in six months and see how everything is going with your training Pablo. Let me know if you need anything else and we'll try and make it happen. Okay?"

"Si Si Señor Lago! I'm overwhelmed with your generosity."

"You're welcome Pablo. Now go and make your dreams come true now that there is nothing holding you back." said Paul.

Paul got into the car and waved goodbye as they drove away. Oso whinnied and shook his head alongside Pablo, who waved enthusiastically, grinning from ear to ear!

"What did you say to Señor Susaniche and Pablo?" asked Celeste.

"I simply asked Señor Susaniche if he would allow Pablo the

time off to go to school to become a trainer for his horses, and that if he agreed, I would pay the tuition for him to become a certified horse trainer. It's an offer that he couldn't refuse, as it would benefit him as much as Pablo.

"Thank you for being so generous with Pablo. I can tell he's a good kid, and without Rafael around to torment him, he will soar. You saw a promising future in him," said Celeste.

"Yeah, he's a natural with the horses and has a passion for the work. Initially, when I spoke with Señor Susaniche about the case, he mentioned what a hard worker Pablo was and how much his family depends on him for their support. This training will not only give Pablo a much-needed title change here at the Ranch, but will also benefit his family monetarily once he earns his credentials. It's a win-win situation that will bless him and his family for many years to come."

*****

The time came to return home to the United States. Celeste looked back in sadness as they boarded the plane, as she was once again leaving the country and people that she loved so very dearly. "I feel a bit melancholy leaving today, kind of like Eva Peron. I know that is an odd comparison, but I think I understand just a bit of what she felt like."

Paul nodded in agreement and couldn't resist telling her all about Eva (Evita) Peron. "Did you know that she is Argentina's most famous woman? It is Eva Peron, who had a significant impact on Argentine politics. She was loved by the Argentine working class, mocked by the aristocratic women of Buenos Aires society and misunderstood by the military establishment. She came to symbolize a wealthy Argentina, full of pride and with great expectations immediately following WWII."

"She met Colonel Juan Domingo Peron at a 1944 fund-raiser, and assisted her husband in his rise to power. When Peron became Minister of Labor and Welfare, she convinced him to institute minimum wage, better living conditions, salary increases, and protection from employers. She established the Social Aid Foundation, which built hundreds of schools, hospitals, trained nurses, and dispensed money to the poor. She was a champion for women's rights and was known as the people's heroine. She died in 1952 of uterine cancer with 'Don't cry for me Argentina, I remain quite near to you' written on her tombstone."

"Okay, Mr. Google. I know she was pivotal in making Argentina what it is today; I understand that one person can and does make a difference. Now, do me a favor and just kiss me!"

"THAT I can do, my future Mrs. Lago," Paul said enthusiastically. He held her face in his hands and tenderly kissed her lips over and over until her sadness subsided as they flew off into the sunset with great hope in their hearts as they moved forward together in faith.

Eva Peron's words became their own sentiments. "Don't cry for me, Argentina, for I remain quite near to you."

Celeste and Paul would always have Argentina, as you may leave, but it will never leave your soul.

The End of the Beginning!

CHAPTER 11

Las Rectas!

Loralee Lago

Milanesas – Serves 2

Ingredients

- 1 lb. of thin-cut U.S. Sandwich Steak or Round Steak (thinly cut)
- 1 t. Salt
- 1 t. Garlic Powder
- 1 ½ t. Parsley
- 1 t. Oregano
- ½ C. Italian Bread Crumbs
- 1 Lemon cut in wedges to squeeze over top of Milanesa before serving
- 2 Eggs (Fried) to put over top

Instructions:

1. Tenderize the steaks by pounding them as thin as possible with a meat tenderizer. Lightly beat the eggs with a fork and add: salt, garlic powder, and chopped parsley
2. Pass the meat through the egg mixture and then through the breadcrumbs. Coat well.
3. Fry in Olive Oil until done, usually a few minutes on each side. Drain on a paper towel.
4. Before serving, squeeze a lemon wedge over Milanesa; place a fried egg on top. Eat with French bread, either as a sandwich or on the side.
5. 1 Lemon – Cut in wedges (to squeeze over the top of fried Milanesa)
6. 1 Egg (Fried sunny side up and put on top of cooked Milanesa)
7. Serve with French Fries or make into a sandwich

Gnocchi Sauce – Serves 10

Ingredients

- 1.5 lbs. of Round Beef Steak cut into small 1" cubes (for more tender meat, marinate a few hours in Coca Cola before frying up. You could also cube and cook meat semi-frozen in a crockpot for extra tender pieces for 8 hours on low).
- 2 t. Salt
- 2 t. Pepper
- 1 Large White or Yellow Onion finely chopped
- Fry in 2-3 T. Olive Oil until Brown. Don't drain oil. Fry until meat is nearly done, then add Garlic Cloves and sauté for a minute, then add rest of ingredients
- 4 Garlic Cloves
- ½ Jalapeno Pepper (finely diced) Take out seeds if you don't want it hot
- 6 Roma Tomatoes (Diced)
- 2 (8 oz.) Cans Tomato Sauce
- 1 C. Water
- 3 Bay Leaves (keep whole as you will take out before serving)
- 3 t. Oregano
- 5 Cubes Beef Bouillon or 2 T. Better than Bouillon
- 3 T. Basil

Simmer for at least an hour and pour over Gnocchi Dumplings. Sprinkle with fresh Parmesan Cheese and eat with sliced French or Italian Bread.

Loralee Lago

Gnocchi Dumplings

Ingredients

- 2 Eggs Beaten
- ¼ t. Garlic Powder
- 2 Eggs (beaten)
- 2 t. Soft Butter
- Whirl this at low speed in a food processor.
- In another bowl mix:
- 4 C. Instant Potato Flakes
- 2 C. Flour
- 1 t. Salt
- 2 t. Parsley

Instructions:

1. Add this mixture to process and mix at low speed until dough forms.
2. Flour hands and table and knead the dough, then roll into long one foot ropes and cut with kitchen shears into 1" pieces. Roll each piece with tines of the fork (optional for the Gnocchi look)
3. Put in 4 Qt. Pan with boiling salted water. Carefully hand drop individual Gnocchis into boiling water. Don't overcrowd them. They are done when they float to the top in about 3-5 minutes. Drain with a slotted spoon rather than with a colander, because they are delicate. Continue cooking until all are cooked and place in a separate bowl.

Ensalada Rusa (Russian Salad)

Ingredients

- 2 Medium Potatoes, peeled (boiled w/ 1 t. salt until slightly soft and diced up). Let cool before mixing in with everything.
- 2 C. Mixed Vegetables (steam/cooked until slightly firm and salt to taste)
- 1 Celery Rib (diced - Optional)
- 1 Green Apple, peeled and diced
- ¼ C. Chopped Walnuts
- ¾ C. Mayonnaise
- 1-2 t. Parsley
- 2 T. Apple Cider Vinegar
- Salt & Pepper to taste

Instructions:

1. Peel, dice and boil the potatoes with salt until slightly tender. Drain water and let cool completely.
2. Steam vegetables until slightly tender. Let cool.
3. Add remaining ingredients and let set in refrigerator for at least 2-3 hours to let the flavors marry.

Loralee Lago

Chimichurri Vinaigrette

Ingredients

- Used as a marinade for meats as well as a table sauce.
- 1 Onion, finely diced
- 1 T. Minced Garlic
- 2-3 T. Minced Parsley
- 1-2 T. Minced Jalapeno Pepper or 1 t. Cayenne (optional)
- 1-2 T. Fresh Oregano
- 2 Bay Leaves (take out before serving)
- ½ t. Ground Black Pepper
- ½ C. Vegetable Oil
- ¾ C. White Wine Vinegar
- 1 ½ t. Salt

Instructions:

Finely mince the onion, garlic, jalapenos, and oregano. Mix with all remaining ingredients (use blender for better mixing). Refrigerate for at least 2 hours or overnight is better to allow flavors to meld.

Empanadas – Makes 24

Ingredients

Dough: (If you don't want to make the dough, buy premade pie crust dough or puff pastry and cut with an extra-large rimmed cup) I like to use Puff Pastry, as it is faster! (Use the precut round-shaped ones, as it is easier to roll out)

- 6 ½ C. All-Purpose Flour
- 1 T. Baking Powder
- 2 ½ t. Salt
- ¾ C. Butter or Lard
- 2 Eggs
- 1 ¾ - 2 Cups Warm Water

Instructions:

In a large mixing bowl, rub together the flour, baking powder, salt, and butter with fingertips until it resembles cornmeal. In a small bowl, beat the eggs well with a fork and add ½ cups warm water. Mix into the flour with a wooden spoon and then your fingers to form moderately soft dough, adding more water as necessary to incorporate all crumbs. (Don't be afraid of making the dough hard by touching it too much as this isn't like pie pastry.) Knead several times so that the dough is smooth. Cover with plastic wrap and set aside to rest for an hour while you prepare the filling. Roll out **as thin as possible**. You'll need to flour both sides to roll out. Place on a lightly greased baking dish after cutting with a large mouth cup. (Approx. 10" circles)

Loralee Lago

Empanada Filling – Makes 12 Empanadas

Ingredients

- 2 White/Yellow Onions, diced
- 3 Garlic cloves, chopped
- 1 lb. Ground beef (ground sirloin is best) or use Round Roast that you've semi-thawed.
- 1-2 Tbsp. Beef Bouillon
- 2 t. Oregano
- 2 t. Paprika
- 1/2 t. Cumin
- 3-4 Tbsp. Apple Cider Vinegar
- ½ t. Salt and Pepper to taste
- ¼ t. Garlic Salt
- 1 Pinch of Nutmeg

Instructions:

Brown the onion and garlic in 2 T. Olive Oil. Add ground beef and brown – medium-high heat. Drain off the fat. Add the spices and cook until the meat is done.

IMPORTANT: Make the filling a day before, or at least a few hours before serving as the filling needs to cool and flavors meld so that juices do not leak out the dough once they are filled and baked.

Other popular fillings are Queso Fresco-you can find it as most major chain stores, or fill empanadas with Queso Fresco with thin ham slices for filling.

1. Prepare and put these ingredients into separate bowls
2. 1/2 C. Whole Green Olives
3. ½ C. Whole Raisins
4. 3 Hard-boiled eggs cut into slices.
5. Individual Empanada assembly:

6. 1 T. Meat mixture
7. 2 whole Green Olives per empanada
8. 3-4 Raisins per empanada
9. 1 Slice of Hard-Boiled Egg per empanada
10. Scoop 1 Tbsp. of the meat mixture onto ½ of a 10" dough circle.
11. Next, add the green olives, raisins & eggs on top. Brush edges with beaten egg then fold the circle in half, forming a semi-circle. Close the empanadas by pressing dough with a fork to seal the open edges or pinching the ends with fingers like a piecrust.
12. Brush the tops of the empanadas with a bit of milk or beaten egg.
13. Lightly Sprinkle with sugar (optional)
14. Bake in over at 350 for 20 minutes or until golden brown or fry in deep fryer until golden brown.

Loralee Lago

Argentine Chimichurri Bread

Ingredients

- 1 C. Water
- 1 ½ T. White Wine Vinegar or Balsamic
- 3 T. Olive Oil
- 1/8 t. Cayenne Pepper
- ¾ t. Oregano
- 2 Cloves of Garlic
- 3 T. Chopped Onions
- 3 T. Parsley
- 1 ½ t. Salt
- 1 T. Sugar
- 3 T. Wheat Bran or Flax
- 3 C. Bread Flour
- 2 t. Active Dry Yeast

Instructions:

1. Put ingredients in a bread machine. Select basic white cycle and press start. I like just to have the machine do all the mixing and kneading for me, and then I put the dough into my own regular bread pans and bake in the oven.
2. Bake at 400 Degrees for 30 minutes. (Makes 1 large or 2 small loaves)

Alfajores (Shortbread Cookies with Caramel Filling) – Makes 24

Ingredients

- 1 2/3 C. Flour
- 1 C. Corn Starch
- ½ t. Baking Soda
- 2 t. Baking Powder
- 1 C. Butter (2 Cubes)
- 3 Egg Yolks
- 1 t. Lemon Zest
- 1 t. Vanilla (I prefer Molina Mexican Vanilla)
- 1 C. Sugar

Instructions:

1. Sift together dry ingredients. Add the rest and mix. Roll out dough and cut into circles using a uniform cutter.
2. Bake at 375 for 10 minutes
3. Let cool completely, then spread Dulce De Leche between two cookies. Let dry. You may dip in white or dark chocolate with edges rolled in coconut if you'd like. I usually just eat them w/o chocolate and coconut, though.

Loralee Lago

Dulce de Leche

Ingredients

- 2 Cans (14 oz.) Sweetened Condensed Milk

Cover 2 UNOPENED cans of Sweetened Condensed Milk in a large pan half filled with water. Bring to a boil, and then continue cooking over medium heat for 3 hours. DO NOT LET THE WATER GO BELOW THE TOP OF THE CANS OR CANS COULD EXPLODE.

Let them cool in refrigerator completely and then open as usual. (Preferably overnight so that it is thicker when spreading on cookies).

Churro's – Makes 12

Ingredients

- 1 C. Water
- 1 C. Milk
- 1 tsp. Salt
- 2 t. Lemon Zest (optional)
- Bring this mixture to a boil. Take off heat and add:
- 2 tsp. Vanilla (Molina Mexican Vanilla preferable) - Can get at most grocery stores or Latin stores.
- 2 C. Flour & mix well (It will be a semi-stiff thick glue-like mixture)

Instructions:

1. Put into a cookie press and press out, then deep fry until golden brown a few minutes on each side. Once they are cool, sprinkle with Cinnamon & sugar mixture. Serve hot or cold. Yummy! Makes about one dozen.
2. Dip in *Dulce de Leche* or Nutella, or Drizzle with Chocolate Syrup.

Loralee Lago

Postre de Manzana (Green Apple Pie)

Ingredients

- 6 Medium Green Apples (peeled and cut into thin slices)
- 1 C. Flour
- 1 C. Sugar
- 1 Egg
- 2 tsp. Vanilla
- 1/2 C. Butter (cold so you can easily cut into mini butter cubes/chunks)

Instructions:

1. Peel & cut apples into thin slices.
2. In a separate bowl, mix the flour, sugar, egg and vanilla. Cut butter into very small cubes, then add butter and mix to a crumbly consistency.
3. Grease the bottom of a 9x13" dish.
4. Then add apples and squeeze a bit of lemon juice on top.
5. Next, sprinkle flour mixture over all the apples.
6. Sprinkle with cinnamon & sugar on top.
7. Bake at 350 degrees for 25-30 minutes.

Papas de Crema (Potato Frittata)

Ingredients

- 10 Potatoes cubed and fried in 4 T. Butter
- 2 Tbs. Parsley
- 2 Tsp. Flour
- 2 Egg Yolks
- Salt & Pepper to taste
- 2 Cups of Milk
- 1-2 C. Grated Cheese (Provolone or your favorite cheese)

Instructions:

1. Cut up potatoes into small cubes and fry in butter until slightly soft and then take off the heat.
2. Add Parsley
3. In a separate bowl, mix milk, flour & egg yolks, and season with salt & pepper than pour over potatoes. Put in a 9x13"- baking dish.
4. Cover with grated Cheese
5. Bake 375 for 25-30 minutes, or until cheese is melted.

Loralee Lago

Pastel Flore (Jam Pie)

Ingredients

- 2 Eggs
- 1 Cube of Butter - (1/2 cup)
- ½ C. Milk
- ½ C. Sugar
- 1 tsp. Vanilla
- 2 C. Flour
- Favorite Jam or *Batata* (Sweet Potato Spread)
- Cinnamon & Sugar

Instructions:

1. Roll out and knead the dough until it is nice a smooth.
2. Roll out piecrust, but keep it thicker than the regular crust. Put in a pie pan.
3. Save some dough to put crisscross strips over top.
4. Spread your favorite Jam/Jelly on top.
5. Cut crust strips and crisscross over top of the pie.
6. Sprinkle with cinnamon & sugar.
7. Bake at 375 for 15-20 minutes

Pastel de Papa (Potato Pie)

Ingredients

- 1 lb. Stew Meat (Cooked and cut up or shredded in small pieces)
- 1 Yellow/White Onion – Finely diced (sautéed in oil then add to meat if cooking in the crockpot or just add when frying up meat)
- 2 Tbsp. Oil

- Set-aside in a bowl until ready to assemble the dish.
- 6 Potatoes-Cooked & Diced (seasoned with salt, pepper)
- 2 boiled eggs - diced
- 1 C. Queso Fresco – shredded
- 1 Box of Puff Pastry/Pie Crust

- White Sauce:
- ½ C. Butter (1 Cube)
- 1/2 C. Milk
- 2-4 Tsp. Flour
- Salt & pepper

Instructions:

1. Cook White Sauce over stove until a nice semi-thick sauce forms.
2. 1 Box of Puff Pastry.
3. Make a piecrust and put it at the bottom of a 9x14" pan, then add meat, Potatoes, Eggs, Queso Fresco and then pour the White Sauce over the top.
4. Optional (put another sheet of Puff Pastry over the top)
5. Cook for 350 for 30 minutes or until crust browns.

Loralee Lago

Torta de Durazno's con Queso (Peaches & Cream Pie)

Pie Crust (Make your favorite pie crust, or use 1 Box Puff Pastry, or a Graham Cracker Crust is also great.

Filling:

2 C. Canned Peaches (drained) or 4 Peaches (thinly sliced) – Place in bottom of piecrust right before pouring cheese mixture on top. **Save a few slices for garnish.**

Mix:

- 1 8-oz Package of Cream Cheese
- 1/3 C. Milk
- 1/3 C. Sugar
- 1 t. Salt
- ¼ t. Vanilla
- 2 Eggs
- 1 t. Lemon Zest

Instructions:

1. Blend Cream Cheese & Milk, then add all ingredients except Peaches with mixer until smooth and pour over Peaches in piecrust.
2. Dust with Nutmeg & garnish top with a few Peaches.
3. Bake 350 degrees for 30 minutes.

Buñelos (Apple Fritters) – Serves 6

Ingredients

- 2 Red Apples – (Peel and dice into small bite size pieces)
- 3 C. Flour
- 1 t. Baking Powder
- 2 Eggs – Beaten
- 1 t. Vanilla
- ¾ C. Milk
- 2 T. Sugar (to taste)

Instructions:

1. Peel and dice apples
2. Mix all dry ingredients and then add apples
3. Roll or hand shape into circles and fry in Canola oil or Lard for extra flavor until browned. Serve hot.
4. Combine 2-3 t. Cinnamon & ¼ C. Sugar (To sprinkle on top of hot Buñelos)

Loralee Lago

Argentinean Style Ribs –
Serves 6
Ingredients

- 1 C. Salt (CORRECT)
- 6 Pounds of Beef Short Ribs
- Coat meat in Salt and let the meat remain in salt for at least 40 minutes before cooking.
- 6 Limes, Quartered

Instructions:

1. Coat ribs heavily with salt (this brings out the fat)
2. Preheat outdoor grill on medium-high and lightly oil grate.
3. Take ribs out of salt and lightly brush off excess salt.
4. Grill for 5-7 minutes on each side or until done.
5. Remove cooked ribs to a large glass dish and squeeze lime juice over them.
6. Serve Immediately.
7. Serve with *Chimichurri* Vinaigrette

Orange & Chocolate Flan

Ingredients

- 1 C. Sugar
- 1 T. Water
- Put ingredients into a saucepan and boil until it begins to turn light brown. Take off heat and pour into a metal loaf pan or tempered bread loaf pan that has been sprayed with oil & sugared and set aside.
- In a blender add:
- 6 Eggs
- 1 1/2 C. prepared Orange Juice
- 1 t. Orange Zest
- 1 Can Sweetened Condensed Milk
- 1 T. Sugar
- 2 t. Corn Starch
- 1 t. Vanilla

Instructions:

1. Blend until everything is incorporated.
2. Pour into a loaf pan that has been sprayed with oil & sugared.
3. Add ½ C. of Semi-Sweet Chocolate Chips evenly over the top.
4. Place bread pan inside of a larger casserole dish and then fill sides with water for a water bath.
5. Cover bigger pan with Aluminum Foil
6. Cook for 40 minutes at 375 degrees
7. Wait for it to cool for at least 10 minutes before inverting onto another plate.

Loralee Lago

Filet Mignon in Egg Batter –
Serves 8

Ingredients

- 1 ½ C Sifted Flour
- 4 Egg Yolks (beaten) – Save whites for later in recipe
- ½ C. Milk
- 2 Garlic Cloves (Minced)
- 1 ½ t. Salt
- ½ t. Pepper
- ½ t. Crushed Marjoram
- ¼ t. Crushed Dried Chili Pepper
- 4 Egg Whites (beaten until stiff but not dry)
- 8 Beef Filet or Boneless Sirloin Steaks (1/2" thick & trimmed of fat)
- 1 C. Olive Oil
- Sweet Paprika
- Garnish with Watercress or Parsley and serve with Chimichurri Bread and Vinaigrette.

Instructions:

Add flour to the beaten egg yolks all at once and beat until smooth. Add milk to the mixture and stir in Garlic, Salt, Pepper, Marjoram and Chilies. Carefully fold in the beaten Egg Whites. Dip the Steaks in the batter coating well. Heat the oil in a skillet until it smokes. Fry the coated Steaks in the hot oil for 3-5 minutes per side, depending on how you like your meat. Remove to a serving platter, dust with Paprika and garnish with Watercress or Parsley.

Sopapillas (Fry Bread) – Makes 24

Ingredients

- 4 C. All-Purpose Flour
- 2 t. Baking Powder
- 4 T. Lard (You can use shortening, but the Lard gives it that signature flavor)
- 1 t. Salt
- 1 1/2 C. Warm Water
- 1 Egg (beaten)
- Lard or Vegetable Oil for Frying
- 1 C. Powdered Sugar

Instructions:

1. Sift the flour and baking powdered together twice. Place lard and salt into 2-quart measuring cup and add boiling water. Allow it to cool until it is luke-warm, then stir in egg and mix well. Work the sifted flour mixture into the egg mixture and knead until you have a smooth, elastic dough. Add flour a little at a time if necessary. Roll out the dough to about a 1/8" thickness and cut with cookie cutters or pizza cutter into any shape that you like.
2. Heat the fat in a deep skillet or deep fryer until it's almost smoking. Add the sopapillas to hot oil one at a time. Fry until both sides are golden and drain on a paper towel. Put Sopapillas on to your serving dish and sprinkle with powdered sugar and serve warm.

Loralee Lago

Pastellitos de Mil Hojas
(Thousand-Leaf Pastry)
Ingredients

- 1 Package Pepperidge Farm Puff Pastry (Cut into 9 squares per sheet)
- 1 ½ C. Quince Paste or Dulce de Batata (can buy at Latin Markets)
- 4 C. Shortening - Divided between 2 Deep Fryers

Assembly Directions:

Place 1 t. filling in the center of the 18 squares (put both sheets of 9 squares together to form 1 Pastel). Lightly moisten the dough around the filling with cold water. Top each filled square with an <u>unfilled</u> square, rotating it so that its 4 corners are offset from the corners of the filled square, forming a total of 8 consecutive corners. With a fork, firmly press the dough around the filling to secure it. Then pinch the corners toward the filling to achieve a flower-like shape with 8 petals.

Syrup

- 1 C. Sugar
- ¼ C. Water
- ½ t. Vanilla

Rainbow Sprinkles (Add after you've fried them)

Combine the sugar and water in a saucepan. Stir until sugar is dissolved. Bring it to a boil over high heat, stirring constantly. Boil steadily without stirring until syrup reaches a temperature of 230 F on a candy thermometer. Remove the pan from the heat and stir in vanilla extract. Cover the syrup to keep it warm while you deep-fry the *Pastellitos*.

Deep fry (several at a time) P*astellitos* in 2 deep fryers. Make sure that the shortening reaches a depth of 3" at 375 F and the other is at 175 F." Add more shortening if necessary. Fry for 3-4 minutes in first fryer and baste constantly until petals begin to separate. DO NOT LET THEM BROWN. Immediately transfer to 2nd deep fryer (175 F) and fry on both sides for 2 minutes or until golden brown. Carefully remove from the fryer and drain on paper towels, then drizzle them in the warm syrup, add rainbow sprinkles and put on a serving dish. Serve at room temperature.

Loralee Lago

Matambre (Rolled Steak & Vegetables) – Serves 4

Ingredients

- 2-Pounds of Flank Steak (Butterfly the steak and trim off fat)
- ½ C Red Wine Vinegar
- 3 Garlic Cloves (Minced)
- 1 t. Thyme (crushed)
- 2 T. Oregano (crushed)
- ½ Pound fresh Spinach leaves, washed and dried with stems removed
- 4 Carrots (cut in half length wise) If more than ½" in diameter boil them for 3-4 minutes to soften or microwave for a few minutes)
- 4 Hard Boiled Eggs (cut lengthwise into quarters)
- 1-Pound Veal, cut into narrow strips
- ½ Pound Bacon cut into narrow strips
- 1 Large Onion (sliced 1/8" thick and divided into rings
- ½ C Parsley – Chopped
- 1 T. Crushed Chili Peppers
- 1 T. Coarse Sea Salt
- 2 T. Grated Parmesan Cheese
- 8 C. Beef Stock
- 1 Bay Leaf
- 4 Black Peppercorns – Crushed

Instructions:

1. Preheat oven to 325 F. Butterfly the steak lengthwise and sprinkle both sides with vinegar, garlic, thyme and oregano. Cover and marinate for 12 hours in the refrigerator. Drain the steaks and lay them side-by-side, overlapping by about 2". Pound the overlapping edges together to make a seal. Cover the meat with a thick layer of spinach leaves. Arrange the

carrots with the grain of the meat in rows about 2" apart. Place eggs, veal strips and bacon strips between the carrot rows. Scatter the onion rings over the filling and sprinkle with parsley, chili pepper and salt. Sprinkle the onion rings with Parmesan cheese and roll up the meat carefully with the grain (like a jellyroll) Secure the roll with skewers and string.

2. Place the Matambre in a 12-quart flameproof casserole or roasting pan on stove. Add stock, bay leaf and crushed peppercorns. Cover and bring just to the boiling point. Turn off the heat and then place the casserole in the middle of the oven. Cook for 2 hours or until meat is tender, but not falling apart.

3. To serve warm, let the *Matambre* rest on a cutting board for 10 minutes. Remove the string and cut the Matambre crosswise into 1-inch slices. Arrange the slices on a platter and moisten with some of the pan liquid.

4. To serve cold, remove it from the casserole after it has cooled. Press the Matambre under weights until the juices drain off. Wrap it in plastic wrap and refrigerate. Once thoroughly chilled, cut it cross wise into ½" thick slices and serve on top of a thick slice of French bread.

Loralee Lago

Ensalada de Naranja (Orange Salad) – Serves 4

Ingredients

- 4 Medium Oranges (Peeled and separated into sections of 2 or 3 pieces each)
- 1 Small Head of Romaine Lettuce (Torn into Large Pieces)
- 1 Small Red Onion (Chopped)
- Boiling Water
- ¼ C. Olive Oil
- 1 T. Red Wine Vinegar
- Salt & Pepper to Taste
- 1 t. Dry Mustard

Instructions:

Place orange and lettuce pieces in a salad bowl. Blanch the onions in boiling water for 30 seconds. Drain and squeeze the onion and discard the water. Add the onions to the salad bowl. Chill in the refrigerator for at least 1 hour. Just before serving, beat oil, vinegar, salt pepper and mustard together with a wire whisk until slightly thickened. Sprinkle over salad and toss.

Budin de Mango (Mango Pudding) – Serves 4

Ingredients

- 3 Ripe Mangoes (Peeled, sliced and cut into small pieces)
- 2 T. Fresh Lime Juice
- ¼ t. Salt
- ¼ C. Sugar
- 3 Eggs, separated
- Zest of 1 Lime
- ¼ t. Nutmeg (optional)
- 2 T. Cornstarch

Garnish with

- 1 Mango cut in wedges
- 10 Strawberries - Sliced
- Whipped cream

Instructions:

1. Preheat the oven to 375 F. Mix the mangos with the lime juice and salt. Sprinkle the mixture with sugar and let set aside for 10 minutes.
2. Beat the egg whites until they hold a peak. Puree the mango mixture in the blender and add the egg yolks and lime zest. Mix well, and then blend in the cornstarch. Pour into a mixing bowl and carefully fold in the beaten egg whites. Spoon mixture into a liberally buttered 1 ½-quart mold.
3. Bake for 10 minutes @ 375.
4. Reduce the heat to 350 F and bake for an additional 30 minutes. Remove the pudding from the oven and let it cool in mold. Carefully unmold onto a serving dish and chill in the refrigerator until ready to serve.

5. Garnish top of Mold with Mango and Strawberries or decorate top of each individual serving with Strawberries and extra pieces of Mango on top with whipped cream before serving.

Panqueques (Crepes) – Makes 4

Ingredients

- ¼ C. Sifted Flour
- Pinch of Salt
- 2 Large Eggs
- ½ C. Milk
- 2 T. Butter (Melted)

Instructions:

1. Sift the flour into a mixing bowl and stir in the salt. Mix in the eggs and then the milk. Beat the batter until it's smooth; the consistency should be like light cream. Add more milk as needed. Stir in the butter and set aside to rest for 30 minutes. Stir just before using.
2. Heat a nonstick pan and brush the bottom with a little butter. Ladle in just enough batter to coat the bottom of the pan, pouring off any excess. Cook for 2 minutes or until browned, then turn over and cook for 1 minute more. Continue cooking the crepes and stacking them on a plate until all the batter has been used up.
3. Serve with Dulce De Leche spread on top, with cut up bananas or thinly sliced apples.

Loralee Lago

Kreutzer Potato Salad –
Serves 20

Ingredients

- 5 lbs. of Potatoes (any kind)
- 2 Medium Dill/Sweet Pickles (chopped)
- 1 Jar of Pimentos
- 1 Can of Large Olives (chopped)
- 1 Medium Onion (Diced finely)
- 2-3 Stalks of Celery (Chopped)
- 1 lb. of Sharp Cheddar Cheese (cut into small cubes)
- 8 oz. Philadelphia Cream Cheese (cut into small cubes)
- 1 32 oz. Bottle of Best Foods Mayonnaise
- 5 Hard Boiled Eggs (Sliced and used for topping)
- 1-2 t. Paprika

Instructions:

1. Wash and boil potatoes about 55 minutes or until a fork goes through easily.
2. Cool, peel and dice potatoes
3. Add all Ingredients in a large bowl and mix gently
4. Add sliced Eggs on top and lightly sprinkle with Paprika

Spanish Candied Peanuts

Ingredients

- Using a large Skillet over medium heat add:
- 2 Cups Shelled (Raw) Spanish Peanuts
- 1 Cup Sugar
- 1/3 C. Water

Instructions:

1. Using a wooden spoon to stir mixture until everything is dissolved
2. Keep stirring until it boils (about 2-3 minutes)
3. Keep stirring - Once water evaporates and the candy seizes and turns gritty
4. Keep stirring until sugar begins to melt down again (caramelized part- 30 seconds)
5. Keep stirring until nearly all crystalized sugar is no longer crystalized (2-3 minutes)
6. Take pan off of the heat
7. Add a Splash of Vanilla
8. ¼ t. Cinnamon to taste
9. Dash of Salt (optional)
10. Other optional flavors would be chili powder or chocolate powder
11. Pour everything over parchment paper/wax paper, spread out evenly with spatula and let them cool.
12. Serve in a cone shaped bag or any favorite serving dish that you'd like.

Loralee Lago

BBQ'd Sea Bass with Vinaigrette – Serves 2

Ingredients

- 2 Whole Sea Bass - Gutted, scaled and cleaned
- ½ of a Lemon – Thinly Sliced
- Handful Thyme Sprigs
- For Vinaigrette:
- ½ C. Extra Virgin Olive Oil
- 1 Shallot, thinly sliced
- 1 Pinch of Salt
- 2 Cloves of Garlic, halved
- 2 Sprigs of Thyme
- 1 T White Wine Vinegar (put this in after simmering)
- Add – 1 Tomato - diced

Instructions:

1. Heat the BBQ to a medium heat. Cut 3 slits down each side of each fish, through the skin and the flesh but not quite down to the bone and stuff cavities with lemon slices and thyme.
2. BBQ each side for 3-4 minutes, then check to see if cooked through. It should appear opaque and easily come off of the bone (145 degrees on meat thermometer.
3. For Vinaigrette, put the olive oil, shallot, garlic and thyme in a small cold saucepan with a pinch of salt. Place over low heat and warm gently, just long enough to poach the shallot, around 20 minutes. You'll know it is done when both the garlic and shallot are soft and clear looking. Take the pan off of the heat and stir in the vinegar and then let it cool completely.
4. When you are ready to serve the fish, take thyme and garlic halves out of the vinaigrette and discard. Stir in diced tomatoes and spoon over the cooked fish right before serving.

About the Author

Loralee Lago is a native of Las Vegas, who is proud to call Nevada home. She will enthusiastically sing the state song, "Home Means Nevada," upon request. She was recently spotted singing "The Sound of Music" while fulfilling a scavenger hunt requirement on a street corner (and also achieving a lifetime goal of being a headline singer on the Las Vegas strip) by the Bellagio Hotel and Casino. She was invited to dinner on the spot by a passing tourist and asked by another tourist to take over performances at Caesar's Palace for Celine Dion, but declined due to a previous engagement;-)

Loralee has been the Controller/Human Resources director for a local advertising agency, Robertson + Partners for the past 25 years and for The Warren Group. She served an 18-month mission for The Church of Jesus Christ of Latter-Day Saints in the Bahia Blanca, Argentina Mission, where she taught the gospel, served, learned Spanish, and gained a great love of the Argentinian people, culture and cuisine.

Loralee is known as the big kid in her family for not being too grown up to go outside to play with her nieces and nephews. She especially loves spending time with her family. She is married to the love of her life, Paul Lago. They have a cat-child named Daisy Blossom and a tenacious desert tortoise-child named Toby.

Loralee would be pleased to hear from you about your positive thoughts and experiences reading "A Tango to Die For!" Please email her at loraleelago@yahoo.com and put "Tango" in your email's subject line.

Bibliography

"With the Strength of the Lord" by Loralee Lago & Jay Powell. If you would like a copy of this music, please email me at loraleelago@yahoo.com. Please include in the subject line "With the Strength of the Lord Tango music."

"To Become as He" by Loralee Lago & Jay Powell. If you would like a copy of this music, please email me at loraleelago@yahoo.com. Please include in the subject line "To Become as He Tango music."

"Be Still my Soul" by Katarina Von Schlegel & Jean Sibelius

The Holiday (movie) starring Cameron Diaz, Jack Black, Jude Law & Kate Winslet - 2006

Butch Cassidy and the Sundance Kid (movie) starring Paul Newman & Robert Redford – 1969

That Touch of Mink (movie) starring Doris Day & Cary Grant - 1962

Gojira (Godzilla) by Terry Morse & Ishiro Honda

Cinderella "So This is Love" written by Jerry Livingston, Al Hoffman & Mack David

Star Trek by Gene Roddenberry - 1966

Bob Ross "The Joy of Painting" – PBS

"The Sound of Music" written by Rodgers & Hammerstein

Argentina Cooks by Shirley Lomax Brooks

Made in the USA
Monee, IL
13 November 2020